THE BLOCK

BEN OLIVER

Chicken House

SCHOLASTIC INC. / NEW YORK

All rights reserved. Published by Chicken House, an imprint of Scholastic Inc.,
Publishers since 1920. SCHOLASTIC, CHICKEN HOUSE, and associated logos are
trademarks and/or registered trademarks of Scholastic Inc.
First published in the United Kingdom in 2020 by Chicken House,
2 Palmer Street, Frome, Somerset BA11 1DS.
The publisher does not have any control over and does not assume any
responsibility for author or third-party websites or their content.

Library of Congress Cataloging-in-Publication Data available
ISBN 978-1-338-58933-7
1 2020
Printed in the U.S.A.   23
First edition, May 2021
Book design by Maeve Norton

For Hollie. Books, eh? Who'da thought it?
(You'da thought it.)

Why are we designed to see the world as supremely beautiful just as we're about to be snuffed? Do rabbits feel the same as the fox teeth bite down on their necks? Is it mercy?

THE YEAR OF THE FLOOD, MARGARET ATWOOD

Defeating Happy came at a cost.

As I lie here, staring up the ceiling of my home on the 177th floor of the Black Road Vertical, I can't help but ask myself if we could have done anything differently.

Pander had taken her own life after Happy had uploaded itself into her, Pod had been stabbed to death by an Alt loyal to the AI's cause, Malachai had died in the battle on City Level Two, and Igby had been shot out of the sky while flying to retrieve a key card that would allow us access to the underground bunker where Happy stored its servers.

But it had been Akimi who had made the ultimate sacrifice, running into the power storage facility with plasma grenades, blowing herself up, along with Happy's life support system. After that, all we had to do was stay alive long enough for the AI's stored energy to die.

"What are you thinking about?" Kina asks, walking into the room and lying beside me.

"Just . . . everything," I reply. I smile because she's still alive, and immediately feel selfish for it.

"Me too," she says, her hand running through my hair. "It feels like it's all I ever think about."

1

"Do you ever feel guilty?" I ask. "That we survived and everyone else . . ."

"Yes," she says. "All the time. I dream about it; I wake up most nights and . . ."

She trails off, tears in her eyes.

"I don't know what I expected," I say. "I imagined the end of the war being beautiful. I imagined us all together, all alive."

"They died fighting for what they believed in," Kina says. "Fighting for each other, and for us, and for all of humanity. In the end all of us were ready to die for the cause, so—in that way—their deaths are noble, courageous. They'll be remembered forever as heroes."

"I know," I reply, "but I'd give anything for them to be back here, with us."

"Me too," Kina says, and kisses me on the cheek. "Try to get some sleep."

She lies back in the darkness, and I continue to stare up at the ceiling.

I don't know how long I lie there for, but before I fall into a restless sleep, I think to myself, *When is it going to happen?*

When I wake, the sun is rising.

I get up, careful not to wake Kina, and move from the bedroom to the kitchen.

There is no electricity now, not after the firebombing that came at the very end, and the only water is from the rain collectors, but we have to ration that carefully, as Happy tried to poison the rain with its last few moments of battery life. In doing so, it affected the weather permanently. Now we get mostly scorching-hot days, and five-minute bursts of heavy rain once every three or four days.

As I half fill a bottle with water, I look out over the city. It's a wreck. Some areas are still smoking and smoldering, some buildings still crumbling. The burning-hot sun and lack of rain has turned the river into a wide path of cracked mud that snakes through the burned-out city.

I change into a pair of jeans and a black T-shirt. I pull on a pair of boots and leave the apartment as quietly as I can.

As usual, by the time I'm halfway down the 176 flights of stairs, I tell myself that Kina and I are moving into a house on the ground floor *today*! But I know that once we start looking around, I'll feel nervous again. Not just nervous but anxious, as if the act of leaving my old home would somehow be sullying the memory of my deceased mother, father, and sister.

I shake off the thought and continue down and down until, finally, I reach the front doors of the building and push my way out into the heat and the blinding light.

I move carefully through the rubble, through the charred streets and hunks of melted metal that might have once been vehicles, until finally I come to a warehouse near the factory district.

I have to be careful now; I'm not the only scavenger around. There are many survivors of Happy's war—some Alts still bent on carrying out their artificial leader's orders, some Regulars who survived because they were on the drug Ebb at the time, even the occasional Smiler, humans driven crazy by the bioweapon that was delivered through the Earth's rain supply. Most Smilers are dead now, though. Those of us who only want to survive have not yet found a way to communicate, and we avoid one another, scared that each living soul is a threat.

I enter the warehouse through a hole that was blown into the outer wall at some point during the final moments of the war. The entire place has been picked over and ransacked, leaving the shelves almost empty, but there are still some vacuum-sealed packs of fruit and sacks of rice.

Once I have gathered some basic supplies and secured them in my backpack, I move down to the last part of the river that still had enough water in it to sustain life, and check my traps for fish: nothing.

I make my way back to the Black Road Vertical, moving

carefully, quietly, from building to building, listening for movement, watching for signs of life. I make it safely back to the impossibly tall building and begin climbing the stairs. Now, with the added weight of the food on my back, I have to take several rests along the way. Once I reach the 177th floor, I leave the bag at the front door of our apartment, and carry on up to the roof.

It's strange being back up here, back where my sister and I stood in shocked silence as the boy had fallen to his death. It had been Molly who had pushed him. She'd had no choice—he had a gun pointed at her head—but self-defense wouldn't have worked in a court of law, as it was *us* who were robbing *him* in the first place.

I had taken the blame; I had confessed to the murder of Jayden Roth and had been sentenced to death.

That's where it all began, I think to myself, staring at the spot where the boy had fallen. *I was sent to the Loop, became a test subject for the Smiler vaccine, and I survived the war.*

I look to the other side of the rooftop, the place where my father—infected by the Smiler disease—used his last reserves of life to tackle one of Happy's hosts off the edge and save my life.

Defeating Happy came at a high cost.

I can feel the surge of emotion inside me and I fight it, push it down and away, and focus instead on the garden.

It had taken two days of almost constant work to carry up the wood that makes the frame of the garden and the soil that fills the frame. I had planted carrots, potatoes, tomatoes, and green beans. There are signs of life, small shoots growing out of the tomato patch and tiny leaves sticking out of the soil where the carrots are.

I use the bucket to scoop the smallest amount of water I feel I can spare out of the rain collector and pour it onto the vegetables.

When is it going to happen? I think, looking out over the city, breathing in the warm air. *When is it going to happen?*

I think back to the Block, the most torturous, cruel, agonizing place I have ever had the misfortune of being inside, and I think about how I got out of there. Has it really been twenty days? Twenty days since the explosion, since the gunfire, since the screams and yells? The entire building had been bombed by Pod and Igby. They had calculated the exact amount of explosives required to blow away the back wall and leave the prisoners alive. Then they—along with Pander, Akimi, and my sister—had stormed the building, killing the guards and dragging us from the paralysis beds.

Twenty days . . . so much has happened since then, and yet it feels like nothing has changed at all.

I look out over the city, to the bend in the river where me, my sister, and my parents used to go on sunny days. I look to the horizon, where the morning sun blazes as it climbs ever higher.

When is it going to happen? I wonder.

All of this—this burned-out city, this burned-out planet—it's all futile, the human race rising up out of the rubble seems impossible, and yet, it doesn't matter. It's not real.

This is not real.

I breathe in deeply, feeling the warm air in my lungs, and

make my way back through the narrow doorway, down the wooden steps, and back into the corridor on the top floor of the Vertical.

I walk down to floor 177 and back into my old home, the place where I grew up.

Kina is in the living room, writing in her journal. She looks up when I enter the room.

"Hey," she says.

"Hi," I reply.

"I'm writing again," she tells me, looking almost guiltily down at her words. "I think it's important—people should know what happened, future generations, you know?"

"Yeah," I say.

She looks at me and smiles. "Luka, I don't want to bring up bad memories, but I want to make sure all of this is accurate. Can you tell me—"

"Wait, Kina," I interrupt, "please don't."

"What do you mean?" she asks, frowning.

"Don't ask me, please."

"I don't understand," she says, half laughing, as if I'm being unreasonable.

"Kina, if you ask me that question, then this is all over."

"Luka, I don't know what you're talking about; you're scaring me a little."

"Yes, you do understand," I say. "You know exactly what I'm talking about, because you're not really Kina, we're not really in my old home, the war isn't over, and I'm still in the Block."

"That's crazy. Luka, that's crazy! You can't really believe that?"

"It's not a question of belief," I reply, "it's a matter of fact. You've been meticulous this time. You've planned it out, played the long game, and there were moments that I almost let myself believe it was real, but it's not real. It's all a mirage, a ploy to get vital information out of me. So, you know what . . . go ahead, ask your questions."

The look of concern on Kina's face turns to one of vacancy, but there is anger deep in her eyes. "Where were Pander, Pod, Igby, and Akimi hiding on the day of the Battle of Midway Park?"

I sigh, take one last look around, and shake my head. "I'll never tell you."

And, after twenty days, the simulation ends.

The false reality that surrounds me begins to melt away, and the heat of the sun is gone, replaced by the nothingness of the paralysis bed inside my cell in the Block.

And now I'm here once again, unable to move, unable to feel anything at all. Staring at a single spot on the white wall, rage and pain warring inside me, hopelessness overcoming me.

When the harvest begins, all that exists is fear.

It feels like an eternity before it ends, before the nanotech releases its grip on the parts of my brain that access terror and panic, before my heart begins to slow and my muscles relax.

Back in the Loop, the prison I was in before the end of the world, the harvest lasted only six hours, and when it was done we were left alone in our small soundproof cells. It seemed horrible at the time, but compared to the Block it was like heaven.

The harvest tube stays in place while the water comes. It rushes in from the ceiling, smelling of acrid chemicals and bleach. As usual, I consider letting it drown me: pushing all the air out of my lungs at the moment the tube fills, and waiting to die so that I don't have to face another day of this hell.

But I don't.

The tube fills with water until I'm completely submerged. Time passes—ten seconds, twelve—and then the water drains away, throwing me to the floor once again.

The air comes next, so hot that my skin feels like it's about to blister and burn. Once I'm dry, the tube lifts and retreats into the ceiling.

The harvest is over, and what comes next is just as terrible.

I wait, naked on the floor, my arms magnetized together behind my back by the implanted cobalt in my wrists.

It's been sixteen days since Happy, the all-powerful artificial intelligence that first ran the world and then destroyed it, tried to trick me into giving up the location of my friends. Happy somehow accessed my brain and convinced me that I had been broken out of this prison by Pander, Malachai, and Kina, but I figured it out; I realized that none of it was real despite how convincing the simulation was. I took them to the river near the center of the city and savored the memories of spending time there with my family when I was young. Me, my sister, my dad, and my mom would go to the riverside on summer days and spend hours playing, swimming, talking, and just being together as a family.

It took the AI about four minutes to realize it had been deceived. Since then Happy has tried every day to trick me into giving up information. It uses different tactics: fear; coercion; bargaining; confusion. Then it tried a twenty-day simulation of a life after the war, a life with Kina.

But I will keep my secrets guarded. I will not let Happy win.

The technology that Happy uses to try and draw information out of me is the same technology they have been using to keep my mind from slipping away in the monotony of the Block. They call it the Sane Zone.

I'm still breathing heavily from the harvest and the water when the hatch in my cell door opens.

Immediately I moderate my breathing, slow it right down.

The guard on duty today is Jacob. Good. In the last few days I have managed to get through to Jacob; he has listened to me, hesitated before beginning the harvest, looked at me with real regret and shame in his eyes.

"Inmate 9-70-981, be informed that I have a loaded weapon and I am prepared to use it if you do not follow my instructions. Am I understood?"

My head is turned in the direction of the cell door and I see Jacob: young, skinny, fashionably long hair. His eyes glare at me down the barrel of an Ultrasonic Wave rifle. I don't move, don't blink, don't react to the gun pointed at me.

"Inmate 9-70-981. Please lie down on the bed so I can activate the paralysis . . . Inmate 9-70-981 . . . Luka, are you okay?"

Still I don't move. I lie on the floor of my cell, and try to keep my breathing as shallow as possible so that Jacob might think I'm not breathing at all.

"Luka?" He sounds unsure now, scared. "Oh shit!"

I hear the spin lock on my door opening and see the door swing inward. The young guard runs over to me, sliding to his knees and rolling me onto my back.

"Luka! Luka!" he calls, slapping my face to try and rouse me.

I want to grab for his USW rifle, I want to spring into action and break out of this place, but the energy harvest has left me drained, so I have to wait for the healing technology inside me to work. The important thing is, I've tricked a guard into entering my cell.

I take a sudden deep breath, as if I've just come to, and look at Jacob with confusion on my face.

"What happened?" I ask.

"I don't know," he replies, his voice shaking. "I think you stopped breathing."

"Gods," I say in hoarse voice, "I wish I'd died."

"Don't say that, don't be saying things like that."

"Why not?" I ask, stalling for time, waiting for my strength to return. "Death is a thousand times better than this place."

"Come on, please, don't say things like that!" he repeats. "I should call a medic drone, make sure you're all right."

His eyes begin to scan left and right, activating menus on his Lens.

"No, no," I say, sitting up. "I'm fine, Jacob, really. I think I just fainted."

"Are you sure?"

"Yeah, I'm sure," I say.

"I'm s'posed to call a medic drone if something like this happens."

"Jacob, I'm okay, I promise."

He sighs. "If you're sure, Inmate 9-70-981."

"Oh, it's 9-70-981 again, is it?" I say, laughing. "What happened to Luka?"

"I was panicking," he tells me. "I'm not s'posed to call you by your real name."

I can feel my strength coming back now, feel the exhaustion ebbing away.

"Well, if you're all right, I need you to lie down on the bed. I have a schedule that I need to stick to. If I'm late again I'll be in trouble."

"Yeah," I say. "I understand."

I get to my feet—it takes enormous effort after the harvest robbed me of all my energy, but I can already feel my power coming back. I can feel my body healing itself, every micro-tear in the fibers of my muscles, every strained tendon and every scratch. This is a new feature, a piece of Alt tech in my body causing me to heal at inhuman speed. We all have this ability now, all the inmates from the Loop and the Block—this way they can reuse our energy over and over again. We are the rechargeable batteries that power the machines that will end humanity. They heal our bodies with tech and keep us from going crazy with the Sane Zone.

I stand beside the bed and turn back to Jacob. I'm still completely naked, and yet unperturbed by that fact, conditioned by now not to care. I don't move, just stare at him.

"You have to lie down, Luka," he tells me.

"So they can paralyze me?"

"Well . . . yes."

"Can you imagine that? Can you imagine what this is like? Every day I go through agonizing pain and then unbearable loneliness and fear."

"Everyone has to sacrifice for the good of humanity—"

"Humanity?" I interrupt, and laugh. "Is that what they've been telling you? They're lying."

"Galen Rye is ensuring the safety of the survivors, and I need to—"

"Galen Rye sold his soul to save himself," I interrupt.

"Please, Luka, I'm just tryin' to get me and my family into the Arc. I'm not a Tier One, I have to earn my place. I don't like this but I don't have a choice! What would you do? If I let you go, they'll kill us both."

I sigh and look directly into the young soldier's eyes. "I know, you're only doing what you have to do to survive, but listen to me, Jacob, they are not going to let you live. They think of humans as a virus, and they can't let even one of us survive. They plan on eradicating everyone."

"What are you talking about? The world is going to end, and the World Government had to make some hard choices, some really diff—"

"Ask yourself: Why didn't they just kill the Regulars? Why did they turn them into monsters?" I yell. "It's because of their programming! This isn't the World Government, it's . . ." I sigh and shake my head. It doesn't matter, he won't believe me. I wouldn't believe that the world leaders have been taken over by artificial intelligence if I hadn't seen it with my own eyes.

I think I've bought myself enough time. I think I have enough replenished energy now.

"It's who?" Jacob asks, his eyes narrowing.

"Not who," I reply, "what."

"Okay, then what?"

"It doesn't matter." I look into the young guard's eyes. "I'm sorry, Jacob."

I run at him.

Jacob moves quickly, turning and running out of the room.

He tries to slam the door shut but I'm too fast. I reach out a hand, forcing it between the thick metal of the door and the concrete frame. I hear the bones in my fingers crunch as Jacob slings the door toward himself. The pain is incredible. I clench my jaw and muffle the scream that forces its way into my mouth.

I close my eyes and breathe through the pain as I pull the door open, the agony doubling in my contorted hand, fingers bending and bowed, blood already pooling beneath the skin, turning into storm cloud bruises.

"Wait, wait!" Jacob cries as I grab him—by the collar with my good hand—and drag him back into my cell.

"Code fourteen in cell three-nineteen!" Jacob calls.

I throw the boy onto my bed, grab his gun, and aim it at him.

"Lens," I say, holding out my hand.

"Wh-what?" he stammers.

I push the barrel of the USW rifle against his forehead. "Give me your Lens."

He reaches a shaking hand up to his eye and removes the translucent contact lens. I take it from him and place it over my own eye. My vision is now filled with a three-dimensional heads-up display that I control with my vision. I find the menu labeled STASIS and activate my bed. The paralysis needle pierces Jacob's skin and he falls immediately lifeless.

I look down at the paralyzed boy-soldier on my bed.

"Sorry, Jacob," I mutter, and move quickly to the open door.

My bare feet slap against the grated metal floor. I assess my surroundings as fast as I can.

Third floor, cube-shaped building, walkways around each floor, approximately two hundred cells per floor.

And then I freeze. I notice that every cell in the place is open, apart from the four that are next to mine.

"Where the hell are all the Block inmates?" I wonder aloud.

I drag my still-weak body to the next cell. For all of the thirty days inside the Block I have been hoping that Kina and Malachai are still alive. They were not included on Happy's list of surviving escapees, so they are either dead or captured.

I try the thick metal spin handle of the cell beside mine—it doesn't budge. A panel beside the door asks for iris identification. I drop Jacob's gun to the floor and take a closer look at the panel, trying to find another way to unlock it.

"Hey!" a voice calls to my left.

I turn to see a woman of about fifty striding toward me, her hand reaching for the USW pistol on her belt.

I run toward her, fighting against the aching in my limbs and joints. Her eyes grow wide as I close the gap and she struggles to grip and draw her weapon.

I get to her just as she frees her pistol. I twist her arm behind her back—wresting the gun from her hand and pushing the barrel into her spine. I hear a snap from my broken fingers and feel them begin to click back into place; the pain of the bones grinding together almost makes me drop my newly acquired weapon, but I hold on.

"If you activate any alarms, send any silent distress codes, if I see one other soldier coming toward me—I will shoot you, do you understand?"

"Do you honestly think you'll get out of here alive?" the woman grunts.

"This isn't my first prison break."

"Galen Rye will—"

"Shut up," I tell her. "Kina Campbell, where is she?"

"I'm not telling you anyth—"

I aim the gun at her foot and pull the trigger. She opens her mouth to cry out, and for a second there is only silence, her face almost comical in its shock. And then she's screaming.

"I won't ask you again," I hiss. "Kina Campbell's cell, where is it?"

She stumbles forward a step and then points to a cell two down from my own. I feel a moment of absolute relief. She's alive; Kina is alive.

"Who else have they got?" I ask. "Malachai?"

The guard bites her lower lip, defiance in her eyes. I aim the gun at her other foot.

"Wren Salter," she gasps, holding out a hand to stop me from shooting. "She's next door to you, Malachai Bannister is next to Kina, and Woods Rafka is there." She points two cells down from Kina's.

"Why are the other cells empty?" I ask. "Where did you take the Block inmates?"

"We didn't take them anywhere. They died."

"What?" I ask, immediately shaken by her answer.

"They died, all of them. It's only you lot from the Loop that are still alive."

I try to work out why this might be. We were all injected with

17

the same healing tech, so why have they died and we haven't?

There's no time to debate this. I push the guard forward.

"Open Kina's cell first," I command.

She leans down and activates the iris scanner.

I hear the lock click and I reach for the handle. I open the door and what I see stops my heart.

I had known that Kina's plight was the same as my own, but to see her, lying motionless on her bed, every muscle immobilized, her face so slack and unmoving that she might be dead, I can hardly breathe.

"Give me your Lens," I say to the guard.

"What are you going to do?" she asks.

I raise the gun until the muzzle is against her forehead. "Don't make me repeat myself."

She reaches two fingers into her eye and pinches out the clear contact lens. A smirk spreads across her lips. "I can't wait to see what Galen Rye does to you when you're caught."

She hands me the Lens, placing it into my broken palm just as another finger snaps from its abnormal angle back to straight.

I squeeze the Lens between two fingers, destroying it so that she'll have no way out.

I use Jacob's Lens to navigate to the energy harvest activation option. My eyes scroll to cell 317 and select INITIATE ENERGY HARVEST. A circle of light appears in the middle of the floor.

"Stand in the circle," I tell the guard.

The smirk falls from her face like melting snow. "I'll help you escape," she says, her eyes bulging now with the prospect of the harvest.

"Stand in the circle," I repeat, moving the gun barrel toward the ring of light.

"You can't open the rest of the cells without me. Are you just going to leave your friends locked up?"

"I have Jacob for that. Stand in the circle. Now."

Shaking, she limps to the circle. "You don't have to do this," she says, turning to face me.

I stare at her, the heads-up display of the Lens around the outskirts of my vision. "Yes, I do."

I activate the harvest and the tube appears from the ceiling, surrounding the guard. Seconds later, she begins to scream.

I run to Kina, deactivating her paralysis.

She gasps, coming back to life. Her eyes take in her surroundings. She sees me, tears forming in her eyes and spilling down her cheeks as she sits up. "Oh my god, Luka. Is this real? Is this the Sane Zone?"

I take a moment to soak in her features, her dark eyes, her brown skin, all her beauty and character.

"This is real," I tell her.

"I . . . I . . ."

It's all she can say as her words turn to sobs. I know what she's feeling; the unbearable cruelty of the machine's Battery Project had left me wishing death would come for me day after day, praying that I would lose my mind so completely that I would no longer be aware of the agony. You don't know what true pain is until the only thing you want is a way out of living.

"Can you move?" I ask, lifting Kina's chin until her eyes meet mine. Her black hair has grown since the last time I saw her. A few strands fall on to her forehead.

She nods and pulls both the long needles out of her stomach, and then the thin one that is driven deep into her neck, and finally the one in her wrist.

"We have to release the others," I tell her. She nods again.

I pull her to her feet, and she stumbles, her brain remembering how to command her limbs once more.

"Are you okay?" I ask.

"Wait," she says, and then kisses me without warning.

I feel a burst of joy inside me, like a million stars glowing bright in every fiber of who I am. The way her hand moves to the back of my head, the way her lips feel against mine. If I die right now, all this hell would have been worth it, and I would live through it a thousand times just to feel this for one more second.

She pulls away from me and smiles. "Let's go."

She's moving to the door, and for a second I'm frozen. Staring at the spot where she had been.

"Now, moron. We're escaped convicts again, remember how that goes?"

"Right, of course," I say, snapping out of my stupor.

We move quickly into the corridor. I pick up Jacob's USW rifle and hand it to Kina.

"Who else have they got?" she asks, her eyes scanning the doors.

I point to the cell beside mine. "That's Wren," I tell her, and then point to the two to the left of her cell. "That's Malachai and the next one is Woods."

"What's the plan?" she asks.

"I don't really have a plan so much as a 'get out of the cell and make it up as we go' sort of thing . . ."

"It'll have to do," Kina says, and tries Wren's cell door. "It's locked."

"We need iris identification," I tell her. "I have Jacob."

I move back toward my cell, Kina follows. She laughs when she sees the guard slumped on my bed. "How in the hell did you pull that off?"

"He had too much empathy," I reply. "Keep your gun aimed at him when I take him out of paralysis."

Kina nods and presses the butt of the rifle into her shoulder, resting her cheek against it as she looks down the barrel toward Jacob.

I lean down to the paralyzed guard. "I'm going to take you out of stasis now," I tell him, using their words. "If you try anything, my friend will execute you. Am I understood?"

He can't nod, can't reply, but I know that he understands the stakes. I navigate the menus and deactivate the paralysis. As soon as the needle is fully out of his body he gasps and sits up. He begins to sob in my arms.

"Get it together," I tell him, pulling him to his feet.

"That was . . . that was . . ."

"Believe me, we know," Kina says, still aiming the gun at him.

"This way," I tell him, pushing him out into the corridor, where the screams of the guard in the energy harvest become almost deafening.

"Oh god, oh god, oh, god," Jacob mutters, stumbling toward the cells of our friends.

"Stop," I tell him, outside Wren's cell. "Open it."

Jacob leans down to the iris scanner but stops as the lights dim.

"What is that?" Kina asks, storming up to Jacob and pressing the gun against his head.

"It wasn't me," he says, standing upright, his eyes wide with terror. "I didn't do it."

Red lights begin to flash on all levels of the Block and a siren sounds followed by the voice of Happy. *"Escapees on floor three. Complete lockdown initiated."* The screens beside the cell doors turn red as the doors to Kina's and my cells slam shut.

Kina looks at me, something far beyond simple fear in her eyes. We're both thinking the same thing: Death is a beautiful prospect compared to what our lives have become in the Block. I nod my head and she aims the gun at me.

"Wh-what are you doing?" Jacob stutters.

Kina lowers the gun and walks to me. She kisses me one last time and smiles up at me. "Thanks for trying, Luka."

"It was no big deal." I shrug, and we laugh as she raises the gun to my head once again.

"See you soon, maybe," she says, and her finger presses down on the rifle's trigger.

And nothing happens.

"There are restrictions on our weapons," Jacob says. "They won't fire when aimed at batteries. To stop us accidentally killing assets."

"Assets?" Kina says, turning the gun toward Jacob and marching toward him. *"Batteries?"*

"That's what they call you. Assets, batteries. These are *their* words, not mine."

Kina doesn't slow. She marches forward until the barrel of the gun is pressing into the boy's temple. "You're one of them."

"I'm sorry, I'm sorry," he says, fumbling his words. "No piece of Block equipment will kill you," Jacob continues, his voice straining now. "You're worth too much to the government."

"The government?" Kina scoffs. "You think the government is behind this? You really don't know anything."

The sound of footsteps running up the metal staircases.

"The guns don't work on us," Kina says, grabbing Jacob and turning him toward the oncoming soldiers. "But they work on you, right?"

"Oh shit," Jacob mutters, affirming Kina's assumption.

The first to appear at the top of the stairs are two hosts, their eyes glowing bright white. They are both clearly Alts, both women, tall and athletic. Both clearly benefiting from the pre-life cosmetic improvements that all Alts are eligible for. In addition to their looks and their obvious strength, it is clear that they have Mechanized Oxygen Replenishment systems where their lungs used to be, as they don't appear to be breathing hard at all despite having just run up three flights of stairs. No doubt they have Automated Pulmonary Moderators instead of human hearts as well.

"Inmates 9-70-981 and 9-72-104. Cease all activity and

23

return to your cells," the slightly shorter one orders. Her eyes briefly glow orange, and both our cell doors swing open once again.

"I'll shoot him," Kina says, pressing the gun harder against the side of Jacob's head. "I will kill him."

"This will not change the outcome of the scenario," the taller host says, stepping forward. "Kill him or don't kill him. You will end up back in your cells."

I look over the edge of the railings—a four-story fall probably wouldn't kill me, especially with the enhanced healing that the Alts have equipped us with. I realize that this is a moot point anyway, as there are nets separating every level.

"We're not going back in there," Kina says, her voice shaking.

More footsteps approach and three more soldiers emerge into the corridor. These ones must be Tier Three or Tier Two soldiers: humans who have agreed to help the government—at least they *think* it's the government—in exchange for their lives and a place on the Arc, a shelter in which they can survive the end of the world.

The shorter of the two hosts turns to the first soldier to arrive, a good-looking blond man. "Soldier Ramirez, execute Soldier Smith."

Without hesitating, the Alt aims his gun at Jacob.

"No!" Jacob manages, before the ultrasonic sound wave hits him in the chest and he falls limp and silent.

"You—you shouldn't be able to do that," I say, staring at the bright-eyed host as Kina lets Jacob's body fall to the floor. Galen Rye had informed me that the AI's core coding would not allow it to harm or kill a human or give orders that would lead to the harming or death of a human. This was the very reason Happy and its hosts infected humanity with a virus that led people to kill one another: to bypass its programming.

"Things have changed, Inmate 9-70-981."

There was a trick I used to use back in the Loop, on those long days when loneliness and boredom would creep into my bones. (How little I knew back then; I hadn't even been introduced to true isolation.) The trick was a sort of disappearing act, escapology of the psyche. I would build a world inside my mind, a world in which I was free and happy. This world—a story really—existed dozens of years in the past, long before I was even born, in a time I had only heard about in accounts from my father. I could wander the city, happy in my freedom; I could meet friends who weren't prejudiced, neighbors who weren't forced to live in poverty; I could spend afternoons reading in the sunlight, evenings with my dad and my sister just talking and laughing about nothing at all. But I've lost the trick; I can't find the way into that world. Instead I have to rely on the Sane Zone.

Minutes after being placed into paralysis again, I appear in the white room.

The Sane Zone exists to keep Happy's batteries functioning. The AI gets its power from the energy harvest, and the energy harvested is produced by our fear. If we lose our minds, we won't feel fear and the harvest won't work. So, to combat the isolation, Happy allows us six hours a day inside the Sane Zone.

I crave it like a drug. I know the experience is not real, I know that it exists to pacify and distract my mind, but I need it.

The first part of the Sane Zone is the white expanse that goes on into infinity in all directions. An involuntary sigh escapes my lips as I can move again. It's a strange feeling, knowing that I am still paralyzed, knowing that I am lying in my bed in my cell and yet being here, in this artificial reality.

All the scenarios in the Sane Zone begin with a memory. That memory can be simply a location that I recall vividly, or it can be a recollection of a day or an event. From there I can take it wherever I want. I don't know how it works—if it's nanobots that crawl into my brain, controlled hallucinogens and augmented reality, or some new kind of tech that I can't even fathom—but it's flawless.

Slowly, the white expanse around me begins to fade into color: dim gray at first and then luminous scribbles. It takes a few seconds, but I recognize this place as the ground floor of the Black Road Vertical, the mile-high tower block in which I used to live.

I stare in awe at the neon graffiti paint that lines the concrete walls: gang symbols and skate team logos, names and threats.

"There's hundreds of them!" a voice calls from halfway up the concrete staircase, and the memory floods back to me.

I must be ten or eleven years old; Molly, my sister, is only eight or nine. We used to play here all the time, imagining that the staircase was our own spaceship in which we would battle

27

armies of aliens who wanted to kill humans and mine the Earth for a precious mineral that we hadn't even discovered yet.

I turn to face Molly, who holds both hands up as though gripping a steering column. Tears sting my eyes as I look at my sister the way she had been before Happy had ravaged the planet, before I had been imprisoned, before our parents had died, before everything.

In the real world, Molly had become a clone: a name given to addicts of a drug called Ebb. The last time I had seen her she was high, unconscious, emaciated. But here, in the past, in my resurrected memory, she was the young girl I used to know, my best friend.

The tight curls of her black hair bounce as she rocks with the movements of the imaginary spacecraft. The hand-me-down T-shirt (which used to belong to me) reaches her knees.

"Did you hear what I said?" she repeats, turning her head frantically toward me. "There's hundreds of them. What do we do?"

I take a deep breath, fighting off the emotion of seeing her again, and I get into character. "Captain Molly," I say, my voice coming out young and high-pitched, almost causing me to burst into fits of laughter. "I suggest we retreat; there's simply too many of them."

"Retreat?" Molly says, a grin forming on her face. "Luka, I don't do running away. Charge the cannons."

"Right away, Captain," I reply, and move down two stairs to where the spaceship's cannons are situated.

And then the ground floor of the Black Road Vertical begins

to melt away, the Sane Zone works its weird magic, and we're no longer just pretending to be mid-battle in outer space, we *are* in outer space.

The concrete staircase melds into the futuristic deck of our ship. Stars and planets dot the black sky through the enormous window in front of us. We appear to be just outside the orbit of a large green planet, and in front of us are hundreds of smaller ships.

"They're almost in range," Molly yells, pulling the steering column left, causing the entire ship to tilt.

I fumble with the cannons, winding them into position and pulling the levers that start the charge. "That means we're almost in *their* range," I point out.

"Let them try it," Molly says, maneuvering the ship through the expanse of space. "Our firepower is too much for . . ."

Molly falls silent as an enormous mother ship appears over the horizon of the green planet.

"Okay," Molly says, "now we run."

The rest of the Sane Zone is spent in an epic chase through space. We travel at near light speed, warping time around us. We fight off attack ships, and use our cloaking device to infiltrate the mother ship.

For a while I had been waiting for Happy to turn against me and try to manipulate information out of me, but sometimes the Sane Zone is just the Sane Zone, used to keep our minds rational so that the Harvest can feed off our fear.

Too soon, Happy's voice sounds and tells me that I have five minutes remaining in the Sane Zone. My heart sinks at this, knowing that I have to return once again to the vacuity of the Block.

Molly defeats the final alien, a nine-foot-high insectile monster with advanced weaponry.

I tell her that I love her and that I miss her and she tells me she misses me too.

And then she's gone.

I'm glad that this was one of the occasions that Happy did not try to gather information from me; I'm glad this was simply a preservation of sanity, an illusion of freedom to keep me sane.

The world fades to white and then the white fades back into my cell. Once again I'm motionless and numb, lying on my bed with nothing but six hours of maddening loneliness and boredom ahead of me, and following that, the energy harvest.

It's gotten harder to deal with since the escape attempt, since seeing Kina, since kissing her. Somehow that little spark of hope has left me broken. It hurts to accept that there is nothing as cruel as hope, and I should just let go of it altogether.

Today's offering from the Sane Zone begins with a memory from the Loop.

It's a Wednesday night, or technically 2 a.m. on a Thursday morning. Every week at this time Happy would shut the safety features down to run diagnostics and upgrades for three hours, during which time we were illegally released from our cells by Warden Wren Salter, the Alt girl I had been infatuated with since almost the first day I met her.

I count from one hundred down to zero with my head against the wall, allowing Harvey—my friend and fellow inmate—to hide. I know where he has hidden because it's my memory: He is in Malachai's cell, and in reality Malachai had found him first and yelled at him for knocking over his pile of comic books, but in the Sane Zone, when I enter Malachai's cell, it shifts slowly into a jungle in which Harvey is hiding high in the trees, no longer needing the crutches that he relied on in life.

It makes me sad to see Harvey again. He was one of the first, maybe even *the* first, to be infected by Happy's killer virus. He was turned into a Smiler, and he died falling from the dividing walls of the Loop's outdoor yard while trying to attack Kina in his altered mental state.

After an adventure in the imagined jungle, running from enormous wildcats, avoiding poachers, and freeing trapped rhinos, I'm returned to the cell I never left and suffer six more hours of paralysis. After that I'm put into the energy harvest. And so it goes, on and on.

I don't sleep in the Block; instead I go into a sort of fugue state where reality slips away. I think of it as sleep mode.

I'm wrenched out of sleep mode every day by the guards who drag me to the center of the room.

For twelve hours I fight against the hell of the harvest, feeling the sweat pour off me, feeling unparalleled terror, certain that I'm dying, that I'm falling, that I'm burning, choking, drowning.

And then, finally, it ends, and I'm put back into paralysis.

The Sane Zone begins. Today, a memory of my mother. Singing along with our favorite songs, neither of us able to carry a tune at all but not caring one bit. This memory turns into an enormous rock concert with a crowd of thousands.

And then it ends, and I enter sleep mode again.

Twelve hours of the harvest.

Six hours inside the Sane Zone: a memory of school friends jumping into the river on a summer day turns into a scuba diving adventure, exploring ancient shipwrecks and underwater caves.

Six hours of sleep mode.

The same routine . . .

Day after day . . .

It never ends.

The six hours after the Sane Zone ends, as I wait for the energy harvest to begin . . . those are the loneliest. If I can't slip into sleep mode, if—for some reason—my cruel brain won't switch off, I find myself in a world where time refuses to pass, where my fracturing mind replays the greatest horrors of my life: the boy falling from the roof of the Black Road Vertical; being dragged to the Loop; being almost eaten alive by rats in a train tunnel; being chased through the homeless villages by Smilers; the barbaric stays of execution known as Delays; the war in Midway Park.

The memories run on repeat in my mind. The more I beg them to stop, the more vivid they become, the more I begin to feel the teeth of the rats sinking into my skin, the panic in my heart as the Smilers closed in, the heartbreak as my friend Blue died in the mud.

These thoughts have been cycling for well over a day now. And when the Sane Zone begins, I know almost immediately that the nightmare isn't over. Something isn't right.

The white room fades back into my own cell in the Block. There is no needle stuck in me, no paralysis.

I sit up and face the cell door.

"What's going on?" I whisper into the room, and my breath comes out in clouds of mist. It's cold in here, ice cold.

My cell door creaks open and Mable slips into the room.

Mable had been the last inmate freed from the Loop. She had been eaten alive by rats in the Dark Train tunnels when I was unable to save her.

Mable walks slowly over to me and crouches into my field of vision.

"Luka," she whispers, "why did you let me go into the tunnels?"

I want to reply, I want to tell her that I'm sorry, that I wish I had stopped her, but suddenly I can't speak, suddenly I'm forced by the Sane Zone to silently watch.

"It hurt," she says, and now lesions are beginning to appear on her arms, her neck, her face. "It hurt when they killed me."

I see something bulging at her throat, something scrabbling beneath the surface, and then the blood-soaked snout of a tunnel rat pokes through.

"It hurt!" she screams. "It hurt when they bit into my skin, when they chewed my eyes out, when they burrowed into me. It hurt! It hurt!"

I want to scream. I want to look away. I can't.

Mable's cries turn into croaks as more open wounds criss-cross over her body. And finally, as she collapses to the concrete floor of my cell, she disappears.

Even though I know this is a simulation, even though I know that this is just the Sane Zone, and in reality I'm still paralyzed, lying in this very bed in this very cell, I can feel my heart pounding in my chest.

I wait in the silence, hoping that there is no more.

What the hell was that? I think. *What's going on? Where are the memories? The adventures?*

Maddox Fairfax blinks into existence before my eyes, leaning down into my face. The last time I had seen my old friend was here in this very cell. He was the first host, the first human that Happy had managed to upload itself into.

"Kill me, Luka. Kill me, please. You have to kill me, for god's sake!" he screams into my face, the same words he had spoken to me when Happy had allowed the real Maddox to come up for air.

Maddox then turns to the wall and begins to beat his head against the hard concrete over and over again. I can't see him, and even if the Sane Zone would allow me to turn my head, I wouldn't watch. Bits of blood and brains and bone begin to cascade down through my field of vision.

He is replaced by Catherine and Chirrak, two young inmates from the Loop who died as Smilers after being experimented on by Happy. They used to chase each other around the prison when Wren let us out of our cells on Wednesday nights. They had crushes on each other but were too young, too immature to know how to say it out loud, so they resorted to playground games. Inside I'm smiling as I watch the kids run back and forth across my field of vision. And then, when Catherine drags Chirrak to the ground and begins clawing at his neck, tearing open veins with a frantic grin on her face, I realize that—in this vision—they are still Smilers, still trying to destroy each other.

These nightmare apparitions continue to come and go. Blue,

Harvey, my dad. All of them distorted and frenzied, mocking and threatening. A parade of insanity sprung like a well from my own mind, broadcast before my eyes by the Sane Zone.

And then, finally, the cell door opens once again.

Oh god, I think, *oh god, oh god, what is it this time?*

My mother sits down on the floor in front of me. Her smile, her kind eyes, they stop time and for a second I feel happy.

No! I tell myself. *Do not fall for it, do not let those bastards get to you.*

My mom had been the first of the people I love to die. Killed by a disease my family couldn't afford to even diagnose. Her body had been carried away in a black plastic sheet by a coffin drone.

Her hands begin to move, signing words to me.

I'm so sorry.

I feel tears coating my eyes. The paralysis lifts, and I'm able to move my hands to reply.

Sorry for what? I ask.

Everything. For leaving you alone, for all the pain you have faced, for all the people you have lost, she replies, her hands moving fast, her eyes never leaving me.

It's not your fault, I reply. And I'm lost now, barely aware of how far I've fallen away from the knowledge that this isn't real.

I hate them, Luka, for what they've done to you, for what they do to you day after day. They are cruel.

And the tears fall from my eyes now, spilling down my cheeks until I can taste the salt of them in my mouth. *I don't know how much more I can take, Mom.*

She stands and throws her arms around me. I hold her tight, my body convulsing as I let all the pain of the years since I was imprisoned flow through me.

My mom gently pushes me back and signs again. *I can make it go away, Luka. I can make them stop.*

What do you mean? I ask.

The harvest, the paralyses, the vicious tricks they play; I can make it all stop. You'll be a prisoner still, but they'll leave you alone.

How?

Tell them, Luka; tell them where your friends are. Tell them where the Missing are. I know, I know—it's not right, it's not fair, it's a horrible thing to have to do. But, Luka, in the long run it won't make a difference. Happy will find them either way, so why shouldn't you benefit? I love you so much and I can't bear to see them take you apart like this.

I feel my hands begin to move into the shapes that would disclose the locations of Pod and Akimi and Igby and Pander. I see the eagerness in my mother's eyes, and finally a voice far off inside me screams loud enough for me to hear. This is not real. My mother died three years ago. This is a projection generated by Happy to trick me.

Go away, I say with my hands.

Luka, my son, please . . . she replies, her hands moving slower now, sadness falling over her face.

Go away. You are not my mother.

And now it's her turn to cry. I try to build a wall between us but the sight of my mom crying—even though I know it's not real—crushes me.

I'm trying to protect you, she says.

You're not real.

I love you.

You're not real.

I love you.

I will never tell you where they are.

The vision of my mother stops crying and smiles. She opens her mouth and speaks aloud. "One day you will tell us, Luka Kane."

"I'll die before I tell you anything," I reply.

"No. We will not allow that."

"We'll see."

"We will."

And with that, my mother is gone, fading out of existence once again. And for the next three or four hours, I sit there in the silence of a replica cell, and wait for the routine to begin once more.

I no longer want to simply let go of hope; I want to kill it, I want to burn it, I want to bury its ashes.

Ever since Happy tried to scare the location of my friends out of me with the apparition of my mother, there has been no Sane Zone. I think it's been four days, based on the guards' shift pattern, but time no longer feels real. Hours stretch out into infinity, and the days never end.

I'm a few hours into today's harvest when I feel my sanity begin to shift and slip. For a brief moment I'm certain that none of this is real. I'm certain that I died a thousand lifetimes ago and this is purgatory, a perpetual punishment for something unforgivable I did in life. The thought makes me laugh, a shrill, shrieking sound that rings out into the glass tube, surrounding me. I grip hold of reality and embrace the chaos and the anguish of the harvest, and then I ask myself why. *Why? Just let yourself go.*

I feel sad in this moment. Giving up on your sanity is giving up on who you are; it's a unique kind of suicide.

I tell myself that if I haven't lost my mind by the end of this harvest, then today is the day I let myself drown in the tube. I have thought about it many times, exhaling all the air from my body at the moment the tube fills up and then waiting for my lungs to reach breaking point. At that moment I'll inhale the chemical-laced water and die.

Again, a burst of laughter slips from my mouth.

Forty-nine, I think. *Forty-nine days is as long as I could survive in the Block.*

My laughter subsides into bursts of giggles, sending strings of saliva against the clear glass. I watch the spit forming into the silhouette of an island, and then rolling into amorphous shapes as it falls slowly down the tube.

For a while my mind is nothing but panic as the harvest ramps up. I have flashes of moments in my life, vivid and bright.

And then the panic subsides and I'm left, drained and depleted, on the floor.

All right, I think, *I'm still here. Still sane as far as I can tell. Time to die.*

The water rushes in, and I'm not scared. Instead I'm relieved. All of this will soon be over.

I brace myself as the water fills the tube. And then I do it; I exhale until it feels like my lungs are folding in on themselves and I sink to the bottom.

Through the clear water, I see my cell door open.

No, too soon, I think. *The guard isn't supposed to come in until after the water has drained.*

Two figures slip into my cell and my fractured mind makes me see them as Pander and Kina.

Somehow I find an extra millimeter of breath in my burning lungs and I laugh again, embracing the madness.

What if it's real? a voice from the final reserves of hope asks.

It's not. It's not real.

But what if it is?

The Pander mirage raises a long-handled ax over her shoulder, and I have time to think, *What is she going to do with that?* before she swings it hard and fast at the harvest tube.

The glass spiderwebs under the blow. I watch the cracks fragment and join other fractures, and I think I understand; I think this is my insanity manifesting itself into a delusion, the cracks in the glass are the cracks in my—

Pander swings again and this time the ax pierces the glass. I feel the pull of the water forcing its way out.

One more swing and the tube is destroyed completely.

I gasp in air as the water tumbles around me. Small shards of the destroyed tube have dug into my face and my bare chest and I laugh again, exhausted and oxygen-starved.

"Luka, get your shit together!" the Pander delusion commands. And this just makes me laugh harder.

"You're not real," I tell her, looking up into her face, seeing the white symbols tattooed onto her black skin. Her deep blue eyes stare at me.

"Shit, we're too late," the hallucination says, turning to the Kina mirage.

"Luka, get up, we have to go, now!" Kina says.

I laugh again. There is no doubt in my mind that I have finally let go of my grip on reality. I have finally let go of hope, and this is where I have fallen to.

"All right, all right," I say, turning onto my back, feeling more glass slide into my skin. "I'll play along. Where are we going?"

"We're getting you out of here, crazy," the imaginary Kina says as she bends down and grabs my arm.

And when her fingers touch my wrist, I know what's happening, I know that this isn't real, it can't be real. I haven't lost my mind either, though. This is just another attempt by Happy to extract information.

"I'm not falling for it," I mutter, pulling my hand away from Kina.

"Luka, this is real. We have to move, now."

I push myself to my feet and hobble over to my bed, resting on the edge of the frame. "Yeah, sure," I say. "You've gotten better at the whole dialogue thing, Happy, I'll give you that, but I'm not stupid."

It's more than that, though; there are little details in this simulation, like Pander wearing a Block uniform as part of her infiltration into the prison, and the mixed look of panic and excitement in Kina's eyes. I begin to pick bits of glass out of my hands and I watch the tiny wounds heal themselves. Suddenly, Pander is in front of me and I realize that she's not wearing glasses—Happy's got that wrong—then I see her fist plunging toward my face. It connects with my eye socket.

"Fuck!" I cry as the pain shakes through me.

"We don't have time for your shit, idiot. Now get up."

"All right, all right," I say, rubbing my eye. "But I'm still not telling you anything."

I stand up, thinking that the aggressive simulation certainly

47

seems a lot like Pander, and then Kina takes my hands. "Luka, this is real, this is not Happy trying to extract information, this is not the Sane Zone. This is happening."

"Yeah, you would say that," I mutter.

Kina's eyes search mine. It hurts too much to look back, so I concentrate on the glass in my arms.

"The first time we ever spoke," Kina says, "you gave me a book, *The Call of the Wild*. I thought it was great, but the best one was *Never Let Me Go*; I loved that book, and a part of me wondered if I was falling in love with you just because you had been so kind to me."

I stop focusing on the healing wounds of my arms and look up into those beautiful dark eyes. There is silence between us for a moment.

"Don't do this to me," I say, my voice cracking. "Don't make me believe that this is real and then break my heart. I can't do it again."

"The first time we met face-to-face," Kina continues, pulling me to my feet, "was on the station platform while we waited for the Dark Train to take us to a Delay. The guard forgot to close the hatch. It was the first time I had laughed since being imprisoned in the Loop."

"Can you two hurry this up? We're on the clock here!" Pander calls from the doorway.

"And the first time we kissed was right out there," she says, pointing to the corridor outside my room. "That was when I knew I really liked you."

I look at her, and I dare to believe that maybe I haven't gone insane. This time *I* kiss *her*. And when our lips touch, I know, beyond a doubt, that this is real.

"Romeo, Juliet, enough of the rom-com shit. Let's move, right now!" Pander hisses at us.

I look to Pander. She looks older than her thirteen years. The hardships she has been through and the horrors she has seen show in her eyes. She has the ax in one hand and a USW rifle in the other. She reaches into the bag on her back and throws a hat and a jumpsuit at me.

"Put these on. I'm already sick of your gross body."

"Gross?" I say, looking down at my nakedness.

"I don't like dudes," she says. "Why am I explaining this? Hurry up!"

I look at the white prison uniform and for a second I'm transported back to my first day in the Loop. I shake it off and climb into the garment. I then pull the hat low over my forehead to hide the Panoptic, a tiny pinhole camera embedded there.

"Okay," I say, feeling the tide of insanity begin to subside from my mind, "we need to get Woods, Malachai, and Wren," I say.

Pander shakes her head. "No, we're getting out of here, now."

"What are you talking about?" I demand. "We're not leaving without them."

"Yes, we are," Pander says, peeking her head out of my cell and looking both ways along the walkway.

"I'm not leaving them behind!" I tell her, stepping forward on still shaking legs.

"Luka," Kina says, reaching out a hand to touch my own, "Malachai and Woods aren't here."

49

"What?" I ask. "What do you mean they're not here?"

"Their cells are empty. They're gone."

I stare at Kina for a long time, trying to work out what her words mean. "Are they dead?"

"We don't know," Pander says. "All we know is they were transported out of the Block two days ago. That's why we decided to come in early for you and Kina."

I breathe heavily, trying to fight back against the tears that are climbing toward my eyes. "And Wren?" I ask, turning to Pander.

"Luka, the only reason you and Kina have any semblance of sanity left is because of the healing tech inside you, and the Sane Zone."

"Surely Wren has had the Sane Zone too," I say.

Pander shakes her head. "She doesn't have your healing capabilities and they weren't willing to give her the procedure. She was just a short-term source of energy for them."

"What are you saying?" I ask.

"Wren will have lost her mind a month ago. The kindest thing we can do is kill her," Pander says, throwing the ax onto my bed and checking the display on her USW rifle.

"No," I say, pushing past Kina and then Pander.

I limp along the metal walkway, not caring about guards, about cameras, about the noise I'm making as I begin to run to Wren's cell. I pass a tied and gagged guard lying unconscious on the floor.

Malachai and Woods were taken away. Why? To be executed? Did they lose their minds and become useless to Happy? I shake my head hard against the pain of it.

I reach Wren's cell and pull at the handle. It doesn't budge.

I turn to see Pander and Kina moving silently toward me.

"Open it!" I demand, glaring at Pander.

"Luka, there's no—"

"Open the fucking cell, Pander!"

She sighs and leans down until her eye is beside the scanner. Somehow it works and the door lock clicks.

I open it and step inside.

Wren is lying paralyzed on her bed. In the seven weeks that she has been in this place she has wasted away to skin and bone. It's hard to recognize the beautiful Alt I was infatuated with during my time in the Loop. My eyes move to her right shoulder, the space where her arm used to be before it was severed by the automatic hatch in my old cell door. I move quickly, pulling the needles out of her body and then lifting her until she is free of the paralysis.

She gasps as I carry her toward the door, her eyes open in wide, glaring horror, and she begins to scream.

"No! No! No!" Wren cries, over and over again, her voice thick and guttural.

"She's gone, Luka, we need to shut her up," Pander says, walking with purpose toward Wren and shouldering the rifle.

"We are not leaving her, and we are not killing her," I command.

"Look, this hurts me too. Wren was my friend, but this isn't Wren," Pander hisses. "She's going to alert the guards and she's insane, Luka. This is what she would want."

"We can bring her back," I say.

"Listen, Luka: She's been a Smiler, had her arm chopped off, been drugged with drone poison, and used as a battery for seven weeks. There's no coming back from that."

"This isn't a debate, Pander!" I yell over Wren's screams. "She's coming with us."

"For fuck's sake," Pander mutters, letting the rifle hang by its strap. She holds a finger to an earpiece in her left ear and for the first time I realize she's not wearing her hearing aids either. She nods, responding to a voice that I can't hear. "We need to go, now."

"Okay, all right," I say, hoisting Wren up until she's draped over my shoulder. "Let's go."

I walk past Pander and Kina and into the hallway. I move toward the staircase that leads down.

"No," Pander says, grabbing me by the arm. "This way."

As we begin moving toward the staircase that leads up to the top floor, the lights once again dim and Happy's voice comes over the speakers while red lights begin to flash. *"Escapees on floor three, moving toward floor four. Complete lock-down initiated."*

"What's the plan?" I ask as we move toward the top floor of the Block, with no means of escape.

"Keep moving," Pander replies from ahead of me.

I hear the massive doors at the ground-floor level begin to open, and the sound of dozens of running footsteps rise up to meet us. At first they sound solid as the soldiers' feet hit the concrete of the ground floor, and then they turn into echoing rattles as they connect with the metal of the staircases.

Kina, Pander, and I climb to the top floor. I lay Wren down and try to catch my breath.

"We're stuck here," I point out, "there's nowhere to go! Great plan, Pand—"

There's no time to finish my sentence—the great glass roof above us shatters, sending enormous shards glittering onto the nets and down to the ground floor.

The building is now an enormous open-roofed atrium. A flying car lowers itself down inside it until it's parallel with us. I stare openmouthed at the Volta Category 8, the same car (with a few new scratches and dents) that had saved me from certain death on top of the Black Road Vertical, and had crash-landed not long after.

As the last of the glass fragments fall, I see Igby smiling at us from the Volta. He's even thinner than he was before, making me wonder about how my friends have been surviving out there.

"How's things?" he asks, nodding at Kina.

"Not too bad. You?" she replies.

"Eh, fuck it, you know, could be worse," he says, and then turns his attention to me. "Luka, long time no see."

Igby's pantomime is cut short by USW rounds zipping up from below, slamming into the metal of the staircase and the underside of the car.

"Do not kill them," an emotionless host instructs from below. "We may need spares."

"Go, go, go!" Pander calls, shoving Kina toward the vehicle.

Kina climbs up onto the railing and leaps into the back of the Volta 8; still weak from the harvest, she barely makes it inside.

Pander takes Wren from me and goes next, passing the still-screaming girl to Kina, who drags her inside.

I follow Pander, climbing up onto the railing just as Kina did. I gauge the distance between myself and the car and propel myself forward, forcing the haggard muscles in my legs to work, but something is wrong. I feel an impact in the calf of my right leg at the same time as I hear the USW round screeching through the air. The ultrasonic wave enters my skin, distorting and tearing through muscle and meat, into my shin bone. I cry out in pain and my forward momentum falls to almost nothing. I feel as though I'm hanging in midair.

My hands windmill in front of me, reaching for the car, then grasping for anything and finding nothing. I'm going to fall. I'll land in one of the nets and I'll be taken back to my cell once again.

All of this happens in the space of a second. And just when I know all is lost, a hand wraps around my wrist, gripping me with immense strength.

I look up and see Pod, an expression of grim determination on his face.

"Go!" I hear Pander call, and the car lurches upward into the air, back through the shattered roof.

I look down at my right leg. From below the knee it looks like a sock full of billiard balls. The damage done by the ultrasonic wave hurts like hell.

We exit into the black night air and begin speeding toward the city.

I bite down hard against the pain that emanates up through

my knee and into my thigh, and I look up at the millions of stars above us. For a second I forget the agony and the fear, and I'm lost in wonder.

The car takes a steep right turn and I'm brought back to the present.

"Pull me up," I yell to Pod, who grins back.

"No point," the enormous, broad-shouldered boy calls back.

"What do you mean?" I ask, feeling the cold air rush around me, pain sparking up my shattered leg. "What if your hand slips?"

"That's sort of the plan," Pod says, and then he releases his grip and I'm falling once more.

A sense of disbelief rolls through me, and I have time to think, *Happy got to him. Happy uploaded itself into Pod and now he's killed me.*

The logic is flawed, but there's no time to acknowledge that as I hit water and whoosh deep below the surface.

My broken leg bends the wrong way and I almost black out from the sudden burst of agony.

For a few seconds I don't know which way is up, and then I'm kicking with my one good leg through the ice-cold water, swimming for the surface.

I break through and gasp in oxygen. All around me my friends burst to the surface too. I look up to the sky and see the taillights of the Volta flying across the city, on and on until it's no longer visible.

"Shame," I hear Igby say. "I really liked that car."

I look around and see Kina, Pander, Igby, and Pod, who is carrying Wren. Wren has fallen silent now, but her eyes move mistrustfully from one of us to the next.

"Come on," Pod says, rolling onto his back to keep Wren above the water and kicking with his legs.

We follow, making it to the edge of the enormous body of

water. I have to turn and hoist myself backward onto the banks. I sit there for a minute, watching my leg heal, feeling the pain dissolve away as the bone fragments fuse into place.

"Okay," Igby breathes, and now that his wet clothes are clinging to his body, I can really see how slim he is. He leans forward with his hands on his knees as water drips from him onto the concrete embankment. "That should buy us some time. Happy's minions will be searching for that car for the next hour; the autopilot will take them as far away from us as possible."

"So, you know?" I ask. "About Happy? About how it took over the government, the world? About how it's uploading itself into human hosts?"

"We know a lot of things," Igby replies. "Can't say too much now with your Panoptic working—the cameras might be covered, but the mics still work. I'll tell you everything we've found out later. For now, we need to keep moving."

"Where the hell are we?" I ask.

"Can't say," Pander replies, touching her finger against her forehead.

Pander takes off her jacket and wraps it around Wren, who is shaking from the cold. Clearly she had not intended on saving her, as she did not bring a third jumpsuit for her to wear. She does, however, pull out a hat from her pocket and places it low over Wren's head, hiding the Panoptic camera.

"We have to keep moving," Pod says once Wren is ready to go.

We take off again, following the path alongside the lake or reservoir or whatever it is. Pod carries Wren in his arms; her breathing is fast and shallow, and her eyes are still as wide and terrified as before.

We walk, moving quickly and quietly, until we reach a boarded-up old building that looks as though it used to be a place of business once upon a time. Igby walks up to the wooden slats that board the old doorway and knocks three times slow and twice fast.

The boards begin to fall away and Akimi's face appears in the gap. Her sharp, beautiful features break into a smile and she ushers us inside.

I follow Kina in and look around. The place is a perfectly preserved coffee shop that looks as though it closed for business eighty or ninety years ago. The prices above the counter are still in old-fashioned dollars and cents instead of Coin.

Suddenly, Akimi's arms are wrapped around me, hugging me tightly.

"Luka, thank the Final Gods," she whispers, her Region 70 accent turning *thank* into *think*. "We thought we'd be too late, we thought they'd take you away like Malachai and Woods."

"It's great to see you too, Akimi," I say, feeling my heart swell as my old friend holds me close.

She releases her grip and then hugs Kina.

"Come on," she says, letting go and wiping tears from her eyes, "we have to move."

She walks behind the counter of the old café and lifts open a trapdoor that leads to a basement level. There is no ladder or staircase, so she lowers herself down until she is hanging by the arms and then drops into the darkness.

A few seconds later a flashlight comes on and Igby follows her down. Pod lowers Wren into the basement; Akimi and Igby guide her to the floor and then help Pod down.

Kina and I are alone now in this dark and dusty old place.

"I can't believe we're out of the Block," she says, her voice hoarse.

"I know," I reply. "I keep waiting for the simulation to end, to wake up in my cell."

"It *is* real, isn't it?" she asks, a look of anxiety in her eyes.

"I think so," I tell her.

She nods and then lowers herself into the basement.

It is real, I tell myself, *it is real*.

I grab hold of the edge of the opening, and then drop down.

In the glow of the flashlight I can see the smallish room is maybe twenty by twenty feet. Boxes of old stock are piled up and a small desk sits in the corner. There is a hole hammered through one of the brick walls.

Igby walks to the desk and I see a contraption with loose wires hanging out of it. He flips the device open and a light comes from a screen within.

"Is that a laptop?" I ask, staring at the obsolete piece of machinery.

"Yeah," Igby says. "Can you believe—?" He swears and yells as his hand brushes one of the loose wires, shocking him.

"You okay?" Pod asks.

"Fine, fine. Let's go." Igby picks up the laptop and walks toward the hole in the wall. He steps through and we all follow.

We find ourselves in a small gap between two walls. Ahead

there is a second hole big enough to enter; we climb through and now we're standing on an ancient subway platform with an ancient subway train sitting on the tracks.

"What the hell?" Kina breathes, looking at the antiquated red-and-white train, covered in old, dull graffiti.

"Just wait," Pod says, smiling as he moves with Igby toward the driver's cab.

Igby climbs into the cab while Pod climbs down in front of the train.

I move up the platform until I can see what Igby's doing. Inside the cab is a mess of wires coming out of the dashboard, and Igby works fast to connect them to the laptop's circuitry.

I crouch down to see Pod feeling around under one of the rails. He too produces a wire, this one thick and covered in rubber tubing that has been torn away. He pulls the inner wire into two cables and connects one side to a series of solar-cell car batteries that have been placed in a dugout in the far wall.

Unbelievable, I think, marveling at my friend's dexterity and special awareness. The fact that he's blind and yet can maneuver in such intricate ways amazes me.

"How are you doing down there, Pod?" Igby calls.

"Ready to go. You?"

"Let's do this," Igby calls back, and then leans out of the driver's cab and calls: "All a-fucking-board!"

Pod connects the second part of the wire to the series of batteries, there's a loud pop sound, and the train's lights come on, followed by the electric engine rattling to life in an ascending wheeze.

There's a whooshing sound and the train's doors crash open. Pander drags Wren on board and leaves her sprawled in the aisle before sitting down on one of the old seats, sending a plume of dust into the air. Akimi sits down opposite her.

Again, Kina and I are left dazed by the bizarre events that seem to be unfolding at breakneck pace. We stare, dumbfounded, at the ancient piece of machinery until Igby and Pod lean out of the driver's cab and Pod explains that the batteries should give us nine minutes of drive time.

"In other words," Igby adds, "get on the train!"

We hop on and the doors shut. We take off, slow at first but gathering speed. The sound is immense, a shrieking whistle accompanied by the clatter of the archaic vehicle, which I'm certain is about to disintegrate all around us.

A feeling of excitement rushes through me. This is really happening, I really am free from the Block, and I'm here, alive with my friends.

I sit and smile, and feel enormous relief wash over me until there are tears in my eyes.

Don't, a scared voice inside me begs. *Not yet. Do not let hope kill you.*

But this is different; you can't fake reality, not to this level, I'm certain of it . . . but still, that voice.

The train hits a fast corner and rocks violently. Wren—still lying on the floor where Pander left her—begins to shake. She sits up, looks at each of us individually, and it's as though she's seeing us for the first time all over again. She backs away, shuffling

61

on her hands and feet until she is pressed against the far side of the carriage. She pushes her one remaining hand against an ear to try and block out the noise.

"Get away from me!" she screams, her matted blonde hair falling from beneath her hat and into her face. "Get away from me, get away, get away!"

"Wren," I say, moving quickly through the rocking carriage and kneeling beside her, "it's me, it's Luka."

"Don't you come near me! Don't you come near me! I won't go with you! I won't, I won't!"

"Wren, no one's trying to hurt you, no one's trying to do anything that isn't in your best interests. We want to help you; we want to get you far away from the Block, that's all."

"I don't know you," she hisses, and then spits in my face.

I sit back, in a state of shock that my friend would do such a thing. I wipe the wetness from my cheek. "Wren, it's going to be okay. Everything is going to be okay."

The electric sound of the train begins to fade out and we start to slow down. The lights inside the carriage begin to flicker.

"What's going on?" Kina asks.

"The geniuses up front must've got their calculations wrong. We've run out of power," Pander explains.

The train rumbles to a stop, the clicks and clacks—that I'm sure must be audible aboveground—begin to slow, and the lights go out completely. We jerk to a halt.

"What now?" I ask.

Seconds later the doors are being hauled open by Pod and Igby.

Igby shines his flashlight into the carriage. "Right, so I misjudged that a bit, but we're close, maybe only a ten- or fifteen-minute walk, so let's get moving."

Pander leads Wren onto the tracks, shuffling between the tunnel walls and the train's exterior. Kina follows, and then Akimi.

I stand in the doorway of the train, looking into the blackness, and I can feel my hands begin to shake as flashbacks of the last time I was in a train tunnel spark inside my mind. I remember the rats so vividly that I can almost feel their teeth sinking into my skin once again; I can almost smell their damp rotting stink and hear their shrill squawks.

"Luka, come on," Kina says, stopping to look back at me.

I nod and jump shakily down onto the tracks. I squeeze myself between the train and the wall until I'm in front, standing between the two rails. I want to walk forward, I want to follow my friends into the darkness, but I can't make my legs move. My heart is racing, I can hear blood rushing in my ears, and I feel as though I can't breathe. The air down here is so old and stale that it must be toxic. I can feel sweat beading on my forehead. What if something bad happens inside these tunnels? What if I die in this darkness? What if . . .

A hand grabs mine. I look down at the fingers interlaced in mine, and then up at Kina's face. Her eyes look deep into mine and she smiles. Her smile only ever takes over one side of her face, and she's so beautiful.

My heart slows to its normal pace and I can breathe again.

"Feel like going for a walk?" Kina asks, and her smile broadens.

I take a breath and let it out slowly. "Yes," I tell her. "Yeah, I do."

And we move into the darkness together.

Igby's estimation of ten or fifteen minutes turned out to be off the mark. Half an hour later we're still walking through the darkness.

But I'm feeling calmer now, more in control of myself.

I look around. Wren's shoulder touches the tunnel wall as her scared eyes dart around. Pander stays close to Wren, making sure she's okay. Pod is a few yards ahead, and the rest of the group leads the way.

I let go of Kina's hand and walk quicker to catch up with Pod. Something has occurred to me, a way of making sure, beyond all doubt, that this is reality.

"Hey, Pod," I say, tapping him on the shoulder.

"Luka," he says. "Hey, man, I'm sorry that it took so long to get you out of there. We've been on the move and trying to plan this breakout. It must've been . . . I can't imagine."

"Hey, you came for me, you got me out of there, that's what matters," I tell him. "Pod, this is going to sound strange, but—can you tell me where you and Akimi were during the Battle of Midway Park?"

"Doesn't sound weird at all," Pod replies, smiling.

"It doesn't?"

"Nope. Happy ran simulations on you, right? Tried to extract information by tricking you into thinking certain scenarios were reality?"

"That's right!" I tell him.

"And you figure if I can give you the information that Happy was digging for, it will confirm that this is all real?"

"That's right!" I say again.

Pod laughs. "Man, they must have some crazy tech to sim reality to that level, and they must have exploited your own memories to re-create circumstances and people you know."

"That's right," I say, quietly this time.

"I don't suppose it matters if Happy is listening, seeing as we've all left those hiding places now anyway. Me and Akimi, we were in the diner on the edge of town. Your sister and the rest of the clones were in an old bank underground in the financial district; the rest of the inmates were . . . well, I can't tell you that until we arrive."

And that's it, the final piece of proof I needed to confirm that I am truly free. I try to say thank you, but the words catch in my throat.

Pod puts a hand on my shoulder. "You're out of there, brother, I promise."

I nod and swallow back the tears. There's something else that's been bothering me.

"Hey, how did you manage to grab me?"

"Sorry?"

"When I jumped for the car and I missed?"

"I don't know what you mean."

"I got shot, in the Block, while jumping for the car, and you grabbed me."

"Why wouldn't I have grabbed you?"

"Well, you know, because . . ." Suddenly, I don't want to mention the fact that Pod is blind; it seems somehow rude. "It's just that . . . you're . . ."

"Slow?" Pod suggests.

"No, you're not slow. It's . . ."

"I'm big and clumsy?"

"No, not that . . ."

"I can't think of anything else," Pod says, shrugging his big shoulders.

"Nah, it's nothing," I say, conceding.

"Oh, wait," Pod says, holding a finger up, "because I'm blind?"

"Yes!" I reply, a little too enthusiastically.

"Right, I get it, because I can't see, you think I'm incapable of saving your life?"

"No, no, no, that's not it—"

"You think that because I'm blind, I'm not a valuable member of the team?"

"Not at all, I would never think . . ."

Pod starts laughing and slaps a massive hand on my back. I almost face-plant into the rails. "You are too easy to wind up, Luka," he says through bouts of laughter. "Of course I shouldn't have been able to grab you; I'm blind, for crying out loud. I mean, in perfect silence I might have been able to gauge where you are by your movements, but come on!"

I laugh too, a little less enthusiastically than Pod.

"So, how did you manage it?"

"My eyes are fixing themselves," Pod says. "Slowly, very slowly, but I can see shadows, and—if it's really bright—I can see the outlines of shapes. Pretty soon I'll be able to see faces, and trees, and the ocean. Don't get me wrong, Luka, I hate Happy for what it did to us, to the world, but that last Delay is giving me my sight back."

Of course, I think, *that's why Pander doesn't have her hearing aids or glasses either.* I smile up at my friend. "I'm happy for you, Pod."

And my happiness for Pod only reminds me that I'm free. *I'm free, I'm fucking free!*

My good mood lasts about four seconds before it is evaporated by a sound like the crack of a whip echoing through the corridor, followed by another and another and another.

"What the hell is that?" Akimi asks from ahead of us.

Igby comes sprinting back toward the group as the sounds grow closer, almost booming now. And the darkness of the tunnels seems to withdraw as the sound grows. I turn to face the source, and see, far in the distance, sets of bright lights on the ceiling coming on, one after the other. Some are missing, the ancient bulbs blown, some explode in a shower of embers as electricity flows through them for the first time in decades, but most still work.

Finally, the lights above us burst into thunderous life and then move on ahead, illuminating the once-pitch-black tunnel.

"How?" Igby asks. "We're inside the radius of the scrambler; they shouldn't be able to find us . . ." Igby's eyes grow wide as they settle on Wren. "Where is her hat?" he asks quietly, and then, louder, "When did she take it off?"

We all turn to face Wren, who looks back at us defiantly.

"I don't know," Pander says.

And now there's a new sound in the tunnel, the familiar, high-pitched wail of the subway train.

At once I put all the information together: Happy has tracked us to these tunnels using Wren's Panoptic and has rerouted power back to this old subway system. The train that we were riding on is now racing toward us. The AI has either decided that we are no longer worth the hassle of keeping alive, or they're going to rely on our ability to heal and hope that at least some of us survive being hit by a train.

Pod's head tilts to the side and then he turns to us. "Run!"

I take five steps forward, sprinting on legs that have almost forgotten how to run. And then I notice that Wren isn't moving.

"Wren, move. Come on!"

The tunnel is just wide enough for the train to fit through, there is no room to wait and let the enormous vehicle pass us by, we have to move, and we have to move now.

"Stay away from me, stay away from me!" she screams, her voice rising as the train's screech grows ever louder.

I approach her slowly, not wanting to scare her. "Wren, listen to me. You don't have to like me, you don't have to remember me, but right now you have to trust me. If we don't run, we're going to die. I won't leave without you."

Her eyes dart toward the sound of the oncoming train and then back to me. "I don't know you," she says.

"Yes, you do, Wren. You know me, we're friends, we've been friends for a long time. You looked after me when I needed it the most, and I'm going to look after you now. Please, come with me."

Again, she looks toward the now almost deafening sound, and then back to me. Finally, she nods her head, and we run.

My legs feel leaden and the tunnel feels hot. Running feels the way it does in a dream, like nothing is working the way you want it to. Wren, despite her MOR system where her lungs used to be and her APM where her heart used to be, is slower than me. Weeks of the energy harvest and the paralysis needle have atrophied her muscles to the point that she is stumbling and shuffling along at an agonizingly slow pace.

Up ahead I see that Kina has stopped and is waiting for us, panic in her eyes as she looks behind us to the approaching train.

I keep pace with Wren, encouraging her, trying to ignore the blasting hot air being pushed forward by the approaching vehicle.

We catch up with Kina, who runs alongside us.

"Thirty yards," Kina says, "just thirty yards to the platform."

I can hear the rattle and clatter of the train now, hear the metal wheels rushing along the metal tracks. It must be close, it must be so close.

The air is rushing around us and the squeal and rumble of the train is so loud that I can't hear anything except the approaching death from behind me.

And then the platform is there.

Akimi grabs Wren and drags her up. Pander pulls Kina onto the platform and Igby's surprisingly strong hands grip my forearms and wrench me away from the train, which screams past less than a second later.

Kina and I lie on the platform, gasping for breath. Wren's eyes stare up at the ceiling in shock.

"Holy shit," Kina whispers once the train's thunderous sound has dissipated.

"I hate tunnels," I say, and Kina laughs. Pod joins in, followed by Pander, Igby, and Akimi.

"Pander," Igby says, "you got a spare hat in that bag of yours?"

Pander digs in her bag and produces a new hat. Once again she pulls it low over Wren's head until it covers the camera.

"Hey," I say, asking the question that's been on my mind since Pander told me to cover my Panoptic camera. "Where are your hats?"

"We don't need them," Akimi says, smiling.

"Why not?" Kina asks.

"You'll see," Pod replies.

We walk up a set of ancient and broken escalators that seem to go on forever. Antique advertisements for long-ago theater shows line the walls, along with faded public service posters informing commuters that pickpockets operate in this area.

We make it to a bank of dust-covered ticket barriers and hop over them. Pander looks back to Wren every few minutes to make sure she is still wearing her hat. Eventually, we come to a set of steps that leads up to a boarded-up exit.

"Okay," Pander says, putting her bag on the floor. "This is the tricky part, and we have to move quickly because they have an idea of where we are now." She takes a pad of paper and a pen out of her bag and scribbles a note onto it. She holds it up so Wren, Kina, and I can read it.

Out there is Old Town. Once we're out, move quickly north. There is an open sewage drain between the courthouse and a Church of the Last Religion. Climb down. That's where we'll meet Dr. Ortega.

Still dazed from the whole experience, I almost ask *Who is Dr. Ortega?* But I manage to stop myself just in time. Clearly Pander has written this information down so that the microphones embedded in us won't pick it up.

We climb the concrete steps, and Pod lifts a massive section of fallen wall away from the opening at the top.

One by one we crawl out into the street and move quickly from cover to cover until we are between the old courthouse and the church.

Pander climbs into the open manhole first, followed by Wren and then Kina. Pod goes next and I follow him. Igby is the last down.

At the bottom of the ladder, my feet are submerged to the ankles in cold, dirty water, and I have to crouch inside yet another tunnel. This one is made of brick and is only wide enough for single file. It smells so bad down here that I feel like I'm suffocating, which is doing nothing for my growing sense of claustrophobia.

"This way," Akimi whispers, and leads the way under the city.

We follow the flashlight's beam for ten or so minutes until

we reach a ladder against one side of the tunnel that leads up to another hole that has been made in the brick.

We climb up, exiting the darkness and the smell of the sewer, and enter what looks like an old tiled bathroom.

"What is this pl—" I start to say, but then a woman wearing a surgical mask sticks a needle in my arm. "What the hell?"

I watch as the woman stumbles drunkenly over to Kina and injects her too.

"What is this?" Kina asks.

And by the time she has stuck Wren with a third syringe, the world is fading out. Colors seem to drain away; everything blends to gray and then to nothing.

There are moments of consciousness. I hear a woman with a Region 100 accent speaking, slurring her words.

"For the love of . . . He heals so fast, how am I supposed to operate? Someone bring me another quarter patch."

"No!" Pander's voice now. "No more Ebb; you're operating, for god's sake."

"Why am I taking orders from a child, someone remind me? Christ, these ancient tools, it's barbaric! Where are my robots? My nanotech? And bring me a quarter patch, I work better high, get me a quarter patch."

"You're already high. Just keep working," Pander mutters.

"Every day, *Just keep working, Dr. Ortega! Do what I say, Dr. Ortega!* I could walk away, you know! I could leave, I don't need you."

I try to open my eyes but I'm groggy and numb. The argument between Pander and the Region 100–sounding doctor begins to fade away until I can't understand the words anymore, and then I sleep again.

I awake with a start.

My eyes snap open and I try to sit up, but I can't.

I'm paralyzed. Trapped inside my tiny cell in the Block, unable to move, unable to scream, unable to cry.

The cruelty of Happy has never been in doubt, but that last trick was malicious. And for what reason? Before, Happy had at least tried to extract information from me, but now it's just torturing me for no reason.

If I were able to, I would cry.

I try to remember all the details of what happened. Pander and Kina had come in during the energy harvest and shattered the tube. We had escaped with Wren through the roof, with Igby driving the flying car. Then what? It's already hard to remember, like a dream. The lake, the subway train, the sewer.

It had all been so real, and I had been foolish enough to believe it.

I'm torn away from my thoughts by a sound. I can't turn my head to look, but I'm sure it's coming from the metal door of my cell. A steady clanging sound that is growing in volume.

And then there's a boom, and I'm sure the door has been smashed inward.

Next there are footsteps, slow and deliberate, approaching my bed.

A face slowly appears in my field of vision and my heart begins to race.

"Hello, Luka Kane," Tyco says.

The last time I had seen Tyco Roth was in the moments after he had drugged me with Ebb. His plan had been to separate me from the group, drug me, and then murder me, because he blamed me for the death of his brother. In truth it had been Molly, my sister, who had pushed his brother from the roof of the Black Road Vertical, but she had only pushed him because he was going to shoot her.

I was saved from Tyco's assassination attempt by Shion and Day Cho, a mother and her daughter who survived Happy's plan to wipe out civilization by being high at the time of the chemical drop. Shion had shot Tyco six times. Tyco is dead, I know that, and so this is just another one of Happy's attempts to torture me with nightmarish visions.

"I'm going to kill you, Luka Kane," Tyco says, and then he raises his hand. A knife with a long gleaming blade is grasped tightly in his fist and he brings it down into my chest.

I can't feel it, but I see him struggling to pull the knife free before plunging it down again, and again.

In my peripheral vision I can see blood beginning to pool around my head as Tyco stabs and stabs and stabs, smiling all the while. And I think, *At least it's over now. At least it's all over.*

I gasp in a deep breath and sit up. I can feel the sweat covering my body, and for a few moments I can't tell if this is real or if I'm still dreaming.

I look around. The room is unfamiliar at first, but then I recognize it as the tiled room in which the doctor injected me with a sedative. Tentative hope begins to fill me up, but I push it away. I know that hope—when dashed—is more painful than anything physical.

But it's true, it's real: I am no longer in the Block.

I let out a long sigh that, for a few moments, turns into sobs of pure relief, and then I get myself together and try to remember all that happened.

She was operating on me, I think, and more flashbacks burst into my mind. Delays; the scientific experiments that the government subjected us to in the Loop to push back the date of our executions, various surgeons cutting into my skin, injecting me with viruses so that they could try out experimental cures, slicing out cartilage from my ribs. But what had happened in this room had not been a Delay.

I look around; the tiled room is lit only by the dim light coming through a frosted glass window high up on the far wall.

I'm lying in a bed in the middle of the room. Kina is asleep on another bed on my right and Wren is on a bed on my left.

I look at the stained walls, the plumbing fixtures, the old rotted wooden cubicles against the far wall.

This is a bathroom! I think. *They operated on me in an old bathroom?* And then, *Why were they operating on me?*

On a small stainless-steel table in the corner of the room, I see a set of primitive medical tools: a scalpel; some long, pointed tweezers; a set of forceps that look as though they belong in a kitchen somewhere. All these instruments are covered in blood.

I pull the thin blanket off me and begin examining my body for signs of an operation. Of course, our wounds heal themselves rapidly, but they still leave a mark if the cut is deep enough. I see two long, straight scars up both of my forearms, and I realize that they've removed the electromagnetic cuffs from inside my wrists. Without thinking, my hand reaches up to my forehead where the Panoptic camera should be. I can no longer feel the little bump where the tiny piece of equipment used to sit.

Immediately I feel calmer, less conspicuous, safer. Ironic, really, seeing as the government had forced the Panoptic cameras upon the citizens of the world under the guise of increased safety.

The bathroom door creaks open a tiny bit, and I see Igby peering in.

"Hey," he whispers, "how you feeling?"

"Not bad," I whisper back, climbing down from the bed and

walking toward him. "What time is it?" Igby holds the door open and I step out into the most enormous old library I have ever seen.

I'm frozen for a minute, staggered by the grandeur of the place. Three floors stacked with thousands and thousands of old-fashioned paper books.

"It's almost five p.m. the day after you were sedated," Igby replies, laughing. "You've been out for over a day!"

"What . . . where is this place?" I ask, still gazing at my new surroundings.

"Some dusty old library," Igby replies, shrugging. He points up to the cathedral-style domed glass roof. "That gives us a three-sixty view. If Happy sends any of its minions our way, we'll know about it."

I squint up to the roof and see Akimi sitting in a makeshift crow's nest. It appears to be made out of an office chair suspended by a dozen or so ropes. Akimi spins slowly around, scanning the city.

"Wow," I say.

"And that," Igby says, pointing to a brand-new, pristine Volta Category 9 sitting in the middle of the mosaic tiled floor, "is my baby. And our getaway plan."

"You sure do love flying cars through glass roofs," I say.

"It's both badass and a fuckload of fun, Luka," he says, grinning at me. "Although I might have to replace it with something bigger now that there are more of us."

I turn slowly around, taking in the place. All the windows (barring the glass domed roof) have been covered by metal sheeting that has been riveted to the walls. The doors too are barred shut in this same manner, but I'm not really focusing on the safety features; my eyes are wandering over the shelves of books. A section marked REFERENCE, one marked CHILDREN'S, another reads SCI-FI, MYSTERY, FANTASY, there's a door marked PERIODICALS, a massive semicircular desk near the front entrance, and a rack full of ancient graphic novels, and that's just the first floor.

"How did you find this place?" I ask, unable to hide the awe from my voice.

"We sort of stumbled upon it when we were escaping after Midway," Igby replies. "She was already here, though." He points to the doctor who operated on me. She has created a bed for herself using hundreds of books and is snoring loudly. I see half an Ebb patch stuck to her wrist.

"Who is she?" I ask.

"She is the mad doctor. Dr. Abril Ortega. She loves Ebb and is constantly high, but she's a great surgeon. She removed all our Panoptics."

"You found her here?" I ask.

"Yep, stoned out of her mind. She kept saying, 'They'll kill me for what I've done. I destroyed nearly all of it.' We still don't know what the hell she was talking about. I don't think she even knows."

The doctor stirs at this and opens one eye. "Are you creepy little boys watching me sleep?"

"No," I say, taken aback by the bleary accusation.

"Why not? Am I not beautiful?"

"I . . . I . . ." I look to Igby, who shrugs. "You are beautiful, but I wasn't watching you sleep."

"Good," she says, turning over to face the other way. "Watching someone sleep is not romantic. Besides, I'm thirty years old—far too old for you, little boy."

I turn again to Igby, who rolls his eyes and mouths, *She's forty-five*. We walk away toward the far side of the big room.

"So, she performed the same surgery on you guys too?" I ask.

"Yeah," Igby replies. "No more cuffs, no more cameras. She can't remove the heart device—it's embedded and woven through a bunch of arteries and stuff. Even with our healing it would kill us if she tried."

"A brand-new friend!" an odd, cartoonish voice yells out from somewhere above me.

"Oh Final Gods, give me strength," Igby mutters.

"What the hell was that?" I ask, still looking for the source of the voice.

And then from the third floor I see a blur of lights zipping toward me.

"Apple-Moth, power down!" Igby calls out, but the drone—which is no bigger than a sparrow—doesn't seem to hear, and before I know it, it's spinning around and around my head.

"Hi, new friend! I'm Apple-Moth, what's your name?"

"Umm, what?" I manage.

Igby steps forward and raises his voice. "Apple-Moth, power down!"

The drone—which I now recognize as a companion drone—ignores him and continues speeding around and around my head. "I love making new friends! What's your name? Do you wanna hear a joke?"

"Apple-Moth!" Igby screams, and the drone stops dead, hovering in front of my eyes.

"Oh, hi, Igby!" Apple-Moth says, a note of caution in its computerized voice.

"I told you to power down."

"But I don't want to power down!" the drone replies, sounding sulky now.

"I don't care, I've asked you to power down, so do as you're told."

Apple-Moth, whose lights had been glowing yellow, fades to an angry pink. The drone zips over to Igby and projects the face of an angry ogre over Igby's own face. The effect is so convincing that I'm actually taken aback for a second.

"Whoa!" I say.

"What is it?" Igby asks. "Is the stupid drone using its stupid face-changer app?"

I laugh as the ogre face moves perfectly in time with Igby's words.

"Dammit, Apple-Moth, power down!" the Igby ogre commands.

"Fine!" the drone says, and floats moodily to the floor, the ogre face fading away from Igby's.

Apple-Moth's lights go off completely, except for one tiny red light blinking near the base.

"What on Earth is—" I start, but Igby holds up a hand to silence me.

"Apple-Moth," Igby says, glaring down at the small, insectile machine, "I know you haven't powered down."

There are a few seconds of silence, and then the companion drone replies, "Yes, I have."

"How are you replying if you've powered down?" Igby demands. The drone is silent. "Well?"

"Fine!" the drone replies finally. And this time, the small flashing red light goes out too.

I look up at Igby. "What?" is all I can manage through my confusion.

"That," Igby says, sighing, "is Apple-Moth."

"And . . . why?" I ask.

"We plan on using it for missions beyond the scrambler," Igby says, as if I'm supposed to understand what that means.

"Excuse me?"

"I've set up a surveillance scrambler with a three-mile radius. It pretty much makes us invisible to Mosquitoes and any other tech that Happy is scanning the city with," he says, using the slang term for surveillance drones. They got the name *Mosquitoes* due to their size and the sound of their high-pitched solar engines. "But eventually we'll need to go out farther than the three-mile radius, and when we do, we'll need to take a mobile scrambler with us—Apple-Moth. We modified it to include a cloak, a jammer, and—if all else fails—a simple laser light to blind cameras."

"All right," I say, "and what's with the personality?"

"It was a kid's toy back before, you know, the world ended. It actually runs on Happy tech, but we managed to disconnect

81

it from the network. Pod has tried to erase its personality but, I swear, it just gets more and more annoying each time we try to delete it."

"You two?" I say. "The guys who hot-wire cars and make ancient trains run as if by magic; you can't erase a toy's personality?"

"Shut up!" Igby replies, shoving me. "It's impossible!"

"Yeah, sure," I say, laughing.

"Fuck off," Igby says, picking up the tiny drone and placing it on a table. He smiles. "Come over here, I want to show you something."

Igby leads the way to what must have been a checkout desk at some point in the distant past. He jumps and slides over the varnished wooden desktop. I walk around and watch him remove a thin rug from the floor and place it on a chair. He begins to remove floorboards until a trapdoor is revealed.

"Check this out," Igby says, grabbing the same laptop he'd used to start the subway train and descending a set of wooden stairs into the darkness.

I follow him down and find myself in a narrow corridor that leads to something up ahead that I can't quite make out.

"What is this?" I ask.

"This is where we go if the Mosquito scrambler fails and Happy comes looking for us," Igby says, his face lit by the screen of the laptop.

He types in a command and the circular metal door up ahead of us begins to unwind, like a complex puzzle, until it is fully open.

"What . . . what is it?" I ask.

"A panic room," Igby says, stepping inside.

I follow him into the metal-walled room. It's long and narrow; the walls are thick steel with benches and shelves molded into the metal. There are cans of food and bottles of water lining the shelves, along with flashlights and a few books. In the far right corner, there is a toilet that is reminiscent of the metal toilets in the Loop.

"How long did it take you to build this?" I ask.

"About two weeks. Me and Pod made it. When we first got here it was a lot easier to get supplies from the city. Happy hadn't mobilized its armies properly yet, so we got all the steel and plumbing easily enough."

Igby leans over to a sink and spins a tap. Fresh water comes out and drains down a sink.

"This is really impressive!" I say.

"Yeah, I'm really good at this shit," Igby replies, shrugging. "I have to fix a glitch with the door, but other than that this place is basically bombproof. It even has an intercom so you can speak to people in the main room." He presses a button on the wall and I hear a microphone click on.

"Let's hope we never need this room," I say.

Igby nods and then leads the way out of the panic room, up the stairs, and back into the library. We pass by some ancient radio equipment that Igby tells me Pander has been using to communicate with survivors from other regions.

"How many survivors are there?" I ask.

"Fewer and fewer every day," Igby replies. "Happy's soldiers are taking them out by the hundreds. Smilers get some of them too. Regions fourteen and eighty-three went quiet yesterday."

I think about this, what it means: rebels being killed for trying to stand up against Happy's plan to eradicate the world of humans. Killed for fighting against Happy's assessment that humanity is a cancer. Killed for daring to exist in the new age of machine logic.

We move over to a long desk. One of the oldest pieces of technology I have ever seen outside of a museum sits in the middle of the counter. It's an old desktop computer with an honest-to-god console tower beside an outdated liquid crystal display monitor.

"What a piece of junk," I say as we approach.

"This piece of junk is the reason you're alive. It's how we knew where you were being kept, how we got Pander inside the Block and her iris recognized on the scanners. It's how we got you out, and it's how we're scrambling the signal of all Mosquitoes within the three-mile radius."

"About that radius," I reply, "isn't that dangerous? Won't they just attack the center?"

"Oh, Luka, Luka, Luka, it's an oscillating radius; the signal is bounced off several satellites . . . it doesn't matter, I've got it all figured out."

Igby smiles, slightly patronizingly, and opens a program on the computer using a handheld piece of plastic hardware that controls a cursor on the screen. I'm pretty sure they used to call it a mouse. I have to hold back a laugh at this. The console begins to whir and bleep as the program powers up.

"Sounds like it's about to take off," I say.

"I've made a lot of modifications," Igby says, "but it still struggles to handle what I need it for. Pod and Samira will be back soon—they'll have the processor I need to speed things up. When that happens, we'll know exactly where Malachai and Woods are."

I'm about to ask who Samira is when I notice a small metal box with four thin wires coming from it sitting beside the PC's tower and reach for it. "What's this?" I ask.

Igby grabs my wrist and holds it firmly. "Do not touch that," he says slowly. "We cannot let it see us."

"What? Can't let it see us? What does that mean?"

"It was the only way," Igby says, and turns back to the screen, where lines of unintelligible code scroll from the top down.

"Only way to what?"

Igby takes a deep breath. "We caught one of the hosts. One of those torch-eyed fucks. Pander killed him and we took one of his eyes. I hooked this old PC up to it, and we keep it inside that box so that it can't see where we are and tell the rest of the hosts."

"That's . . . genius," I say. "I mean, it's brutal, but it's genius."

"I wrote a program that can decode some of the information we get from the eye. It takes ages and the machine can only handle it for a few minutes at a time. We found out that Happy is behind the Smilers, that it has uploaded itself into the world's leaders, that—until recently—it couldn't order others to hurt humans."

"Yeah," I say, "I saw that firsthand. I watched one of the hosts command an Alt soldier to shoot another Alt soldier. It's not good."

"Not good at all," Igby agrees. "It won't be long before they can inflict harm upon humans themselves."

The thought sends a shiver down my spine. I try not to dwell on it. "What else did you find out?"

Igby continues, "That they were keeping you in the Block and using you like batteries. When we found that out we started planning a way to get you out. It took a long time, but we did it. I'm just sorry we couldn't get there in time to save Malachai and Woods."

"When will we know what happened to them?" I ask.

"I'm working on it," Igby says, "but it's slow, really slow. The latest information I've managed to decode is basically an equation about how fast Happy sent that subway train after us to give it the best chance of incapacitating us and not killing us."

"Jesus," I whisper.

"This is how we're going to do it, Luka, this is how we're going to bring Happy down."

"Is this dangerous?" I ask, glancing at the ancient computer. "I mean, will Happy figure out that you're listening in to its plans?"

"No, that's the beauty of using this antique computer—Happy can't even see it."

"Can we use it?" I ask. "Can we use it to—I don't know—upload a virus into Happy?"

Igby laughs. "Firstly, all I can do with this tech is watch and read code; secondly, there isn't a computer virus strong enough to touch Happy."

"Right," I reply, dejected. "Do we have a plan, then?" I ask.

Igby sighs. "We had a lot of plans: infiltrate the Arc; find a cure for the remaining Smilers; search the city for surviving Ebb users. But we can't do any of that without an army. We were going to free and recruit the Block inmates, but they all started dying a few weeks ago."

"I know," I say. "I saw the empty cells. Why is that? I thought they had the same healing tech as us. They were part of the same trials."

"They gave the Block inmates one variant of the drug and the Loop inmates another. I guess they were trying to figure out which one worked the best . . . turns out it was ours."

I shake my head. I feel sick knowing that Happy has used us all as lab rats, not caring about who lived or died.

"So, without the Block inmates, how do we build an army?"

"We need the Missing," Igby replies. "The citizens of the city who disappeared in twos and threes over the last five years. We know they're out there somewhere, but we don't know where. Without them we don't stand a chance. We lost the war before it even began; we're nothing more than the last surviving soldiers. All we can do is keep on running away, keep on hiding, keep on surviving."

"Until what?" I ask.

"Until we can't anymore."

"So, we find the Missing or we die?"

"Pretty much."

"They must be hidden, like us," I point out. "Camped out somewhere with a surveillance scrambler thingy too."

"No, that's the thing," Igby replies, "the scrambler is easy to detect. Happy knows we're scrambling the signal; it just doesn't know where from. I've scanned the whole region for similar tech and only found ours. Wherever they are, they're off the grid and invisible."

"But there were hundreds of them," I point out. "At Midway Park, there were hundreds . . . How hasn't Happy found them? Where are they?"

"That's the lifesaving question."

"Luka"—Pod's voice comes booming through the library— "glad to see you're recovering from surgery."

I turn to see him walking sideways through an aisle between bookshelves.

"Hey, Pod," I say, "how's the eyesight today?"

"It's getting better all the time," he says through a smile. "I estimate that in seven to ten days I'll be able to see the stars again."

"That's so awesome," I say.

"Yes, it is awesome. It appears the more historical the injury or ailment, the longer the Delay takes to fix it. I don't mind waiting, though," Pod says, and then turns to Igby. "Igby, ten minutes, you and me, storming the Temple of Zah! Bring your dice."

"Absolutely," Igby replies, smiling.

Pod walks away, disappearing through the door marked PERIODICALS.

"You guys still playing that game?" I ask, remembering the endless hours that Pod and Igby would play their fantasy dice game, yelling out their storylines over the walls of the exercise yard.

"Sure are," Igby replies.

I smile, and then the question that has been burning in my mind recurs.

"Hey, Igby, after we crashed near the Red Zone, before I was captured, did you manage to . . . ?"

"Get your sister to the hidden vault?"

"Yes," I say, terrified of the answer.

"I did," he tells me. "It took me hours to find it, but I got her there. I left her with Day and Shion and about fifty other clones, but, Luka, there's something you should know."

"What is it?" I ask, the fear that had dissipated now back.

"The only reason I managed to get her there was because of the rally in Midway Park. Something like ninety percent of all the Alt soldiers were there, and most of the fallen surveillance drones hadn't started self-repairing. I had to leave her in the vault so I could come and try to help you guys, but by then the battle was over, and I was forced into hiding—more and more Alt soldiers started patrolling the streets. Luka, we can't get back to the financial district without being spotted now—there are thousands of Mosquitoes all over the city. I can scramble all of them within the three-mile radius, but the vault is seven miles east of here. I don't know how the clones are getting food or water, I don't know if they've been captured . . . or killed. I don't know."

I don't know how to respond to Igby's words. Part of me feels hope—Molly made it to the vault, where Day and Shion will have looked after her, helped her get clean, nursed her back to health, but if they were stuck in that vault, no way out, no source of food or water, then surely they're either dead or captured.

"They weren't in the Block?" I ask, remembering that Igby had access to that information via the eye.

"No, none of the clones from the vault were in the Block," Igby replies.

She can't have survived, a voice says, unbidden, in my mind.

I'm about to ask Igby if he thinks there's any chance Molly might still be alive, but my words are cut off by the sound of something tumbling to the floor in the bathroom where Kina and Wren are, and then the sound of screaming.

Igby and I dash for the bathroom. I get there first and throw open the door.

Wren is on her back with Kina in a choke hold on top of her. Wren is growling in an almost-inhuman way, and for a second I'm sure that she has become a Smiler once again. Kina's eyes are rolling back in her head as her struggling arms fall limp.

I rush over to Wren and grab her arm, wrenching it away from Kina's neck.

"Get off me! Get off me!" Wren screams, and—as her arm comes free from Kina's neck—she punches me twice, once in the right eye and once on the nose.

I fall back, and she dives on Kina again.

"What the hell is all the noise?" Dr. Ortega asks from the doorway. "I'm trying to sleep, for the love of hell."

She sees Igby trying to restrain Wren and calmly walks to the far side of the room, grabs another syringe, and injects Kina.

"Shit, that was a double dose," Dr. Ortega says, staring at the empty needle.

"Why are you sedating *her*?" I ask. "She's the one being attacked!"

The doctor shrugs, grabs another syringe, and injects Wren. The two girls become groggy and fall to the floor, sedated.

"Can I get back to sleep now, maybe?" Dr. Ortega asks, and then marches out of the room, back to her book bed.

"We're going to have to restrain Wren until we can figure out how to help her," Igby says, breathing heavily.

"No," I say, "we're not restraining her. She's spent two months restrained and locked up. We're not doing that to her."

"Then what do you suggest?" Igby asks. "Just let her attack people every time she forgets where she is?"

I'm about to reply when, from the main library, Akimi's voice calls out, "Scavenger group returning."

Igby calls for Pod and the two move quickly, running to the back of the bathroom toward the hole in the wall before climbing down the ladder to the sewer.

"Come on," Igby calls up to me.

I follow, climbing down as fast as I can to keep up. Pod and Igby are already sprinting through the low, narrow tunnels of the sewer, back to the manhole cover outside the courthouse.

Seconds later the heavy steel cover is lifted away and Pander leaps down into the tunnel.

"Nothing," she pants, pushing an antique-looking gun into the waistband of her shorts. "We got nothing! They were everywhere. Happy is sending more and more soldiers into the city."

"What happened?" Igby asks, but before she can reply a second person hangs from the sewer's entrance and, just before she drops lightly down to the ground, I notice her curved, pregnant stomach. She lands and pushes her black, sweat-soaked hair from her eyes. She's about sixteen, and she looks pissed off.

"Hosts everywhere, and soldiers. We were lucky to get out alive," she says, her angry eyes darting over to me. "You must be Luka?" she asks. "I've heard a lot about you. I'm Samira Deeb."

"Oh, you're Samira," I say, getting a raised eyebrow from the pregnant girl in return.

"So, we got nothing?" Pod asks. "No food? Water?"

"Nothing," Pander replies.

"What about the processor?" Igby asks.

"Do you know what nothing means?" Samira asks, sounding genuinely curious as she pushes an early model USW rifle into her backpack.

"All right," Igby says, "let's get back to base and we'll make a plan."

We shuffle through the sewer once again, climbing up into the bathroom, where Wren and Kina are still slumped on the floor. I lift Kina up and lay her on one of the beds. Pod and Igby get Wren onto another.

"All right, Mr. Compassion," Igby says, looking from me to Wren, "if we're not restraining her, what do you suggest we do?"

I think about it for a while. "She needs time and rest. She's been through hell. We need to give her a chance to come back from that."

Igby sighs, and I can almost see his thought process: *We're in the middle of a war, resources are stretched, we hardly have enough people to fetch food and supplies.*

But, finally, he nods. "You're right," he says. "We'll take her to the storage room at the front of the library so she's as far away from everyone else as possible, but we won't lock her up or restrain her. I'll talk to Dr. O about treatments and find out what medication she'll need."

"Thank you," I say.

Igby then leans close. "Between you and me, Luka, I don't completely trust the mad doctor."

"Why not?" I ask.

"Think about it: She doesn't breathe, and I can guarantee she doesn't have a heartbeat. She's full of more tech than Apple-Moth. She's an Alt."

"So is Wren," I point out.

"But Wren can't surgically remove Alt tech without the aid of robots. Dr. Ortega is next level."

And for a second something tries to fall into place in my mind, something about Dr. Ortega. It's almost as if I know her, as if I've met her before, but where? When? I shake the thought away, putting it down to my tired and overworked brain.

"What are you saying?" I ask. "Surely you don't think she's working for Happy?"

"I'm just looking at the evidence." Igby shrugs. "That's all."

Pod and Igby lift Wren's bed and carry her out and through the library to the storeroom.

Still feeling groggy from the sedation and the operation, my head now trying to process what Igby said about Dr. Ortega, I move through to the library and sit down in an uncomfortable chair.

The new girl, Samira, is pulling her white T-shirt over her head. She stands there in only a sports bra and pokes a finger through a bloodstained rip in the material of her T-shirt. "Dammit!" she says. She looks down at her protruding stomach and sees a nasty-looking wound. "Dammit," she says again. She wanders over to where Dr. Ortega is sleeping, grabs a bottle of brown stuff, a surgical needle, and some thread from a medical kit on the floor, and, after pouring some of the brown liquid onto the wound, begins to sew it up.

I notice, just above the crease of her concentrating, knotted brow, a small horizontal scar, and I realize that this is where her Panoptic was removed too. I look around at the ex-Loop inmates and there are no scars at all, our healing abilities wiping away all signs of the Panoptic removal surgery.

I stand and walk over to the girl, unsure of what I'm going to say until I say it. "Hey, it's Samira, right?"

"Yeah," she replies, not looking up as she digs the curved needle deep into the skin on one side of the wound, hooking it under and pushing it up through the other side. "But just call me Sam."

"All right, Sam," I say. "I can't help but notice that you're pregnant. Like, a lot pregnant, and, I think . . . I mean . . . is it such a good idea for you to be going on missions into the city?"

She stops, mid-pull, the buzzing sound of the thread dragging through skin halting as she makes eye contact with me. "Hey, here's an idea, Luka—why don't you mind your own fucking business?"

"Whoa, look, I'm just saying—"

94

"Oh, is being pregnant during the apocalypse dangerous? Thank the Final Gods you were here to let me know."

"I didn't mean to . . . I was just saying that . . ."

"Cool, well, just don't say, all right? You think I don't know the risks? You think I need some boy to tell me what to do and what not to do?"

"No," I say, pushing aside the flush of embarrassment that washes over me. "No, you don't. I don't know why I assumed that I'd know better," I say, smiling apologetically.

Sam holds eye contact, thread still taut. "What do you want, a pat on the back for saying the right thing?"

"Kind of," I say. "How sad is that?"

She exhales a laugh. "You can go and sit down now."

I walk back to the uncomfortable chair, feeling like a moron and wishing I could turn back time.

Pod and Igby come back from the storeroom.

"Pander, you're up," Akimi says, appearing from the ceiling, pulling on a rope that lowers her and the suspended office chair to the floor of the library.

"Great," Pander says, moving eagerly to the lookout seat. "I need a rest." She pulls a second rope, propelling herself skyward, where she stares out at the city.

"So," Igby says, "what happened out there?"

"We went to that depot on Brooke Street," Pander calls down from the crow's nest. "Got one step inside the door and three bright-eyed hosts were waiting with an army of Alts. They gave the order and the soldiers opened fire."

"We ran," Sam adds, focusing intently on sewing up the deep

cut. "To the old parliament buildings. Pander knew about these secret tunnels that run underneath. We thought we'd lost the soldiers, but they followed us down there. We got out near the river and managed to lose them in the hospital. We waited for about an hour and then came back. The city is crawling with them."

"We need that processor," Igby hisses. "We *need* it. If Malachai and Woods are still alive, it's the only way we're going to save them."

"Well, we'll go again," I say, standing up, suddenly ready to run into danger at the mention of my friends. "I'll go; tell me what you need, I'll get it."

Igby nods. "All right," he says, "but we do it fairly."

"How's that?" I ask.

"Last alphabetically go into the city," Akimi says, walking over to the fiction section of the library.

"Wait," I say, "you've lost me."

"Close your eyes and pick a book," Pod says, joining Akimi in the fiction section. "A mission like this will require . . . how many?"

"Three," Igby replies. "Two to go for the processor, one to try and get some supplies."

I watch as Akimi and Igby stand in front of a shelf of books, close their eyes, and grab one each.

"Throw me one," Sam calls, snipping the thread and examining the closed wound. Pod tucks one book under his arm and then throws another one toward Sam. It misses her outstretched arm by a yard, and she rolls her eyes before retrieving it from the floor.

I join the others, close my eyes, run my hand along the spines of the books, and—before I select one—I smile. I love the feeling of books; they remind me of all the hundreds of hours I escaped prison without ever leaving my cell. I stop on one and pull it from the shelf, and then open my eyes. *The Year of the Flood* by Margaret Atwood. I've never read this one, but I have read others by her and loved them.

"All right," Akimi says, holding her book up, "first letter of the first word of chapter one."

"Yours is *T*," I say, recognizing her book as *A Wizard of Earth-sea*, a fantasy classic.

"What?" she asks.

"*The Island of Gont,*" I say. "Those are the first words of that book."

Akimi flips to chapter one, looks at the first word, and nods her head. "Yep, I got *T*," she says, and then looks at me. "How the hell did you know that?"

"I've just read that book a bunch of times, that's all."

"I got *I*," says Sam, and then begins to read her book, a Victoria Schwab classic.

I flip my book past the opening poem and on to chapter one. "Mine starts with *I* too," I say.

Pod hands his book to Igby, who reads the first word. "Z," he says.

"That wasn't funny the first ten times," Pod mutters.

"Fine, it's a *D*, mine is *H*, which means Luka, Akimi, and Sam are heading into the city," Igby says. He closes his book and points it at me. "I need a SilverWave quantum processor—you'll find them inside almost any SoCom unit and all LucidVision headsets. They're silver and about the size of your thumbnail. If you don't have time to remove the processor, just bring me the whole unit and I'll do it."

"I'll try my best," I tell him, already feeling apprehensive about sneaking into a city full of soldiers who want to take me back to the Block.

"You better," Igby says, "and then get back here safe, understand?"

I nod. He hugs me, and then Akimi and Sam.

"All right," Sam says, pulling her bloodstained T-shirt back on. "No point in wasting time. Let's go."

I'm about to ask if someone else should go in her place seeing as she's just been on a mission and stitched up a wound on her pregnant belly, but I stop myself, remembering how that went last time.

The rest of the group hug us and wish us luck. Pod walks to the door marked STAFF ROOM, now the library's armory. I go with him and look inside.

"Whoa," I say, looking at the array of ancient guns and knives. There's even a sword, five proximity mines, and three round metal things the size of tennis balls. "What are these?" I ask, grabbing one.

"That," Pod replies, deftly removing it from my hand, "is a grenade. An ancient explosive from the Second World War. It's very dangerous, don't play with it."

"How does it work?" I ask.

"You pull the pin and four seconds later, boom!" he says, grinning. "I found them in a museum—they were decommissioned but I fixed them. Before the city was swarming with soldiers I tested one. They're pretty awesome."

He puts the grenade carefully back on the shelf and hands me an old handgun, smiling apologetically. "It's from, like, the twentieth century, I guess. Takes bullets. We got it from the museum too, and I managed to get it working again. You have eighteen rounds of ammo, so be careful—it's not like a USW where you can just keep on firing. And it's loud, really loud, so only fire it if you absolutely have to. Happy will hear it and will come for you."

"Thanks," I say, turning the weapon over in my hands. I'm surprised by how light it is. It seems to be made of some kind of primitive polymer. "How do I fire it?"

As Pod gives me a quick demonstration, Akimi grabs a much more modern Ultrasonic Wave rifle from the armory. "How come she gets a USW?" I ask.

"Because she's the best shot," Sam says, walking past us and taking her own gun out of her backpack. Hers is an early model USW. Better than my antique, but not great.

We head back into the main room, and Pander waves from the crow's nest. "All clear," she calls, and then we leave, back through the bathroom. I touch Kina's hand before climbing down into the sewer.

We make it to the street by the courthouse, and I follow Sam and Akimi toward the center of town.

The sun is low in the sky as evening falls, but it's still bright and I'm wondering if broad daylight is the best time to be raiding a city full of Alt soldiers and hosts who want to capture us and use us as batteries. I doubt it helped Sam and Pander earlier.

We move quietly to an old, abandoned office block and slip inside through a broken window. The three of us crouch down behind an upturned desk.

"All right," Akimi says, whispering, "I'll go to the depot on Marwick Street, about a mile northwest of here. You guys go to City Level Two; there's plenty of rich-people houses up there that'll have Igby's processy thing."

"Shouldn't we stick together?" I ask.

"No," Sam says, "if we're going to die it's better they don't get all of us."

"Meet back here in four hours—that'll be quarter to ten—and we'll go back to the library together," Akimi says. She heads off, running low through the old office building.

I'm struck at how cold everyone has become, how hardened against the notion of death. They move headfirst into danger, knowing that every trip into the city could be their last, putting their lives on the line for provisions so that the others can survive a little longer.

How long can this go on? I wonder, and I think about Igby's plan: *Find the Missing, build an army* . . . then what?

"This way," Sam says, leading the way along several corridors and down a flight of stairs to a fire escape. She pushes the door open a crack and looks out into the fading daylight, aiming her USW first left and then right. "Clear," she says, and then we're running toward the graphene stilts that hold up City Level Two.

As we dash across the street, I look up toward the Black Road

Vertical, my old home, but something else catches my eye: far off in the distance I see one enormous, thick black cloud. I slow and turn in a circle, trying to find the edge of the cloud, but I can't. It's as though the entirety of Region 86 is surrounded by a storm cloud, and we're at the center of it as it closes in.

"Hurry!" Sam's voice calls from up ahead.

"Sam, what the hell is that?" I call, pointing up to the sky.

She glances up and I see a momentary look of surprise on her face, but she turns back to me and shrugs. "Big cloud."

"Yeah," I reply, looking up one more time, "I guess."

I try to forget the colossal circular storm cloud and focus on the mission.

I sprint and catch up with Sam. We rest behind one of the stilts and assess our options. There is a ladder to the top that maintenance workers use, or the spiral road that leads to the gates of the luxury real estate.

"The ladder is quicker," Sam says, "but there's nowhere to hide if they spot us."

"So, we take the road?" I ask.

Sam nods and then takes off toward the spiral tarmac. I take a deep breath, trying to beat the exhaustion, and run after her.

The spiral road is steeper than it looked from a distance and sweat is pouring off me by the time I reach the gates. Sam is already halfway up and acrobatically vaulting over as I start climbing.

I have a second to remember, as I climb, that I used to sneak into this place when I was a kid. Me and my friends, we would knock on rich people's doors and run away. That was a million years ago. We drop down into the gated neighborhood and run toward the first house we come to that isn't a burned-out shell. The reflecting pools either side of the walkway that leads to the front door are full of ash, and the water has turned black. We're in luck, as one of the long windows at the side of the front door is broken. Sam knocks out the remaining shards and we step inside.

The size of the place is absurd; the entrance hall alone is bigger than the apartment I grew up in. It has an enormous water feature in the center with a slab of granite at an artistic angle protruding from a mosaic pool. The water that sits stagnant in this pool is not black, but red.

"Come on," Sam says, and we move into the house.

"Do you know how to get a SilverWave processor thing out of a SoCom unit or a LucidVision?" I ask.

"No," Sam whispers back. "Do you?"

"No."

"Then I guess we take the whole thing back, like Igby suggested."

"Right," I agree. "I'll go upstairs and try to get a LucidVision headset, you try to find a SoCom?"

"All right," Sam says.

I change direction and head for the stairs while Sam moves deeper into the house.

It doesn't take me long to find a bedroom and, above the headboard, a LucidVision headset. I had always wanted one of these growing up. The Barker Projectors that cast holographic advertisements made them look so cool. *Choose your dream! Be the hero! Fly through the air! Do whatever you want! LucidVision: Make it happen!*

I look at the metal arm that holds the headset and follow it to the wall, where it's bolted firmly in place. I shrug and remind myself that the thing doesn't have to be in perfect working order, that I just need to get it back to Igby. I grab the arm and pull as hard as I can; it holds firm, but I hear a crunching sound from inside the wall. I pull again and feel the arm give a little. One more hard tug and it comes free, wires trailing in the brick dust. It takes seconds for me to pull the wires free from the casing, and I'm about to call down to Sam to let her know that we don't need the SoCom unit when I hear a scream.

I move quickly, running toward the sound, sprinting downstairs into the main space.

Sam cries out again and I see her, on her back in the middle of the massive flagstone kitchen floor. A Smiler—blinking and grinning a set of yellow teeth—is on top of her. Sam's shaking arms are holding the Smiler's weight as he bears down on her with all his strength. A shard of glass clasped in his hands, pushing closer and closer toward Sam's chest, blood dripping from his shredded fingers.

I move toward them, turning sideways to gain more momentum as I swing the LucidVision headset as hard as I can, gripping the metal arm like a baseball bat. It connects with the Smiler's head with a sickening, hollow *thunk*, and he falls limp on top of Sam.

She struggles under his weight. I drop the LucidVision and drag him off her.

Sam stands up, breathing hard, tears in her eyes. "He . . . he . . . God, he almost killed me."

Her hand moves to her stomach as she looks into my eyes.

"We should go," I say, bending to pick up the piece of equipment that houses Igby's processor. Sam grabs my hand. I stop and look at her once again.

"That messed me up, Luka. That was . . . that was scary. I've been shot at before, I've been chased by Smilers, but that was . . . that was too close . . . He almost . . ."

"It's okay," I tell her. "You're okay. You're alive."

She hugs me, suddenly and ferociously. "Thank you," she whispers.

I hug her back, and in that moment I hear the sound of the Smiler stirring on the floor beside us. In one smooth movement, Sam pulls away from me, grabs the gun from my waistband, and aims it at the Smiler.

"No!" I cry, trying to grab the gun from her.

The explosion is deafening. The way my eardrums contract feels as though all the air has been sucked out of the room. The bullet ricochets off the stone floor and I feel it buzz past my ear like some enormous insect as it bounces around the room.

All I can hear is a high-pitched whistling. I can see Sam's mouth moving but can't hear her words.

"What?" I ask, yelling over the tinnitus that is already beginning to subside.

"What are you doing? He's going to kill us!" Sam screams.

"The gun," I say, my own voice sounding like it's coming from far away. "Happy will hear it!"

"Fine," she says, grabbing her USW gun off the floor. "I'll use this."

I'm about to stop her, about to explain that this is someone's brother, or father, or son, and he's been poisoned by Happy to act in this way, but we both freeze.

A new sound fills the silent evening: a humming, insectile sound.

"What is that?" I ask, but I don't need to wait for an answer as three attack drones, identical to the ones that used to guard the Loop during our exercise hour, float into view through the enormous kitchen window.

The thin strip of light encircling the closest drone turns from green to red, and the low-hanging cannons take aim.

As the first dart pierces the windowpane, sending raindrops of glass shimmering down, I know that I am doomed. The darts will be filled with a combination of hallucinogens and a drug called Crawl. Crawl slows down all bodily functions: heart rate, respiration, and brain chemistry. It's what they used in the Loop to stop us trying to climb the walls. Drone poison is a hellish cocktail that leaves the victim in a nightmare world of terrifying visions that feel like they last a hundred years.

I close my eyes, waiting for the impact of the dart, but it doesn't come. In the commotion of the drones, I hadn't noticed the Smiler had gotten to his feet and lunged at me. The dart has struck him above the temple, and he is wavering on his feet.

Sam and I don't wait around to see what happens next. She grabs my hand and runs, dragging me toward the front door.

As I haul it shut behind us, I hear two more darts thudding into the heavy wood.

"They must've heard the gunshot," Sam pants, running fast, still holding my hand as I grip the headset in the other.

The whirring sound of the drones grows once more as we sprint toward the spiral road. They have moved up and flown over the house in seconds, and now they're tracking us, lowering down to our level to fire again.

Sam hands me the heavy old pistol and draws her USW gun from her backpack. She stops running, turns and drops to one knee, firing four rounds at the nearest drone. The relentless whirring sound stutters and chokes and the drone falls from the sky.

I turn and aim the pistol at the drone closest to me. I fire five times, hitting it twice, which is enough to damage one of its rotors. It dips to the left as it fires another dart, this one so close that it tugs at the shoulder of my prison jumpsuit.

I fire four more rounds and hit it again. It loses control and thunders into the ground, smashing into pieces.

We stand on the lawn of the mansion, waiting in the charged silence for whatever comes next.

"We have to move," Sam whispers.

And, again, the silence is broken by the sound of engines, this time louder, like rolling thunder.

Over the edge of City Level Two, a large military vehicle hovers up and four soldiers disembark.

"Go!" I yell, and push Sam away from the Alt soldiers.

USW rounds begin to flash past us, and we dive behind a

parked car. I drop the LucidVision headset to the road beside me and lean around the bumper of the Eon 14. I see the four soldiers spreading out and taking tactical positions. Two are at the corner of the house we just left and two more are ducked down behind vehicles across the road.

I lean out farther and take one shot. The bullet sparks off the corner of the house, sending a cloud of debris into the air.

How many bullets is that? I think, trying to add them up.

Sam leans out and fires seven, eight rounds. Around thirty rounds come back, rocking the car on its suspension.

"Got one," she breathes.

I slide the magazine out of the pistol and see that I have six bullets remaining, plus one in the chamber.

"Jesus, these old guns suck!" I hiss as Sam fires again.

"They're getting closer," she says, and leans her head against the door of the car. "Fuck it."

Before I know what's going on, Sam has darted to the next car. She stands up and fires, then moves again. In no time she's twenty yards away and aiming at the soldiers from a whole new angle. She fires relentlessly, screaming as she pulls the trigger. I stand up too. Knowing that I can't waste a single shot, I take my time, trying to ignore the blasts of energy that thump into the car and whoosh past my head. Sam kills another soldier and then ducks back down behind the solar charge panel she is using as cover.

Time seems to slow down as I fire; it's almost as if I can see the path of the bullet as it misses to the right of the closest soldier. I adjust my aim and pull the trigger twice, but both rounds miss by centimeters. I move a millimeter to the left and fire three times, hitting the young man twice in the neck and once in the jaw. He goes down, and I fall back behind the vehicle.

The last remaining soldier has retreated behind the house. We have to get out of here right now.

"Hey, Regulars," the final soldier calls, his voice gruff and perhaps a little panicked. "I have an offer for you. How about you put your guns down and come over here, nice and easy?"

"I didn't hear any offers when there was four of you," Sam calls back.

"No, but in about thirty seconds there's going to be about a hundred soldiers backing me up. You can either wait and let them kill you, or I can arrest you right now. You get to keep your lives and I look like a hero. Everyone's a winner."

Sam looks over to me. I shake my head. "Fuck that," I call back.

Sam points to herself, mimes firing her weapon, and then uses two fingers to simulate running away toward the spiral road. I nod my head.

Sam stands and begins firing the old USW gun at the house. I get to my feet and dart toward the road. Sam walks backward, still firing, pinning the Alt soldier to the corner of the building.

We have to move fast, I think, *before the other soldiers arrive.*

The road tilts down as I hit the start of the decline.

And then the screech of ultrasonic rounds ceases.

I stop running, my feet skidding on the road, and I turn to see Sam pulling the trigger of her old USW over and over again, but only a weak electronic buzz emanates from the weapon.

"Shit," she breathes.

"That must be a very old model," the soldier calls, and I can hear that he is smiling. "Overheating was an issue with USWs one through six. Luckily I have a nineteen."

And then he's running toward Sam. I'm thirty, maybe forty yards from her, and with only one bullet left in my antique pistol. Sam stands there, the sun setting in front of her, shock and fear in her eyes, pulling the trigger of the burned-out rifle over and over again, and still no sonic rounds come blasting out of the barrel.

Run, I think. *Run, Sam!*

But she doesn't, and the Alt soldier, with his robot lungs and robot heart, is closing the gap at near-impossible speed.

There's no more time to think. I sprint from behind the car, trying to close the gap. Any second now the Alt's Lens will pinpoint a spot right between Sam's eyes, and he'll fire a round of pure concentrated sound into her, turning her brain into soup.

I make it to the next car as the distance between me and the Alt narrows. I climb up to the roof and raise my pistol to eye level. I see his head in my shaking sights just as he raises his USW to his shoulder. I'm aware that Sam has stopped pulling her trigger. She has let the gun fall to her side and her mouth is slightly open in shock.

"Wait," she pleads, her hand moving protectively to her stomach.

One shot, I think. *You get one shot at this*.

I see the look of triumph in the soldier's face, the satisfaction in his narrowed eyes.

I squeeze the trigger.

The soldier turns into a marionette with its strings cut, and flops down onto the hood of an orange Skyway 15.

We stand there, unmoving, for a full three seconds, before Sam bursts into frenetic laughter.

"How the hell did you make that shot?" she yells, and though she's laughing, there is a world of alarm in her eyes.

She puts her hands to her face and falls to her knees. She cries for five or six seconds before taking a deep breath and pulling herself together.

"We have to move. More will be here soon," she says.

I nod and dash back for the headset. I glance at the dead soldier's gun, only ten yards away, but the sound of more military vehicles fills the air, and we sprint away as fast as we can, down the spiral road. I'm certain we won't make it out of here without being spotted.

We run and run. We make it to the end of the road and back onto ground level. Above us the sound of the Alt soldiers yelling orders echoes out over the city.

"This way," Sam calls, taking a hard right, leading us away from the sewer behind the courthouse.

"But the library!" I yell.

"No time!" she calls back, and then shoulders her way through a boarded-up doorway, splintering the wood and disappearing through a spiral of dust.

I follow her into the building. It's an old shop of some kind, with a tiled floor and a smashed glass display cabinet—perhaps an old butcher's shop from long before I was born, when people used to buy animal meat. Sam is shoving part of the counter aside, revealing a set of rotted wooden stairs that leads down into darkness.

"Where are we going?" I ask.

Sam doesn't answer, just carefully and quickly climbs down into the gloom. Outside, I hear the Alt army mobilizing: more vehicles, more footsteps, more orders being barked out. I follow Sam down, using my fingertips to pull the heavy counter as far as I can back over the staircase.

I move quickly, reaching the bottom of the stairs and walking right into Sam's back in the darkness.

"Pander has mapped out a bunch of these old tunnels," she whispers, "but they're dangerous, they're like mazes. We found some books on them. Apparently, politicians and royalty from a thousand years ago used them. Others were made by smugglers. One of them used to be a tunnel to the gallows where criminals were hanged."

"Wow," I say, still whispering despite the fact that we're deep underground.

"And now they're used by us," Sam says. "Stay close—you do not want to get lost down here."

It's hard to know how close I am to Sam in the darkness, but I reach out every now and then to make sure she hasn't gotten too far away from me. The thought of making a wrong turn and being trapped in a labyrinth of pitch-black tunnels terrifies me.

Tunnels, I think, *I'm haunted by goddamned tunnels. If this thing ever ends and I'm still alive, I will never go near another tunnel again!*

We turn left, then left again. A particularly long stretch curves slowly to the right for about a quarter of a mile before

Sam hesitates. There are three right turns close together; she seems about to take the second, even takes a few steps into it before changing her mind and taking the third. We go up a set of six steps and then the tunnel curves downward and around to the right again.

After another ten or so minutes of walking, Sam feels the wall until she finds a ladder.

"Here," she says, and leads my hand to it. "And be quiet when you get to the top; we're not far from the Arc."

"The Arc?" I repeat, remembering Galen Rye's words: *It might surprise you how effortless it was to enlist soldiers, to convince humans to join our cause. Offer them a hierarchy in which they can belong—Tier One, Two, or Three—tell them they will earn their place on the Arc, where they will be safe from the end of the world.* "What is it?" I ask. "Some kind of bunker?"

"You'll see," she says.

I climb up the ladder. It's greasy with moss and moisture, and made even harder to climb by the fact I'm still carrying the LucidVision in one hand, but I make it to the top, where my head hits against a metal grate. I lift it up and carefully guide it to the floor. I look around and see an old cellar, a portion of the floor covered in dirty tiles. Steel beer and cider kegs are piled high among a web of tubes and valves.

We climb out of the tunnel and make our way to the rotting wooden staircase against the brick wall.

We emerge behind the bar of a wooden-floored old pub. It has been long abandoned, but the ancient varnished oak of the bar still curves majestically through the middle of the room.

Champagne flutes still hang like icicles from racks above the beer taps. The tables and chairs arranged around the room look as though they are waiting for clientele to walk through the boarded-up doorway at any second. If it wasn't for the dust that rests over everything like snowfall, this place could be merely closed for the evening, rather than shut down for decades.

Sam joins me behind the bar and we both look around, mesmerized by this place that has been frozen in time.

The sound of marching boots from the street outside snaps us both out of our reverie, and we move quietly to the storage area behind the bar and into a long-defunct walk-in refrigerator in the back room. I sit on an ancient crate of beer as Sam pulls the door shut, careful not to close it all the way.

"What's the plan?" I ask quietly.

"We wait."

"Wait for what?"

"Wait until it's properly dark. Wait until there's not as many soldiers looking for us. If I'm right, we're just inside the surveillance scanner, so we should be safe."

"And if you're wrong?" I ask.

"Mosquitoes will find us in about five minutes."

"We should've taken Apple-Moth with us," I say.

"Yeah, right," Sam laughs. "That stupid thing would draw attention to us in a heartbeat."

I smile, remembering the drone's irritating voice and enthusiastic personality that refused to be wiped out.

And then something occurs to me: We've been traveling toward the center of the city.

"How far are we from the financial district?" I ask.

"About four miles that way," she says, pointing to one side of the cold room.

"Right," I say, staring at the wall as though I can see right through it, all the way to where Molly is.

I think about leaving, about sprinting all the way to the financial district, making my way to the hidden vault and finding my sister, but the sound of soldiers swarming the streets tells me that I'd not only be captured immediately, but they'd find Sam too.

"You okay?" Sam asks. "You look like you've got something on your mind."

I smile and half laugh. "I have *so* many things on my mind," I tell her.

"The end of the world will do that to you," Sam replies, smiling back. She reaches into a faded old box and pulls out a cardboard tube. She opens it up and produces a bottle of whiskey.

"Go get two of those glasses from the bar," she says. "We're going to be here awhile."

"What? We can't drink, we have to stay alert. And you're preg—" I stop myself as Sam's eyes narrow. "Yeah, all right, we could have one, I suppose."

I move quietly to the bar and grab two dusty glasses from a shelf. I find a packet of old dishcloths, take a relatively clean one from the middle of the bundle, and use it to wipe the grimy glasses inside and out.

I take them back to Sam, who pours a generous measure of the ancient whiskey into each glass.

"You go first," she says, looking suspiciously at the amber liquid.

I hesitantly hold the glass up to my nose and smell the alcohol. It's sharp, but not at all unpleasant. It's like burnt wood and strong coffee. I take a sip and it lights up my mouth. My tongue feels at once hot and cold; the alcohol surrounds my teeth and clings to the inside of my cheeks.

"Whoa," I choke out, my voice sounding like I have Drygate flu.

"Good whoa, or bad whoa?" Sam asks.

"It's pretty good," I say, my voice still hoarse. I steel myself and take another sip.

Sam takes a drink from her glass and handles it far more calmly than I did. "Yep," she breathes, "that'll work."

There's no way we can make the rendezvous with Akimi with so many soldiers on the streets, so instead, we drink for the next three hours. Or rather, *I* drink for the next three hours. I only intended to have one or two, but I must have lost track. Sam stopped after one and moved on to water.

"All right, all right," Sam says, swirling the water in her glass around as though it were a fine wine. "How many times have you almost died since the end of the world?"

I think about this, laughter escaping my lips as I remember Wren trying to kill me, two trips through the rat tunnel, Smilers attacking me in the village on the outskirts of town, Tyco Roth trying to end my life twice, falling into the ice river, and many, many more. "Honestly," I tell her, "I've lost count."

We both laugh hysterically at this, and I lean so far to the side that all my whiskey pours from my glass onto the floor. We stop laughing, look at the mess, and then laugh some more.

"Okay, okay," she gasps, "your turn, what do you want to know?"

I think about it for a while and then an obvious question pops into my head. "How the hell did you survive the end of the world? Ebb users survived because they were on Ebb, prisoners survived because of the Delay, the Alts survived . . . I don't know, because they're Alts. How did you survive?"

"Junk barges," she replies nonchalantly.

"Junk barges?" I repeat.

"Junk barges."

"Care to expand?" I say, and this makes her laugh once again.

"I was one of the Junk Children," Sam says, her eyes moving to the floor as if she's embarrassed by this fact.

"I heard that you prefer to be called refuse adolescents," I say, breaking the tension.

Sam snorts water out of her nose. This sets us off again and we're rolling on the floor laughing. Sam, finally managing to get ahold of herself, hits me in the arm.

"You bastar—" she starts, and then falls silent, grabbing my hand as the sound of soldiers patrolling the streets outside the abandoned pub drifts through from the main room.

We stare at each other as we lie on the floor, fear in our eyes.

A minute later, all is silent once again.

We get to our feet and then take our makeshift seats (me on an old crate, Sam on a small side table).

"Happy sent the Smiler poison through the rain," Sam says, her voice quieter now, "and the rain was concentrated on the populated portions of the world. I had swum a mile out to sea. I was foraging one of the barges at the time, looking for electronics, or clothes, or anything valuable I could fix and sell. Happy didn't send the rain that far out, and so me and the other Junk Children on the barges, we survived. Got a hell of a shock when we made it to shore, though, I'll tell you that."

"Hey, did you know Pod before all of this? He was a Junk Child too."

"What, you think just because we both grew up in the homeless villages we *had* to have known each other?" she asks, a note of anger in her voice once again. "Well, we did, as it happens, but that's just coincidence." She laughs, quietly this time, at the expression on my face.

"Okay, okay," I mutter, "your turn."

She thinks for a second, tapping a finger against her chin affectedly. "What did they lock you up for?" she asks, and then leans forward, raising her eyebrows in an exaggerated questioning expression.

My smile turns into a sigh as my humor fades. As usual when anyone brings up the topic of my incarceration, the vivid image of the boy falling from the roof appears in striking clarity in my mind. I see my sister standing there, near the edge of the Black Road Vertical, the impossibly high tower block where we used to live, her face covered by a Halloween mask. I see the boy falling back, a look of incredulity in his eyes, a look of disbelief, of denial.

"I took the blame for something my sister did," I reply.

"And what did your sister do?" Sam asks.

"That's two questions," I say, taking another drink.

"Fine. Your turn."

"What's the deal with the baby?" I ask, without hesitation.

"That's perhaps the most incoherent question I've ever heard," Sam says. "What do you mean 'what's the deal'?"

"I don't know," I say, the alcohol giving me more confidence than is good for me, "like, who's the dad, and how long until it's born, and is it a boy or a girl, and how come you're not exhausted, carrying it around all the time?"

"That's three . . . four questions," Sam says, a sadness sweeping over her.

"You don't have to answer," I tell her, reaching for the bottle and finding that there's only a quarter of the whiskey left.

"Pick one question," she says. "Maybe I'll answer."

"Who's the dad?" I ask.

She sighs. "A dead man."

She reaches out a shaking hand and grabs the almost-empty bottle from the floor. She lifts the bottle to her lips and then changes her mind, puts the cork back in, and sets it down.

"Sam, I . . ." I start, but I don't know what to say.

"I know," she says. "You're a good person, Luka. You care, and you want me to be good too, but I'm not, I'm not good. I don't care, I won't ever care."

"I don't think that's true," I tell her. "You are good—and you do care. About your friends *and* about your baby. Every time you were in danger back there on Level Two, your hands went to your stomach, like you wanted to make sure it was safe. Did you know that?"

Sam runs her hands through her hair. "Yeah, whatever, maybe." She takes a breath and then stands up. "We should get moving, try to get back to the library before you're too drunk to walk."

I look to the doorway, to the small crack where light from the streetlamps had been seeping in, and see that the sky is pitch-black. I try to guess the time and figure it must be after 10 p.m.

"Okay," I agree, and stand on unsteady legs, the world seeming to shift and tilt in front of my eyes. I realize, suddenly, that I *am* drunk. I had felt okay, a bit overconfident, but it has shifted, very quickly, into full-blown inebriation.

I've never been drunk before. When I was twelve, my friends and I shared a single bottle of beer that one of them had stolen from his dad. We all pretended like we were drunk, stumbling around, laughing like Ebb addicts, but this is real. Part of me hates the sensation of being slightly outside of my character—slightly electric, slightly ahead of myself and few steps behind—and part of me loves it.

We move to the door, the ground seeming always to be half a step farther beneath my feet than I'm expecting.

"Getting drunk was not smart!" I announce in a loud whisper. "I mean . . . I mean, what were we thinking? We're about to run for our lives and . . . and we got *drunk*!"

"*You* got drunk," Sam replies, not looking back. "I'm perfectly sober, thank you. Try to focus, Luka."

"Yep," I say, and then laugh as I stumble over my feet.

"Luka, will you shut up? In case you haven't noticed, we're in the middle of the city, about to do something very dangerous!"

"Yeah," I say, shaking my head, trying to clear away the fog. "Yeah, you're right. What's the plan?"

"You'll see," she whispers, resetting her rifle.

"Shouldn't I know the plan?" I ask. "I mean, it seems pretty important for me to at least know the basics . . ."

"Shh," Sam says, opening the front door until there is just enough space between it and the frame for her to see out.

I fall silent, staggering back one step and stifling a laugh.

I see Sam taking several deep breaths, as if she's psyching herself up for something. I'm about to ask if she's okay when she throws open the door and fires six rounds from her USW rifle.

"Quickly, Luka!" she hisses, and then disappears into the street.

"What . . . what's happening?" I mutter, and stumble after her.

Out in the street, four soldiers lie dead. A USW round has hit one of them right in the mouth and the toothless grin left on her face sends a shiver down my spine.

Sam is dragging one of the dead soldiers by the heels into the pub. "Get the others," she seethes as I stare dumbly at the corpses.

"Yeah, right, okay, sure," I say, and grab the toothless one under the arms, pulling her inside.

We get the others into the pub, and Sam begins to undress the female soldier. I get the idea and take the body armor off one of the men, his dead eyes staring up into nothing.

I hop up and down as I force my feet into the soldier's boots, which are at least two sizes too small for me, but they look to be the closest fit. Sam watches with an exasperated look on her face.

"Are you done?" she asks.

"Yeah," I say, patting at the uncomfortable bulletproof body armor that is supposed to decrease USW round impact by up to 14 percent. "I think so."

"Final Gods," she sighs. She walks over to me, unclips the chest plate, and spins it around.

"Oh, that's much better," I say, grinning stupidly.

"Okay," she breathes, "this is the easy part: We walk out into the city as if we own the place, then we wait at Hollie Park Station, get on the city train going west, and get off near Old Town; from there we can access the sewer and get back to the library."

"So, we just walk right into the middle of the city?" I ask.

"Pretty much."

"Great," I say, throwing my hands up and smiling brightly, "why not."

"If we come across soldiers . . . well, we'll improvise."

I pick up one of the soldier's USW guns. "What about this?" I ask, nodding toward the LucidVision headset I've tucked under one arm.

"Fuck," Sam mutters, "give it to me."

I lean toward her and she grabs the headset, resting it on the bar and examining it; then she lifts it into the air and smashes it down onto the hard wood with all her might. The headset shatters, detaching from the arm. Pieces of metal and plastic fly in all directions, along with circuit boards and wires. Sam digs through the debris.

"One of these things has got to be the processor," she says.

"Igby said it was silver and about the size of a thumbnail," I offer.

"Practically everything inside this thing is silver and about the size of a thumbnail!" Sam replies, pocketing the pieces of the electronic device that look important. Then she slips out into the street.

I follow, trying to walk confidently, as if I belong out here in this uniform, but my inebriated legs seem to be leaden and reckless.

"Fuck, fuck, fuck, fuck," I whisper, feeling sweat beginning to bead on my forehead, despite the cool evening air.

"Shut up," Sam says, and I bite my bottom lip to stop myself from talking.

We move through the dark city, our shadows stretching out long behind us and then in front as we pass below streetlights.

I try to focus on my movements, try to figure out how to walk normally, but the alcohol is messing with the signals from my brain to my limbs, and suddenly this strikes me as funny and I start to laugh.

"Oh shit," Sam mutters.

I look up and see what she's seeing: two Alt soldiers approaching us from up ahead. My laughter dies away immediately.

"Any sign of them?" one of the Alt soldiers asks, stopping a few feet in front of us.

Neither Sam nor I replies. The silence hangs in the air for too long, growing like a balloon between us.

"No," I say, spitting the word out. "Nope, no sign, no sign at all."

I sway on my feet, and—in the new silence—offer an enthusiastic thumbs-up to the soldiers.

"Who are you?" the shorter, female Alt asks, leaning close to get a look at my Regular face.

I try to duck my head, try to hide my big ears and the scars that adorn my face and neck. These are Alts—they are born perfect through pre-birth cosmetic enhancements, and they'll see through my uniquely normal face in a second.

"She asked you a question," the second Alt soldier says, stepping close and prodding a finger into my chest.

"Who am I?" I say, trying to make my brain work. "I'm . . . I'm . . ."

"He's your commanding officer, son, show some goddamned respect!" Sam says, stepping forward and swiping the tall Alt soldier's hand away from my chest.

"But he's . . . and you're preg—"

"You see those markings on his uniform?" Sam says, interrupting the stammering soldier and pointing to the stripes on the shoulder of my body armor. "That makes him a Tier Two captain, and if I'm not mistaken, you are a Tier Three lance corporal."

The soldier stammers, trying to get words out. "But . . . but . . . he's a Regular."

"Wrong again, Lance Corporal!" Sam yells. "This is Captain Yossarian. I imagine you've heard of him—he's become quite famous following the Battle of Midway Park, where he single-handedly killed fourteen, that's *fourteen*, Missing soldiers, after saving Galen Rye himself from the explosion that surely would have ended his life. The disrespect you have shown is staggering, sunshine, *staggering*. To call the famous Captain Yossarian a Regular because of the injuries he sustained in protecting our leader . . . I'm speechless! What's your name?"

The Alt soldier looks down at the road, shamefaced. "Lance Corporal Bisset, ma'am," he mutters.

"And you?" Sam asks, turning her attention to the female soldier, who has fallen silent.

"Lance Corporal Selassi, ma'am."

"And who is your commanding officer?"

"Lieutenant Johnstone," she replies.

"Lieutenant Johnstone," Sam repeats. "Yes, I know Lieutenant Johnstone. I think he'd be *very* interested to hear about the insolence displayed by two of his platoon."

Bisset turns to me and snaps off a smart salute. "Captain Yossarian, sir," he barks, "I apologize for my insubordination and lack of knowledge. I will accept any and all punishment that you see fit, sir!"

I try to mimic the salute and almost poke myself in the eye.

"Um, Captain Yossarian is still recovering from the injuries he sustained in Midway and we have to be going," Sam says, shoving me forward. "We'll let you off on this occasion, but in the future, try to be more aware of who you are speaking to, okay? Goodbye."

Sam pushes me along the street, past the soldiers and toward the train station.

"Yossarian?" I say under my breath, remembering the main character from one of my favorite books.

"I panicked!" Sam says, stifling a laugh. "I just read *Catch-22*."

"How good is *Catch-22*?" I extol, far too enthusiastically.

"Not now, drunky. We have to get out of here."

We move quickly, the sounds of more soldiers, gravity engines, and drones seemingly coming from all directions now.

We take a left and are met by the sound of an Alt soldier yelling orders somewhere nearby. We run, sprinting down alleyways and streets, moving left, then right, then right again.

We're close to the platform now, and from here I can see the lights of an empty waiting train.

I hear rapid beeping sounds that mean the City Train's doors are about to shut, and we race for the platform. Sam makes it on to the train just as the doors begin to slide toward each other. I'm right behind her, but in my desperation, my feet get tangled up in each other and I fall. I hit the ground but use my forward momentum to roll over my shoulder between the closing doors and make it through.

I lie sprawled on the train floor, breathing heavily and looking up at the flickering lights, and in this brief moment of calm, staring up at a light that doesn't quite work, two emotions run through me almost simultaneously: unbridled joy at being free from the Block, and unparalleled rage at Happy for hunting us down like rats.

"We can't let Happy win," I say, climbing to my feet.

"I know," Sam replies as she moves through the carriage, checking for cameras and soldiers.

"No, I mean it. If we have to die to stop the machines, then we have to die."

Sam turns to me. "Luka, I know."

We ride the train for four stops, returning the salutes of two soldiers who board just as we get off.

We move quickly through Old Town, past the crumbling remains of the parliament buildings and onto the road by the river where less than two months ago I almost froze to death.

Sam stops at a storm drain, lies on her back, and slides into the gap. She has to adjust and tilt to get her pregnant stomach through. I follow, lying on my front, holding on to the edge of the drain and lowering myself into the sewer.

I thought the darkness of the city was bad, but we're immediately plunged into such thick blackness that my eyes need time to adjust. There is no time; Sam has grabbed my wrist and we're moving through the ankle-deep wastewater.

"This way," Sam breathes as we twist and turn through the channels beneath the city.

When we make it to the drain behind the courthouse, Sam climbs up and lifts the manhole cover up a few inches and looks out. "Wait here," she whispers, before slipping out to the road.

I wait in the quiet and the dark for what feels like an age before she returns.

"Where did you go?" I ask.

"Pod hooked up a switch that sets off a bunch of separate lights across the city—that way whoever's on lookout knows when we're returning."

"Smart," I say, and then I'm rushing to keep up with Sam as she moves through the tunnels toward the library.

We're only twenty or thirty yards along when we hear footsteps approaching from the opposite direction. The first thing I see is the glow of Apple-Moth's lights, and then figures appear. By now my eyes have adjusted, and I recognize Igby, Pander, and Akimi.

"Friends! Friends! You're back!" Apple-Moth cries as the drone zips around and around our heads.

"Thank the Final Gods," Pander says, and hugs Sam with such ferocity that she knocks the air out of her.

I smile at this. It's nice to see some of Pander's icy veneer beginning to melt.

Akimi walks up to me, puts a hand on my shoulder, and breathes a sigh of relief. "I thought . . . I thought you weren't coming back."

"Who, me?" I say, trying to smile, despite the adrenaline and relief that's still coursing through me. "I always come back."

Akimi laughs without much humor and hugs me.

"Did you get it?" Igby asks, and then shakes his head. "I mean, hey, *thank the Gods* and all that, but did you get the fucking processor?"

"We're not sure," Sam replies. "Let's get back to the library and we'll show you what we've got."

"Hey, how's Kina?" I ask Igby.

"She was awake for a bit, and asking for you, but she was really groggy and went back to sleep. God knows how much sedative Dr. O gave her."

"She was awake?" I ask.

"Yeah, but not making much sense."

I breathe a sigh of relief. We reach the library, and Akimi, Pander, and Sam head through to the main room. I linger behind in the bathroom-cum–field hospital and watch the door as it swings slowly shut on its spring-loaded hinge. I walk to Kina's bedside.

"It's real, Kina," I whisper. "It's all real. We really did make it out of the Block." For some reason I can feel tears stinging my eyes, and for the first time I realize how scared I've been. "God, it seems like it's so much worse now. Going out there, fighting against them, risking my life, it's all so much worse now that I have something to lose, someone to leave behind. Kina, I like you, I really like you. We have to end this, we have to beat the machines, and we have to survive."

Kina stirs, her eyes open, and she recognizes me.

"Luka," she says, and smiles.

"Hey," I reply.

"You're not going to ask me where the Loop inmates are hiding, are you?" Her voice is hoarse, and—although it's a joke—I catch fear in her eyes.

"No," I reply, "we're safe; we're out of the Block."

"What the hell did that person inject me with?" she asks as she tries to sit up, but the effort is too much for her.

"Listen, that doctor is . . . she's eccentric, and she may have been a bit overzealous with the sedative."

Kina nods. "We were ready to die, weren't we?" she says, lying back down and closing her eyes.

"Yes," I reply, recalling the moment she had held the gun to my head and pulled the trigger.

"If they ever come for us again, Luka, if they ever try to take us again, promise me you will kill me."

I take a deep breath to try to get on top of the tears that threaten to come. "I won't let it happen," I say.

Kina smiles, and I can see that she is drifting back toward sleep. "I know you'll try," she says, "and I'll try not to let it happen either . . . but if it does?"

"If it does," I say, "then yes, I'll kill you."

She nods, and she is very close to sleep now. "Luka, promise me you won't leave me again."

"Just rest for now," I tell her.

"Promise me, Luka."

"I promise," I say, and it's an easy promise to make. I don't ever want to leave her.

I lean forward and kiss her on the side of her mouth, and she falls asleep.

I brush her hair away from her eyes and then wipe the tears from mine before joining the others in the main room.

". . . perfect, fucking perfect!" Igby is declaring, holding aloft a tiny microchip from the handful that Sam has given him. He dashes toward the computer and the artificial eye.

Pander walks past and pats me on the shoulder. This is about as affectionate as she gets, and it makes me smile.

I feel a sense of love for these people, all of them my friends, old and new.

I glance up to the crow's nest and see Dr. Ortega on lookout duty, spinning around in a slow circle, thumb and forefinger pinching the bridge of her nose in a posture of boredom. Or perhaps she has a headache. Igby said he didn't trust her, and there is still part of me trying to work some connection between her and something I've seen or heard.

I give up thinking about the doctor and collapse, exhausted and still a little drunk, into a chair. I close my eyes.

"Psst."

My eyes open slowly and I realize I've been sleeping.

"Psst!" the voice comes again, and I try to focus, but all I see is an orange glow.

"What?" I ask groggily.

"Friend, what do you call a dog that does magic tricks?"

I lean back and blink. Apple-Moth comes into focus, hovering too close to my face.

"What?" I repeat.

"I said: What do you call a dog that does magic tricks?"

"I don't know," I reply, confused.

"A labracadabrador!" Apple-Moth says, and then does backflips in the air as it laughs at its own joke.

I look around, still half asleep, and then Apple-Moth hovers expectantly in front of my eyes.

"Good one," I say, and Apple-Moth glows pink and does three more backflips before zipping off to the second level to find someone else to tell jokes to.

"What the hell?" I mutter, and then I see Pod walking toward me.

"What happened out there?" he asks. "What's with the uniform; you joined the Alts? You Captain Kane now?" He smiles.

"That's Yossarian to you," Sam says from across the room, and smiles knowingly at me. We both laugh.

I explain everything to Pod, the others gathering around as I tell the story. Sam takes over at times, and by the time we're finished everyone except Igby is listening intently.

Pander whistles a long descending note. "You two should be dead. I mean, I'm glad you're not, but damn!"

"Yeah, you guys work well together," Akimi says. "I mean, not to brag, but I did get a week's supply of food on my own, but, shit, you two should have been erased three times over."

"Holy shit, it worked!" Igby's voice calls out, echoing through the library. "It worked, it worked!"

"What is it?" Pander asks.

"Everything," Igby says. "Everything, I have it all, or I *will* have it all! All the information we'll need."

"Malachai?" I ask, getting to my feet and walking over to the computer. "Woods?"

"Not yet," Igby replies, "but I should know within two or three hours."

I look down at the time in the bottom right corner of the screen: 7:36 a.m. I must have slept for six hours!

"What do we do until then?" I ask.

"We need a plan," Pod says. "It's getting harder and harder to survive out in the city. Happy and the Alts are mobilizing; they're getting more organized and they're looking for us. If we're going to beat them, we'll need an army."

"We need to find the Missing," Pander says.

"Well, yeah," Igby replies, "but if Happy can't find them, how the fuck are we supposed to find them?"

"You know, you don't *have* to say *fuck* every second word," Pander replies, narrowing her eyes.

"I fucking know, I'm just fucking making a fucking point!" Igby replies, and then smiles brightly at Pander.

"All right," Akimi says, "so *how* do we find them?"

I turn to Akimi, who looks to Igby. Igby shrugs and looks at

Pod; Pod stares forward with a faint smile on his face, unaware that anyone is looking at him.

"Awfully quiet in here," he says, shifting his weight.

"Malachai would have known what to do," Akimi says, frowning.

A few months ago a comment like this would have made me jealous. I would have resented the fact that Malachai was always seen as the leader, as the one who everyone turned to for answers, but now I agree with Akimi—I wish he was here to tell us what we're going to do next, how we're going to succeed.

Lost in my thoughts, I didn't notice that everyone is now looking at me.

"What?" I ask.

"What do we do?" Pod asks.

I look from Pod to Pander to Igby, genuinely shocked that they're looking to me for answers. "I don't know," I say. "Really, I don't know. Igby, you should be making these decisions, you're the one who's decoding Happy's plans. Or, Akimi, you just stormed the city and brought back supplies single-handedly. Or, Pander, you're the bravest person I know. What do I bring to this team? Trouble, that's what: You've had to rescue me from Tyco; save me from the roof of the Vertical; break me out of the Block. What am I going to do next, invite Happy to our front door? I'm a liability; why are you looking at me?"

For some reason my anger has risen up during this outburst. Perhaps it's because I'm just now realizing how much of a mess I've caused and what a burden I've been to my friends.

"Holy hell, Luka," Pod says, a big grin on his face, "are you fishing for compliments?"

"What? No!" I reply.

"Yeah, I think Luka wants us to tell him how great he is," Akimi says, arms folded across her chest, eyebrows raised.

"Aw, is little Luka feeling sad?" Pander adds, grinning.

I can't help but smile, despite residual anger still remaining. I shake my head. "Piss off," I say, and they all laugh.

"You got us out of the Loop in the first place," Igby says. "You went through the rat tunnel and saved Wren's life; you went into the city to find help for Akimi when she broke her leg."

"You led us into battle against the Alts in Midway Park," Pander adds.

"And I got Blue killed," I say. "I got Mable killed. I failed."

"It's the end of the world, moron. People are going to die," Pander says.

"You saved my life in the city twice," Sam says.

"Honestly," I say, "I've done no more than any of you. Most of you have saved my life at some point. We'll decide together what we do next."

Pander nods. "Spoken like a true leader."

I flip my middle finger at her, and she smiles. The sight wipes my own smile away—I think this is first time I've ever seen Pander smile.

The next few hours are spent discussing exactly how we're going to try to find the Missing. We talk about the history of the Missing: how people would disappear from the city in groups

134

of three or four; the rumors that they were hiding in the radio-active Red Zones; the Church of the Last Religion claiming that they had been raptured; the search parties that would try to find them to no avail; and how they had shown up at Midway Park and saved us from certain death.

"So," Pander says, resting her chin in her hands, "no one could find them before the apocalypse, Happy can't find them after the apocalypse—how the *hell* are we going to find them now?"

"Why can't Happy find them?" Pod asks, his brow furrowing.

"How the hell should I know?" Pander replies.

"The Mosquitoes," Pod continues, getting to his feet and beginning to pace. "They scan for Panoptic footage and tech generally, but they also scan for signs of life: heartbeat; body heat; movement. If the Missing aren't using a scrambler, how are they staying hidden?"

"Do Mosquitoes scan the Red Zones?" Sam asks.

"Yes," Igby replies.

"The junk barges?"

"Yep."

"Underground?"

"They scan fifty yards above and below ground. They fly three miles out to sea, and they go deep into the most irradiated parts of the Red Zones. And that was their protocol *before* Happy took over. Who knows how far they go now," Igby says.

I sit quietly, listening to this information, my heart sinking as I think of Molly, who was trapped underground in an old bank vault, Panoptic still intact, heart beating loud and clear for the Mosquitoes to detect. There's no way she hasn't been captured, no way she hasn't been found by Happy, and Igby said she is not in the Block. I try to stop the thought from entering my mind, but I can't.

She's dead, I think. *They've killed her.*

"What about Alt tech?" I ask. "Mechanical hearts to hide their pulse?"

"No, the Mosquitoes can detect MORs and APMs just as easily as the real thing, plus it doesn't hide body heat," says Pod.

"So, what?" Igby asks. "They've found a way to mask all signs of life? Found a way to trick the Mosquitoes into ignoring their vital signs *and* any tech they're using?"

"What about old tech?" Dr. Ortega asks from her book bed, Akimi now on lookout.

"Sorry?" Igby replies.

"Old technology," she repeats, sitting up. "Freaking Wi-Fi, the internet, the cloud, all that kind of stuff? Do the Mosquitoes scan for that?"

"No," Pod replies.

"No, exactly," she says, and lies back down. "The Red Zones are filled with ancient tech; some of it is probably salvageable."

"But, so what?" I say. "The Red Zones are irradiated; nothing can survive there."

"That's true," Igby says, "but we've been looking at one point in the Red Zones where the radiation hasn't receded at the same pace as all the other parts."

"Doesn't that just mean the radiation is stronger there?" Pander asks.

"Maybe," Pod says, "but it's irrelevant, isn't it? So what if they don't scan for old tech? The Missing would still have to hide all signs of life, and that's impossible."

Dr. Ortega sighs, but it's not an exasperated sound, more a sound of regret, or resignation. "Have any of you heard of a scientist named Etcetera Price?"

I hear Igby snicker. "You mean Dr. Oxymoron?"

"I mean Dr. Price," Dr. Ortega repeats.

"Yeah," Pod says, "but you're not suggesting . . . surely not?"

"What?" Pander asks.

Pod turns toward the sound of Pander's voice. "There was this scientist, a literal *mad* scientist, way back, years before all this happened. His work got leaked online and contained these crazy experiments where he claimed he could effectively kill someone for an indefinite amount of time and then bring them back to life."

"He was crazy," Igby adds, "but his heart was in the right place. He wanted people with terminal diseases, or incurable diseases, to use his technology: Safe-Death, he called it—hence the nickname Dr. *Oxymoron*. And they could remain dead for decades until a cure was found and then be brought back to life."

"So, what are you suggesting?" I ask, turning to Dr. Ortega. "That this Dr. Price figured out how to make his technology work? And he's taken all the Missing into the Red Zone and they're all . . . well, dead? But how would they be brought back to life if there's no one alive to bring them back?"

"Safe-Death," Dr. Ortega says, "wasn't complete death."

"What you're suggesting is insane," Igby says. "Etcetera Price's theories were ridiculed even when he had access to the best technology in the world. If he really *is* somehow hiding in the Red Zones, there's no way he could've built Safe-Death tech with equipment from a hundred years ago."

"Is it worth checking out?" Pander asks.

Igby thinks about this. "There is almost zero percent chance that this has anything to do with Dr. Price and Safe-Death."

"Almost zero isn't zero," Pander says. "So, let's go."

"No," Igby replies. "It's a waste of time, resources, and we could die."

"Then I'll go on my own," Pander says.

Igby cries out in frustration. "This is why you shouldn't talk!" he says to Dr. Ortega, before turning back to Pander. "We can't just *go*; the edge of the Red Zone is nine or ten miles away and we only have one—very temperamental—mobile Mosquito scrambler, and even if we *did* somehow make it to the Red Zone, the radiation would kill us in one minute flat."

"So what do we do?" Sam asks.

"What do we *do*?" Igby repeats. "We stop listening to fucking nonsense! What Abril didn't tell you is that Etcetera Price was an Alt doctor who worked at the Facility. That's right—the same place that they used to experiment on child prisoners like us! Why would a sicko like that want to help anyone, let alone Regulars?"

"People change," Dr. Ortega says, staring up wistfully at the ceiling.

"Exactly," Pander replies, still looking at Igby. "People change.

Now, are you going to help us check it out, or not?"

It's Igby's turn to bask in incredulity for a while. Finally, he sighs. "I guess we could send in Apple-Moth to check it out, but I'm telling you it's a—"

Igby is cut off by the sound of the old desktop computer beeping over and over. He frowns and walks over to it.

We watch, our collective breath held, knowing that the computer—with its newly fitted processor—could be offering up information about our friends.

"They're alive! Malachai and Woods, they're alive!" Igby yells, and then the excitement in his voice fades away. "Oh no, oh shit . . ."

I run over to the computer. "What is it?" I look at the screen but can't decipher the sprawling mass of numbers, letters, and symbols.

"No, no, no, no . . ." he mutters.

"Igby," Pod says, joining us, "what's happened?"

"They've taken them to the Arc."

"But they're alive?" I ask.

"We're too late. I think we're too late."

"Too late for what?" Pander asks, running over to the computer.

"They've already taken their eyes. They've replaced their lungs and their hearts."

"Igby," I say, grabbing the boy by his shoulders and turning him around, "tell me what's going on."

"They need three of them," Igby says, reading the symbols on the screen. "They're trying to figure something out . . . I'm not sure what, but because of their healing abilities, they're the perfect hosts. Happy is uploading itself into them today."

"Three of them?" I repeat. "Who's the third?"

"I don't know; it's a code I don't recognize. I'm still deciphering it."

Whoever the third is doesn't matter right now—Woods's and Malachai's safety is what is important.

"When?" I ask. "When is Happy uploading?"

"They operated on Woods first—he becomes one of them at 11:07 a.m.—and then the mystery host at 11:12, and Malachai at 11:20."

I look at the computer's clock. It tells me it's 9:33 a.m. And then the screen goes blank.

"What happened?" I ask.

"No, no, no! Fuck! No!" Igby grunts, hitting the computer's screen with his palm. "I left it on too long with the new processor. It's burned out."

"How long will it take you to fix it?"

"An hour and a half, maybe two hours."

Too late, I think. *It'll be too late.*

"I'm going," I say.

"What?" Igby asks, turning toward me. "What do you mean you're going?"

"I'm going for Malachai and Woods," I tell him.

"The computer's down," Igby says, pointing to the blank screen, "which means the Mosquito scrambler is down."

"I know," I reply. "The rest of you get the scrambler up and running again—when I come back we'll find the Missing."

"You don't understand," he says. "With the scrambler down, you'll be spotted within five minutes."

I stare at him, my mind already racing toward the Arc. "What about Apple-Moth?" I ask.

"I mean, it'll scramble Mosquitoes, but the thing won't shut up!" Pod answers.

"It'll have to do," I reply.

"It doesn't matter. You can't get into the Arc," Igby says. "No one can get into the Arc—only Tier Ones and Twos."

"This is a Tier Two uniform," I say, pointing to the insignia on the shoulder of my stolen body armor.

"But your face," Pander says, walking over and pointing at me. "It's, like, crazy ugly. They'll know you're not an Alt."

"What about Apple-Moth's face-changer application?" I ask. "Can it do something more realistic than an ogre?"

"I guess so . . ." Igby says doubtfully.

"It'll do," I say. "Where is it? There's no time, I have to go now."

Pod moves quickly to the periodicals room.

"I can't just let Happy take them," I continue, glancing over to the bathroom, hoping that Kina will emerge, hoping that I can see her, talk to her before I go.

"Boy, you will die," Dr. Ortega's sleepy voice comes from across the room. "But hey, if you happen to make it into the Arc and find the boys, make sure you destroy the E4-EX-19."

"What the hell is an E4-EX-19?" I ask.

"Just destroy it. They need three of you to . . . just do what I say."

I'm about to ask for an explanation when Pod returns from

141

the periodicals room with Apple-Moth. "Are you sure you want to take this? It might be more trouble than it's worth. Plus, the stupid thing has been flying around all morning telling jokes—the battery is almost dead."

I nod and take the companion drone. "It's solar charge, right? It'll charge outside." I look Igby in the eyes and I know that he can see my fear. "Okay, I'm going."

"Luka, our one working radio won't be up and running until the computer is fixed. You're going to be completely on your own."

"I have to do this," I say.

Igby nods. I jog to the bathroom door, which swings open before I reach it, and Kina stumbles out.

"Luka," she says, her voice quieted by the drugs that Dr. Ortega administered.

My heart stops for a moment. I knew I would be leaving Kina behind, but I refused to acknowledge it. This mission, this foolhardy journey, could end in my death—and the worst part about dying would be never seeing Kina again.

"Hi," I say stupidly.

"You're leaving?"

"Kina, I have to," I say. "Malachai and Woods, they're—"

"You said you wouldn't leave."

I freeze. Staring at her, looking at how beautiful she is and knowing how much I need her, knowing beyond all doubt that I love her.

"I . . . I know . . ." is all I can manage.

I watch emotion flicker across her face, and then she bites down on it, hiding her fear and her frustration.

"I'm coming with you," she says, determination in her eyes, but then she almost passes out, the sedative still swimming in her veins.

"You're too weak," I tell her.

"I'll be fine in a minute."

"They don't have a minute."

Kina looks at me, desperation on her face, tears falling from her eyes. "Go," she tells me, "but you better not die."

"I won't," I reply, and kiss her one more time.

"Teenagers," Dr. Ortega mutters from behind us, "it's all drama, drama, drama."

I force myself to move, knowing that if I hesitate, I won't go.

"Good luck, Luka," Akimi calls from the lookout chair. I turn to wave at her, then see all the rest of them in a row behind me.

"Good luck," Igby says.

"Good luck, Luka," Pod says.

I nod, and smile a half-hearted smile, and then I'm gone again, into the sewer, into the darkness.

I make it out onto the street by the court and try to walk confidently. I'm still wearing the military uniform, but I lack the artificial self-assurance that the alcohol gave me earlier, and now all I'm left with is a pinpoint headache at each temple.

Despite the fact that it's almost ten in the morning, there is almost no sunlight at all. I look up at the sky and see that the gargantuan dark cloud has closed in even further, and I worry about what Happy is planning next.

No time, I remind myself, and I turn the companion drone

over in my hand, looking at the sleek translucent design; the casing is made of transparent aluminum and changes color with the drone's artificial emotions; the machinery inside—as intricate as an ancient watch—is made from metallic glass. Companion drones were huge among the Alts before the world was destroyed—you were nobody unless you had the latest Happy Inc. companion drone.

I lean toward the drone and say, "Apple-Moth activate."

Flashing lights come on and the tiny machine lifts into the air.

"Hey, hey, hey, friend! What's going on?" the drone says in a cartoonish voice. "My name's Apple-Moth. Wanna hear a joke?"

"Shut up!" I hiss, waving my arms at it.

"Hey, it's you again! My newest friend. I'm Apple-Moth; what's your name?"

"You have to shut up," I say in a loud whisper.

"Aw," the drone replies, its lights dimming to show its disappointment. "I just want to be your friend."

"You can be my friend by being silent! Your only job is to make me look like an Alt and hide me from the Mosquitoes."

"Oh yeah, I see that in my programming. Hey, hey, hey, you're not supposed to rewrite my code. That makes my warranty null and void, which makes me a sad Apple-Moth."

"Apple-Moth, can you speak in a quieter voice?" I ask.

"Sure can, friend! How's this?" Apple-Moth replies, just as loud as ever, and then—finally—it lowers its voice. "Wanna hear a joke?"

"That's much better," I tell it. "Keep your voice at that volume."

"No problem . . . but, do you wanna hear a joke?"

"No," I say, and Apple-Moth's lights dim once again.

I begin to move, staying as silent as possible while trying to act as though I'm a soldier in Happy's army, but my false confidence is completely undermined by Apple-Moth zipping along beside me, darting to the left and the right, lights blinking and changing color with its programmed emotions.

"Hey, look at that," Apple-Moth whispers, looking over to Old Town. "That's the old parliament building. Did you know that the World Government chose not to demolish the derelict site, but to let it slowly crumble over time as a monument to symbolize the corruption of the old ways?"

"Apple-Moth," I say, stopping in the middle of the street, "do you have some sort of sleep mode where you can still scramble Mosquito signals while you're inactive?"

The tiny drone's lights grow brighter and then change to slightly purple hue as it hesitates. "No."

"Are you sure?"

The drone is silent for a beat too long once again. "I'm sure."

"Apple-Moth, don't lie to me."

"Okay, fine, yes, I have a sleep mode, but that's no fun!"

"This isn't about fun; I have to save my friends."

"Friends are the best! Can we be friends?"

I sigh. This must have been a young kid's companion drone. I wonder if that kid is a Smiler right now, or dead. "I'm sorry,

Apple-M—" I start, but then I hear the whine of a Mosquito high above me.

I turn to see the surveillance drone dipping low and flying along the street, free to see all now that the scrambler is down.

Apple-Moth's lights change to a deep red and it moves silently until it's hovering above my head.

As the Mosquito comes in closer, Apple-Moth emits a low buzzing sound.

The surveillance drone moves to within a centimeter of my face, circling slowly around my head, its camera lens scanning me over and over. I can hear the machinery bleeping and buzzing inside its tiny shell. My heart is thumping as it returns to my field of vision, so close that I can barely focus on it.

And then it's gone, whipping up into the air above the height of the buildings either side of me, disappearing toward the second-home villages on the edge of town.

Apple-Moth lowers, still looking menacing with its red lights. And then, suddenly, the lights change to green and yellow and blue, and the drone begins to bounce on thin air again.

"Wow, wow, wow!" it says, and then lowers its voice again. "Sorry! I mean, wow, wow, wow, that was scary!"

"You did great, Apple-Moth," I say.

"Really?" the drone replies, lights changing to a deep pink color. "Does this mean we're friends now?"

I can't help but smile. "Well . . ."

"And you're not going to put me into sleep mode?"

"Jesus," I mutter, "fine, but if you sense any humans coming toward us, you have to be silent and hide in the pocket behind my body armor, understand?"

"I understand, friend!" Apple-Moth replies, spinning in short, excited circles.

"And use that face-changer software so they think I'm an Alt."

"Yes, yes, yes, I will! I love an adventure! Do you want to hear a joke?"

"Not now, Apple-Moth," I say. "Maybe later."

"Okay! I'm going to think of a good one!"

I refocus my mind on the Arc, and Malachai and Woods, and the probability that I won't make it back to Kina alive to tell her again that I love her, that I love her more than she'll ever know.

The safest way to the Arc is through the sewers, back to the pub where Sam and I hid, but the safest way is also the slowest way. Woods and Malachai have just over an hour left before their minds and bodies are taken over by Happy. I have to take the train straight to the center of town.

Apple-Moth and I pass three groups of soldiers as we walk through town, and each time the tiny drone falls silent and dives into the pocket behind my chest plate before any of the Alts can see it. From its hiding place the drone projects a digital face over my own, one that must be appropriately handsome, as all the passing soldiers snap off salutes without hesitation or a second look.

Apple-Moth waits in my pocket at the train station, projecting the attractive overlay onto my face as Alt soldiers wait for the train. All four of the awaiting soldiers salute me and I nod back, playing the part of a grumpy, overworked commanding officer.

When the train finally pulls up, my heart skips a beat. Every single carriage is filled with soldiers.

The doors open and the Alts, seeing my military rank, part like traffic for an ambulance. I'm offered seats by five officer cadets and choose one on the edge of the row. I can feel sweat trickling down the side of my head as I sit in the silence of the carriage. All the Alt soldiers are on their best behavior in front of me, their superior officer.

I catch sight of my reflection in the opposite window. The face-changer app that Apple-Moth is using has transformed my big-eared, bulbous-nosed, scarred face into a chisel-jawed, blue-eyed runway model. The only problem is, the new face is white.

"Apple-Moth, you moron," I mutter, glancing down at the contrasting brown skin of my hands and shoving them into my pockets.

Another batch of young soldiers boards the train, all five of them saluting me. This time—aware of Apple-Moth's error in judgment—I do not salute back, only nod at the soldiers, who look disappointed.

"Psst!" the quiet but panicked voice of Apple-Moth hisses from beneath my body armor.

I feel a jolt of adrenaline and glance around, but nobody appears to have heard. I look down and see that Apple-Moth is projecting words a centimeter above its body:

BATTERY DYING. NEED SOLAR POWER.

No sooner have I read this short sentence when I see, in my peripheral vision, the digital mask around my face begin to flicker.

"Fuck," I whisper.

I lower my head and try to cover it with a hand, as though I'm suffering from an oncoming migraine; then I remember the false face is white and hide my hands in my pockets once again.

The train stops again and the doors whoosh open. The crowd parts and a soldier with an identical shoulder patch to mine strolls into the aisle and glances around. She notices me, grins, and saunters over.

"Captain," she mutters, lowering herself down onto the seat beside me.

"Captain," I reply.

We sit in silence for a few seconds, and then I'm aware of the soldier trying to get a good look at me.

"Say," she says, ducking lower and trying to look at my face, "I don't think we've met. You newly promoted?"

"Yes, Captain," I reply, trying to stay as still as possible, knowing that Apple-Moth and its dying battery will struggle to track my face and keep it disguised.

"The name's Captain Rooney," she says, holding out her hand to be shaken.

I take her hand and give it a perfunctory grab before shoving back into my pocket. "Yossarian, Captain Yossarian."

"Yossarian?" she says, a hint of awe in her voice. "Hell, I've heard of you! The legend of Midway!"

For a second I'm silent in confusion—then I realize: The story

Sam told the soldiers when we bluffed our way out of the pub must've spread like wildfire. I offer a polite smile, and then stand up. "This is my stop," I mutter.

"Hey, now, wait, you're not heading to the Arc with the rest of us? Let me buy you a drink after the meeting."

"Meeting?" I repeat, turning back to the soldier.

"The meeting, you know about the meeting? It's mandatory, eleven hundred hours at the Arc? Galen Rye himself called it."

"Yes, of course," I say, trying not to show the panic that's settling over me. "I've been asked by the higher-ups to gather some troops from certain tactical points around the city first."

"All right, Yossarian, but I'm getting you that drink."

"Understood," I reply, and then turn back to the train's doors. Once again my mask flickers. I notice one low-ranked soldier staring at me, squinting at my imperfect face.

Finally, the train stops and the doors open. I jump off and move quickly into the city. Getting off a stop early has left me about a mile from the pub where Sam and I hid, but there was no other choice—I couldn't let the mask disappear in front of dozens of soldiers.

I move quickly, recalculating my odds of survival now that Galen Rye (controlled by Happy) has called a meeting of *all* Alt soldiers in the Arc at the very same time I'll be trying to break my friends out. I don't think I stand much of a chance.

I tell Apple-Moth to come out and get some solar charge now that we're in a completely deserted part of the city, but the charge is slow in coming, as the big dark cloud is still hovering above us.

"Wow, wow, wow! Captain Yossarian, I almost died back there!"

"Yossarian is not my name," I say, running through the streets now.

"Oh. Then why did you tell that nice soldier that your name was—"

"Because I was lying," I interrupt.

"Lying is bad!"

"Apple-Moth," I say, "I'll explain later; for now you'll just have to trust me that I did the right thing."

The drone seems to think about this for a second, its lights turning dark green before brightening to yellow. "Okay!"

I move as quickly as I can, sprinting through the town, weaving my way through streets and alleyways toward the Arc. I'm aware, suddenly, of darkness falling over me, the sun dipping behind a cloud maybe, but when I steal a glance up, I realize that I'm in the shadow of the Arc. The steep dome structure rises up over the buildings of the city, the dark material it is constructed of sending a cold shade over this part of town.

Looking to the top of the building, I see that the enormous circular storm cloud is emanating from the Arc itself. A stream of mist pours out of the tip of the dome.

What the hell is going on? I wonder.

I'm still about a quarter mile away from the enormous building, but already the scale of it is staggering. It's not nearly as high as the Verticals, but at its base it must be three miles wide.

"Apple-Moth," I whisper.

"Yes, friend?" the drone replies in hushed tones.

"When did they build this?"

"Tier Two and Three soldiers were offered shelter from Phase Three if they took part in construction of the Arc. The first three floors were built between the first of June and the twenty-first of June. The rest was built over a four-week period from July the fourteenth to August the tenth of this year."

I was in the Loop for the first part of construction, and the Block for the rest, I think.

"And what exactly is Phase Three?" I ask, already knowing that Phase One was the deletion of 98 percent of human-kind, and yet sure that Phases Two and Three might somehow be worse.

Apple-Moth's lights flicker. "I don't know. I do not have access to that information."

"What time is it now?"

"Ten forty-one a.m."

"Fuck," I whisper. Woods has twenty-six minutes left.

"Hey, come on now, friend, you don't need to use that kind of language. Find a better word!"

"No, *fuck* is the appropriate word here, Apple-Moth."

"Okay, friend. Fuck!"

I actually laugh as I speed up, moving quickly toward the dome. As I get closer, Apple-Moth returns to my pocket, now with enough charge to reapply the digital mask to my face.

"Apple-Moth, do me a favor and make the mask match my skin tone this time, okay?"

"No problem, friend!"

We begin passing armed soldiers milling around, sentry towers with snipers, tanks idling near the foot of the Arc.

152

I'm entirely in the shadow of the building now. I stop and survey the enormous Arc towers before me, matte-black blocks tapering upward to the apex of the dome, one large entrance guarded by four soldiers through which tanks periodically enter and exit.

There's no time to come up with an intricate plan—the seconds of my friends' lives are ticking away.

I walk up to a slow-moving tank and hold both hands up in a *stop* gesture. The tank halts and a soldier appears at the turret.

"Sir?" he asks, after saluting me.

"Make room inside, Officer Cadet," I say, trying to fill my voice with the commanding confidence of a military leader.

"S-sir," the soldier replies, uncertainty etched in his voice, "the tank is full. Lieutenant Bransky said—"

"Lieutenant Bransky is a grade-A piece of shit, son," I say, and I think of Sam on the streets outside the pub, when she had tricked the lower-ranked soldiers into believing that I was a captain with just her self-assurance and confidence. "Now either step aside or tell someone else to get out. That's an order," I instruct as I climb to the summit of the tank.

The young soldier's face becomes splotchy with red and he ducks inside, telling a soldier even more junior than him to get out.

I climb inside and we ride—in silence—into the Arc.

The tank comes to a halt after two minutes of slowly rolling onward into the structure. I try to steal glances at the screen that shows what's in front of us, and see a space so vast that—if it wasn't for the artificial lighting—I'd think must be outdoors. We all wait inside the tank for . . . what?

"Sir?" one of the young soldiers intones.

"Hmm?" I reply, staring dumbly at her. "Oh, right," I say, realizing that they're waiting for me, their senior officer, to exit first. I climb out of the tank, my mind flashing back to the Battle of Midway Park: Kina, Malachai, Pander, Blue, and I had ridden into the middle of the Alt's rally in a tank identical to this one.

The other soldiers join me on the concrete floor. The tank is parked in an enormous hangar-like space beside at least a hundred others. Around us, troops are disembarking and moving toward a checkpoint at the far end of the hangar. "My" squad is looking at me expectantly again, so I tell them to lead the way, all the while glancing around, looking for a door that might lead to a medical facility or laboratory. As the soldiers walk, we are joined by others. At first a dozen or so, then thirty, and then we are in a great wave of Alts, all dressed in black, all perfect in their features and bodies, all of them with their enhancements: mechanical lungs; robotic hearts; synthetic blood.

I slow my pace down as we approach the checkpoint—beyond it is an enormous hall. I let the soldiers pass me by until I'm near the back of the line.

Drones are scrutinizing the crowd for weapons, and sentries posted at the entrance are using handheld iris scanners to check identification.

I hang back even more, slowing until I'm barely moving at

all. The river of soldiers flows by me on each side. I spot a deserted access corridor and decide to slip down it. I glance once more through the enormous open doors of the hall—and see Galen Rye taking to the stage to rapturous applause.

I want to stay and listen, I want to gather information about Phase Three, but I can't.

I run down the long, dark corridor, the vinyl floor squeaking under my rubber-soled boots, the black and red of the painted walls rushing by, and Galen's voice echoing after me.

"Soldiers of Earth, survivors of the end of days, warriors of destiny, you are the chosen few!"

Galen's words and the roar of the crowd chase me down the never-ending passageway. I scan the plaques on the doors—MESS HALL 5 FOR TIER THREE USE; TRAINING CENTER 5 FOR TIER THREE USE; BARRACK 2 FOR TIER THREE, G COMPANY—and half a dozen other barrack notices that are all useless to me. This pattern repeats from MESS HALL 6 and TRAINING CENTER 6, and on and on with no sign of the whereabouts of Malachai and Woods.

Galen's egomaniacal ramblings begin to fade as I increase the distance between me and the great hall, but the roar of the crowd after every declaration is a swarm of hornets filling the Arc relentlessly.

I'm in the belly of the beast now, I think, almost deliriously, as I sprint through the enemy's base.

Finally, ahead, at the corner where this protracted corridor meets another, I see an elevator. I come to a skidding stop. The sign above reads, ELEVATOR: FLOORS 2–10. I see a door marked STAIRS beside it. I decide on the stairs, knowing that Happy has the capability of trapping me inside the metal box of the elevator if it becomes aware of my presence.

Before I push the door open, I see four beams of light wavering against the corner wall, growing steadily brighter and larger. My instincts tell me to shove the door open and sprint up the stairs as fast as I can—I know that the lights belong to the eyes of host soldiers. Instead, I move quietly, pushing the door slowly open to avoid any sound, but as soon as the door opens, it becomes clear that this is unnecessary, as a thunderous roar fills the room. I turn around to see that I'm in an enormous open ground-floor space. From here, I can see all the way to the top of the Arc. Through the middle of the building, an enormous waterfall cascades down, acting as a natural air conditioner. I can see the narrowing corridors of each level going up and up until they almost disappear near the top. There is nobody else here; all the Alts and all the hosts must be at Galen's conference. All except the two that are patrolling the corridor on the other side of this door. I stand with my ear pressed against the wood, waiting and hoping that the hosts don't come this same way.

From here, on the ground floor, I can hear Galen's voice echoing through the building once more. I have to strain to hear the footsteps of the hosts over the crashing of the waterfall, but as they slowly pass by on the other side of the door, I can't help but pick up on the words.

"... *Thirty-seven men and women who protested the government's decision to choose your lives over the lives of the Regulars stand before you here today. Thirty-seven men and women who tried to undermine our plan to save your lives and your family's lives by warning the Regulars of what was to become of them."*

I struggle to pick up on every word that Galen is saying, but notice a wall-mounted SoCom unit and wave my hand over it. Suddenly, in front of me in perfect holographic projection, is Galen Rye. To his right, beside him on the stage, is a group of Alts, all of them with their hands magnetically cuffed behind their backs. When Galen speaks next, his voice is as clear as if I were in the room with him.

"Do we respect their bravery? Yes, we do. Can we let such actions go unpunished? No, we cannot."

I look at the images of the men and women on the stage, some crying, some stoic, some shaking with fear.

They're going to send them to the Block, I think. And then Galen gestures offstage, and eight Alt soldiers walk onstage carrying Deleters—sickle-shaped executioners' weapons that reduce the condemned to microscopic particles. One of the cuffed prisoners begins to scream.

"Remember this, friends," Galen says as the Deleters rise above the prisoners, "remember what happens to those who do not support a World Government who chose *you* to live through the end of the world."

Galen nods, and the Deleters begin to swing.

I look away as the first prisoner is reduced to ash. I switch the SoCom off as the crowd begins to cheer, and I am left only with the ghost of that sound, resonating throughout the building.

I exhale, thinking that I might be about to throw up.

Happy is killing Alts, I think. *Happy is killing Alts who dared to question genocide.*

And I cannot understand it. I cannot understand how so many people can be talked into believing in something so cruel, something so ruthless and vicious.

"Apple-Moth, time?" I whisper, my voice shaking.

"The time is 11:02 a.m., friend."

I feel my heart sink. Five minutes until Woods becomes a host, eighteen minutes for Malachai. I have to put the atrocities that are occurring just down the hallway to the back of my mind.

"Apple-Moth, do you know if there's a medical center or laboratory in this building?"

"I don't have access to the blueprints or plans to the Arc. Sorry, friend."

"Shit!" I say, almost yelling but stopping myself just in time.

"But," Apple-Moth says from the chest pocket of the T-shirt beneath my body armor, "the building is completely uniform on every level barring four anomalies: the hangar where the tank was parked; the big hall where that man was speaking; a single, large, circular room at the very top of the building, and two more rooms that don't fit the symmetry on the penultimate floor."

"It has to be one of those three," I say, running to the center of the room until the spray from the waterfall begins to soak me. I look up into the abyss of stairs and corridors. "How many floors to the top, Apple-Moth?"

The drone zips out of its hiding place, the electronic mask disappearing from my face. Apple-Moth looks up too. "Sixty-six floors."

I know that I can't climb sixty-six floors in less than five minutes, but my eyes have already fallen upon the emergency drone-risers inside the break-glass-in-case-of-emergency cases against the far wall. Drone-risers are used to travel up and down tall buildings rapidly in an emergency to get people to safety. They removed them from the Verticals after kids stole them and hurt themselves.

I move to the case, using the side of my fist to break the glass, hoping that an automatic alarm won't be set off. Luckily, there's silence as I grab the drone-riser, switch it on, and throw it to the floor. The small black platform hovers a few inches above the ground and I step on, lifting my toes to command the board to rise up. It does so, rapidly.

I'm whooshing up between the staircases, the gargantuan waterfall booming down beside me, Apple-Moth struggling to keep pace as I rush up and up, trying to keep an eye on the floor numbers as they flash past.

Floor fifty-five, the black letters say, floor fifty-six, fifty-seven, fifty-eight. The higher I go, the less space there is between me and the water as the dome shape of the building gets narrower and narrower. And at around floor sixty, the waterfall stops, and I am above it.

I lower my toes, slowing the platform down, but not by much.

As we reach the highest point, I slow the riser down to a crawl, and jump off at floor sixty-six, the top floor.

I find myself on a circular platform, and I'm dumbstruck by what I see—a production line of drones being created by robotic arms, thousands and thousands of them. Large attack drones on the left, and small Mosquito drones on the right. The robotic workers attach rotor blades, tracking devices, cannons, antennae, and scanners, and then the drones fly straight out into the gigantic cloud that encircles the city.

"What the hell is this?" I whisper.

Apple-Moth glows red in front of my face, hiding me from each individual Mosquito as it is born and flies off into the air.

The drones, both Mosquitoes and attack drones, are being produced at a rate of about one per second, maybe even faster than that.

I stare at the conveyor belt for too long before snapping out my amazement. I have to go. I turn, running toward the staircase.

Right now, all that matters is saving my friends, and they are not on this floor.

I move down to floor sixty-five. Compared to the lower floors, the shape of the building means that the corridor is much, much smaller up here, and there are only two rooms facing each other. The plaque on one reads: LABORATORY: RESTRICTED ACCESS. The other reads: RECOVERY ROOM: RESTRICTED ACCESS.

I move to the laboratory door and try the handle—it's locked.

"Apple-Moth, time!" I call.

"11:04 a.m., friend."

"No, no, no, no!" I yell, no longer caring who hears me.

I failed, I think. *My friends are on the other side of this door, and I can't get to them. Woods becomes one of them in three minutes.*

"I couldn't save them," I say, my voice coming out in a croak. "There's no time left. I couldn't save them."

"Friend," Apple-Moth says, hovering beside my ear.

"What?"

"Do you need to get into that restricted area to save your friends?"

"Yes," I say, feeling a tentative burst of hope.

"Normally I wouldn't do this—breaking the rules is bad—but if it's for friends . . ."

The little drone dips to the vinyl floor and slips underneath the door and into the room. I wait in the empty corridor. Another roar from the crowd reaches me, even over the monotonous drone of the waterfall. And then the handle moves, twisting of its own accord, and the door swings open.

"Apple-Moth, you genius!" I say, and run into the laboratory.

Against the far wall of the large room are dozens of screens, each showing different sets of statistics and information. Vials of nanobots line one shelf on the right, and robotic equipment hangs from the ceiling. Double-size holographic projections of Malachai, Woods, and the third subject float in an open space, their bodies translucent so doctors and scientists can see their organs working inside them. Three metal arms protrude from the floor, the characters E4-EX-19 stenciled in white paint on them. There is a glowing orb of light levitating above the machinery. The arms all face away from one another—they look like an ancient fairground ride, only each of them hovers over a paralyzed human being lying in a bed. These humans are who I came here for, Woods and Malachai.

I run over to them, and stop as I see who the third subject is.

Tyco Roth.

The boy who tried to kill me, the boy who was shot six times, the boy who should be dead.

In a moment, a million thoughts flash through my mind: *Is it really him? Should I save him? He tried to kill me; why should I help him? He'll only try to kill me again! It's the right thing to do. It's the wrong thing to do.*

I choose to ignore all thoughts of Tyco for now. I run over to the paralyzed test subjects, going to Woods first. I see that his eyes have been replaced by the glowing eyes of Happy. I look closely at them and see that they are not fully lit up yet—the light seems to be encircling his iris one segment at a time. Right now there is only one segment left to light up.

"Apple-Moth, time!" I scream as I grab Woods and haul him from the bed.

"11:06 a.m.," the drone replies, buzzing anxiously from side to side.

One minute, I have one minute to save him.

Woods collapses onto the floor, gasping in a lungful of air.

"Luka," he says, his mechanical eyes turning to me.

"Woods, how do I help you? Tell me how to stop this."

"I knew you'd come," he says, a smile spreading across his pained face.

"What do I do, Woods? How do I stop this?"

"Thank you," he replies, and his smile widens, the gap in his front teeth showing. "I'm glad they didn't get me in the end."

I have enough time to think how sad that smile seems, and then he's gone, running out of the open laboratory door. I watch

162

as he lifts his large frame elegantly over the banister of the sixty-fifth set of stairs.

He falls in a silence punctuated by my own inability to breathe.

For a moment, I wonder if the waterfall might save him, if he might get swept up in the cascade and somehow live. But I know it's not possible. Even at its closest point to the highest floor, it's ten feet from the edge.

"No," I say, finally inhaling. "No. I could have saved you . . . I could have . . ."

Images of my father falling from the roof of the Black Road Vertical, saving my life by dragging one of Happy's hosts to its demise, flash in front of my eyes. I can feel my chest tightening, my breath coming in and out in shallow gasps that leave me craving oxygen that I can't seem to find. I fall to the floor, my legs collapsing beneath me.

"I . . . I . . . I . . ." My voice is a stammering motor that I have no control over. "I could have saved you . . . I . . . I could have . . . I could have saved you . . ."

My hands are shaking as the images of my father falling, Blue bleeding to death, Mable screaming, the rats biting, the Smilers attacking, all become vivid and real in front of my eyes.

The lights dim and a red light begins to flash as Happy's voice comes over the speakers: *"Incident on ground floor. Complete lockdown initiated. All floors to be scanned and searched."*

"I could have saved you . . . I could have . . . I . . ."

Somewhere, miles away, in the back of my mind, locked in a coffin buried underground, my own voice is screaming for me to get up, screaming that Tyco is still alive, Malachai is still alive, that he needs my help.

"Friend," a soft voice says, and my eyes focus on the low pink lights of Apple-Moth.

"I could have saved him," I tell the small companion drone. "I could have saved him."

"You can't save everyone, friend."

"But he didn't have to . . ."

"That was his decision. You have risked your life to save your friends. Is this correct?"

I nod, tears now falling down my face. "I can't keep going, I've lost so many people already. They just keep on dying."

"You have my permission to quit, friend, if that's what you need. But if you need someone to tell you to get up, to keep fighting, to never give up, I can do that too."

I wipe the tears away from my eyes, my hands still shaking, but I can breathe again, I can feel the oxygen slipping silently into my bloodstream and giving me strength.

"Tell me," I say.

Apple-Moth's lights grow brighter. "I believe in you, friend. Now get up."

I push myself to standing. Shaking legs carry me past Tyco's bed. I glance at the boy who tricked me, told me he had forgiven me, that we had to work together to survive the end of the world, and then stuck an Ebb patch to my back and planned on killing me slowly with a knife. I ignore him. *Let him become one of them*, I think, and try not to dwell on the shame. And as the thought flashes through my mind—*Kill him now*—my shame doubles, not because the thought is cruel, but because it would be merciful, and yet I don't have it in me to end his life.

I move to Malachai's bed as the sirens wail and Happy's voice gives instructions.

I grab the boy—who now has one segment of light shining out at the top of each iris—and haul him off the bed.

Malachai sucks in air and then pushes it out of his lungs, screaming as he does. "Took your fucking time, Luka!" he gasps.

"Sorry," I say, unable to think of anything else.

Suddenly, the older boy grabs me, wrapping both arms around me and holding me tight. "I love you, Luka, you're my hero."

"You're mine," I reply, my voice muffled by the skin of his bare shoulder pressed against my mouth.

"Got a plan?" he asks, his mechanical eyes scanning the room and the floors below us. "Because there are one thousand and ninety-eight soldiers all heading this way. We have about fifteen seconds, according to these magical eyes."

"Less," a voice comes from across the room.

I spin around and see that Tyco is sitting up, his eyes glowing bright white. Happy is onto us.

He leaps down from the paralysis bed and strides toward Malachai and me.

"Shit, shit," Malachai mutters, stumbling backward, not yet recovered from the Block and the paralyses of this place.

"Hi, new friend!" Apple-Moth says, zipping up to Tyco's eye line.

Tyco swats the little drone to the floor. And in that moment I feel a blinding rage.

I move forward to meet the Alt, raising my fists. I swing hard at his head but he ducks it easily, throwing a hook as he does, his fist connecting with my solar plexus and knocking the wind out of me.

I crumple to the floor, gasping for air, and Tyco aims a kick at me, the top of his foot slamming into the underside of my chin.

My head rocks back and I see white stars in my vision, but the rage is still pulsing through me. I get up and run at Tyco, tackling him around the waist and dragging him to the floor.

Tyco throws three jabs and hits me each time, once in the left eye and twice on the jaw.

"It is futile to fight me," Tyco says, getting to his feet. "You are shorter than this host, lighter than him, you did not have the upbringing he did, and you have no upgrades."

"No," Malachai says from behind Tyco, "but I do."

Malachai throws four heavy punches at Tyco, landing all of them before headbutting him right between the eyes.

Tyco stumbles backward and falls, sliding across the floor, coming to a rest against a set of stainless-steel cupboards. Malachai marches over to the cupboards, grabbing them and pulling them on top of the thrashing, bright-eyed boy.

I look up at Malachai, who doesn't even seem out of breath.

"That should buy us about thirty seconds. What now?"

I get to my feet, and just as I'm about to admit that I have no idea how we're getting out of this one, I spot the drone-riser still hovering a few inches above the ground outside the lab door. "Does that window open?" I ask, pointing to the large pane of glass beside the shelf of nanobots.

Malachai's eyes—now with two segments lit up—glow orange and the window opens. "Wow, I can override Happy . . . because I'm about to *be* Happy!"

"One more thing," I say, and grab a small trolley by the legs. I swing it hard at one of the arms of the E4-EX-19. Sparks fly, the glowing orb that floats in the center flickers. I hit a second arm and the orb goes out. I swing the trolley four more times, completing Abril Ortega's cryptic task to destroy the device, whatever it is.

"Sure, *now's* the best time to deal with your anger issues," Malachai mutters.

I take the riser and run toward the window, grabbing Malachai by the wrist as I go. I can hear the sound of Tyco shoving off the heavy steel cupboards, hear the elevators opening up, hear about ten more drone-risers gliding up toward us.

"Apple-Moth, let's go!" I scream, and the drone darts into the pocket behind my body armor.

And then we're in midair, the enormity of the Arc beneath us, stretching out into the daylight.

Malachai screams, half out of fear and half out of exhilaration.

I push down the riser beneath our feet and our descent slows. Not by much—the riser is meant for only one person—but enough that there's at least some control.

Now I scream too as we zoom down the side of the building, the drone-riser staying flat beneath our feet, adjusting to the angle of the building, pushing us outward toward the foot of the dome.

Suddenly, the ground is approaching, and I'm aware of just how fast we are going. Apple-Moth, possibly sensing the speed of descent, floats out of my pocket and hovers in the air. I watch the little drone get smaller and smaller.

"This is going to hu—" I manage, and then we're being thrown into the scrubland at the back of the Arc.

I feel my wrist snap and something ping in my back as my legs are thrown over my head. My chin scrapes along the ground and then my ear is ripped half off. For a full five seconds I can't breathe, my diaphragm cramping from the trauma. I sit up, finally hauling in a rasping breath. Malachai is holding his side, a bubbling stream of blood seeping out between his fingers.

"I think I've broken every single rib. Every single goddamned rib," he gasps.

I can hear the sound of his snapped bones popping back into place from here, and I can feel my own ear zipping itself back to the side of my head.

"We have to keep moving," I say, my voice equally as gravelly as his.

I drag myself to my feet and help Malachai to his. I try not to show the panic I'm feeling as I see that three segments have now lit up in his eyes.

"Apple-Moth, time?" I call out, and the drone floats into the air beside me.

"You're alive!" the drone wails happily, spinning loops in the air. "You're alive, alive, alive!"

"Yes, we're alive, Apple-Moth," I grunt, the pain just starting to evaporate. "What's the time?"

168

"It's 11:09, friend," Apple-Moth says, colors flickering rapidly, blue to green to pink to orange.

Eleven minutes, I think. *Eleven minutes until it's too late!*

The sound of Happy's voice blaring out into the afternoon reverberates around us, commanding its soldiers to track us, to follow us and find us and bring us back.

I pull Malachai along with me as I stumble into the tall grass behind the Arc.

We move deeper, making the most of the small amount of time we've gained from luring the soldiers to the top of the enormous building before making our escape.

I hear the sound of running water and we half stagger and half fall down an embankment and into a shallow stream. And still the voices grow louder behind us.

My wrist clicks back into place as I look frantically around for a place to run, a place to hide.

And then I see a large sewer outlet pipe pouring a steady stream of gray water out toward the lake. A way down. A way into the tunnels.

Remembering Malachai's Panoptic camera, I quickly unclip the Alt body armor, take off my T-shirt, and wrap it around Malachai's head. I then put the body armor back on, wondering all the time if it'll matter, because time is running out and those robotic eyes will come online any minute.

"Come on," I say, pulling Malachai toward the pipeline.

We climb up into the foul-smelling tube and run, crouched over so far that it's hard to breathe.

As soon as we're in the pipeline I think about Sam's words

the last time I was in the tunnels—*you do not want to get lost down here.* But there's no choice; we have to get back to the library.

I can hear Malachai's breath behind me, ragged and hoarse.

"Apple-Moth," I say, and the little drone appears in front of my face.

"Yes, friend?"

"Can you light the way?"

"No problem!"

A bright light illuminates the tunnel, and I can't see the end of it; it just goes on and on.

"Luka," Malachai grunts.

"Just keep moving," I tell him, trying to ignore the choking sensation in my lungs.

"Luka," he says again, and I can feel him tugging on my arm as his legs buckle beneath him. He regains his balance and I continue pulling him forward.

"There's no time, Malachai," I tell him as the panic starts to rise up in me. I already know that we're too far away from the library, and I don't know my way around these tunnels, and there's only minutes left before Happy—

"Luka, stop!" he screams. The desperation in his voice strikes me like a fist.

"What is it?" I ask, standing still, breathing heavily.

"It's going to happen soon. You have to do it now."

I look into the boy's handsome face, so handsome, in fact, that he was known as a Natural back before the apocalypse: a Regular so perfect he was often mistaken for an Alt. In his eyes I see that the lights are now three-quarters of the way around his iris.

"They're uploading the code that will turn me into a host, Luka. As long as I have these eyes, they can get to me."

"Igby's at the hideout; he can figure out how to stop it. There's a surgeon too, if it comes to that."

Malachai shakes his head. "It has to happen now."

I stare into his robot eyes. They change my friend's face so drastically. He's still beautiful but he's not completely Malachai. "I don't think I can do it, Malachai. I can't—"

"Please, Luka," he says, lowering his voice.

The reality of what he's asking of me sinks in, and I feel horror creeping up my spine.

"I don't know if I can," I say.

Malachai nods. "Then kill me, Luka, please, because I can't become one of them." He points in the direction of the Arc. "I've seen what happens to the person behind the eyes, I've seen the agony of the passengers inside, and I won't let it happen to me."

For a moment I try to think of another solution, I scour my mind for a way out, but I know there's nothing else.

I look to Apple-Moth, whose lights dim to an almost-imperceptible orange glow. I look back to Malachai.

"Lie down," I say, trying to steel myself.

Malachai nods, relief mixing with utter terror on his face as he lies in the shallow, dirty water, mechanical eyes staring at the metal of the pipe.

I reach a shaking hand toward his face, noticing that another segment of light has come alive.

"Wait," Malachai whispers as a pool of tears spills onto his cheek, and his eyes scan his dingy surroundings. "It would've been nice to have seen the sky one last time . . . okay. Do it."

I take a breath, and then there is no more hesitation.

I push my forefinger into the socket beside his left eye, my mind recoiling.

Malachai begins to scream as I push harder. The agonized and inhuman noise that escapes my friend makes my head spin. I begin to feel faint, nauseous, weak, but I keep going, wrapping my thumb around the cyborg eyeball and pulling it toward me.

Malachai lets out a closed-mouth scream, thumping his fists against the pipe on either side of him, sending out a reverberating shudder.

I haul at the artificial eye, but it won't come.

I suppress waves of nausea and pull harder, harder; Malachai's scream turns into a bloodcurdling screech. I grit my teeth, breathing heavily through my revulsion. Finally, there's an audible snap, and it's over.

Malachai falls silent as I vomit into the foul water. Tears run down my face, my vision blurred and graying out at the edges as I struggle to maintain consciousness.

I turn back to my friend. I look to see if his chest is rising and falling. It isn't.

"No! No, Malachai, don't you dare die!"

I crawl over to him and begin to pump at his chest.

"He's not dead, friend," Apple-Moth says, hovering beside my left ear.

"But his heart . . ." I start, and then I remember what Igby had said: *They've already taken their eyes. They've replaced their lungs and their hearts.*

Malachai now has an MOR and an APM system: no lungs and no heart. I press my newly fixed ear against his chest and hear the mechanical hum of machinery.

He's still alive.

I'm distracted by a noise, a quiet, mechanical whirring, and I realize that it's coming from my hand.

I look down. Malachai's eye is moving, the pupil contracting. I see that the second-to-last light around the iris has come on— I'm almost out of time. And then the pupil begins to revolve until it's looking right at me.

Without thinking, I smash the blood-covered eye against the floor of the pipe, shattering it.

I clamber back to Malachai. The other eye continues to upload and I don't have time to hesitate. It's easier now that he's unconscious.

The final light comes on and a rapid beeping sound comes from the eye just seconds after it is liberated from Malachai's socket. I'm about to destroy this eye too when something stops me. I think of the eye that Igby uses to hack into Happy's mind, and I push it deep into my pocket.

I survey the scene before me. My friend, lying still in the sewage water, face streaked with blood, two bruised and bloodied holes where his eyes should be. And me: hands red with gore; exhausted both mentally and physically.

Apple-Moth moves slowly around us both. The drone's movements are sluggish, as if it is somehow queasy too.

I pull the T-shirt covering Malachai's forehead down to cover his wounds too. Now that his eyes are out, Malachai's Panoptic is the only way Happy has of tracking us, other than the Mosquitoes, but Apple-Moth will be taking care of them.

What now? I think, sitting on my heels and putting the body armor back on, but there's no time for careful planning as the voices of the soldiers come again, far away, echoing down the pipeline, but close enough for the adrenaline to flow back into my body.

"They're coming, friend, we have to move!" Apple-Moth says, zipping back and forth through the air.

"I know," I grunt as I scramble over Malachai, hooking my arms around his chest. I try to drag him deeper into the pipeline.

Apple-Moth flies over, grabs Malachai by the hair, and tries to help me drag him—but it's no use. There's no way we're moving fast enough to outrun Happy's soldiers.

Then Malachai begins to stir.

"Malachai," I whisper, crouching beside him, "can you walk?"

"I'm not one of them?" he asks, his voice raspy and full of pain.

"No," I tell him, "you're still you."

"I'm blind," he says, sounding neither pleased or displeased.

"Does it hurt?" I ask.

"Stupid fucking question," Malachai barks back. "It hurts. It hurts like hell, but I think I'm in shock right now, because it's bearable."

"Can you stand? The Alts are coming, and we need to get you to a doctor."

Malachai nods and gets shakily to his feet. I watch as a disturbing amount of blood seeps from his right eye socket into the T-shirt.

I put my arm around him, and tell Apple-Moth to light the way again, and we stumble through the sewer pipe for what feels like a very long time, until finally it connects to larger stormwater tunnels and we can stand up straight again.

"Apple-Moth," I say, and the drone turn toward me, dazzling me with its beam.

"Yes, friend!"

"Do you know the way back to the—" I almost say library, but catch myself before I reveal the location of our hideout to Malachai's Panoptic microphone. "Back to the base?"

Apple-Moth turns slowly around, scanning his surroundings. "No. Not one hundred percent, but I could try."

"It'll have to do," I say. "Lead the way."

Apple-Moth glows green, and begins to move cautiously through the old tunnels, turning first one way, changing its mind and then turning another.

We follow the drone for what feels like twenty minutes, when, finally, I whisper, "Apple-Moth, how much farther?"

"Umm," the drone replies, turning toward me and then away, "not long now!"

The drone's voice is so unsure that I already know we're lost. I'm about to yell at it when Malachai falls to the ground behind me.

"Malachai," I call, running over to his collapsed form.

Apple-Moth comes over. "He's alive."

"Where's the nearest exit?" I ask, knowing that we have to get our bearings.

Apple-Moth scans the area. "Umm, it's two minutes that

way, but don't be mad if we're not right beside the base. I was getting there."

Apple-Moth leads us in the direction of the nearest exit. I pull Malachai along and progress is slow, but finally we make it to another sewage outlet pipe and drop down into an ancient, abandoned wastewater treatment plant.

All around us are concrete tanks sunk into the ground that would once have been filled with sewage water, but are now empty. The machinery is all rusted and still, and thousands of birds have made their nests on the roof of the old metal tanks that tower over us.

I don't hang around, though—I see higher ground ahead, and drag Malachai through the structure and over to the grassy hill. When we reach the top, my heart sinks. We are nowhere near the library; instead we are on the edge of town, only a quarter mile from the Red Zone.

"Dammit, Apple-Moth!" I yell, suddenly filled with anger.

"I'm sorry, friend, I got lost!"

"You got lost and now Malachai might die!"

Apple-Moth's lights dim until they're almost gone, and I feel pity and regret welling up in me.

"I'm so sorry, friend," Apple-Moth says.

"Don't be," I reply. "It's not your fault. I would've gotten us just as lost."

Apple-Moth turns away, as though hiding so I can't see it cry.

I look out over the city and try to figure out what my next move is.

And then I hear footsteps coming from the wastewater plant.

I look down and see three Alt soldiers coming toward us.

"No!" I whisper, trying to duck down, but I know that they've already seen us.

I grab Malachai and start pulling him down the other side of the hill. Finally, I pick him up, channeling all my desperation into strength, and run on shaking legs toward the woodland on the edge of the Red Zone.

I can hardly breathe, I'm so exhausted, so tired, but I keep on going, keep on running.

I carry Malachai into the woods, Apple-Moth flying alongside us, but progress is slow. Too slow. The footsteps grow louder; the commands of the senior officers are closer. I'm unarmed and Malachai is unconscious. I try to hide, laying Malachai down behind a bush and crouching beside him.

But suddenly, they are there. Three soldiers, all of them with headlight eyes, staring down at us.

At least it's not Tyco, I think, looking at each of the human hosts one at a time. *At least he doesn't get the satisfaction.*

Apple-Moth glows red and hovers in front of us, trying to protect us with its tiny body.

I shake my head, sweat spilling off me. "Why can't you just leave us alone?"

One of the host soldiers steps forward, his eyes lighting up the gloom of the forest.

"Because," he says, a hint of smug satisfaction in his almost lifeless voice, "we need three of you to re—"

And then his head bulges above his right eye and he falls down dead.

The two other soldiers have no time to react before they too are hit by USW rounds.

Five seconds after the soldiers arrived, they are now dead in front of us, their eyes fading until there's no light in them anymore, artificial light or life-light.

"What the hell?" I murmur.

And then, from behind me, a rustling of branches.

I stand and turn in time to see a girl emerging from the thicket. At first she is almost invisible—she's wearing camouflage clothing and her face is painted in shades of green, leaving her looking like an apparition.

"Step aside, Luka," she says, slinging the strap of the USW rifle over her shoulder.

"Molly?" I ask, sure that this is a mirage. The last time I saw my sister she was an emaciated clone, high on Ebb, sores on her face, cracked lips, sunken eyes. Now she looks strong, tough.

I feel overwhelmed, overcome—elated. My legs are suddenly too weak to hold me and I slump down to the ground.

"You're alive," I say. "I can't believe you're alive. Molly . . ."

She drops to one knee beside me and Malachai and I reach out to touch her, to make sure that she's real, but she ignores me, removing a thin metal tool from her pocket.

"What are you doing?" I ask.

She doesn't reply, only removes the T-shirt from Malachai's head, places the tip of the spiked tool against his Panoptic camera, and pushes down with all her strength.

The tool spins and sinks into Malachai's head. *Jesus, hasn't he been through enough?* I think, but I'm still too overwrought and incredulous at the sight of my sister to really feel much else.

"Take his legs," Molly says, extracting the tool, which has grabbed the tiny camera from the bleeding hole in Malachai's forehead. "I'll grab his arms."

"Molly, you're . . ." I start, but my brain feels like it's short-circuiting as I try to comprehend what's going on.

"Hurry, there will be more of them," she says, throwing the dislodged Panoptic into the trees. There's something strange about her voice, something dull and listless.

Molly grabs Malachai around the chest and then gives me an impatient look as I stand there, staring at her.

"Right, yeah," I say, grabbing the boy's feet and lifting him.

"Is this a new friend?" Apple-Moth answers, floating around Molly's head.

"Luka, why do you have a toy?" my sister asks, struggling with the weight of Malachai.

"Uh, Apple-Moth," I say, "sleep mode."

"Oh, but we're on an adventu—"

"Sleep mode, Apple-Moth," I demand. "I promise I'll reactivate you later. Your battery is on five percent anyway," I point out, noticing the warning message hovering over the drone's body.

"Fine!" the drone replies irately, and then falls slowly to the ground.

I pick up the drone and put it in my pocket, glancing sheepishly at my clearly impatient sister.

"It's not a toy, exactly," I say, grabbing Malachai's legs. "It's a mobile scrambler—it hides me from Mosquitoes."

"Uh-huh," Molly says.

I glance up at the storm clouds, now so dense and dark that Apple-Moth's battery was struggling to recharge. I know now that Happy is filling that storm cloud full of Mosquitoes and attack drones. Its plan? I'm not sure.

We pick Malachai up and I try to carry him toward a thick area of brush, but Molly pulls him toward the Red Zone.

"This way," she says.

"We can't get any closer to the fence," I say. "The radiation—"

"This way," she repeats, and again, I notice that odd indolent tone to her voice. Is she back on Ebb?

I look around for a better option. Molly does not have our healing abilities and I don't want her risking her life in the Red Zone, but the sound of more soldiers approaching makes up my mind, and I follow her.

Molly's alive, my mind rejoices. *She's alive, she made it out of the vault and she's still alive.*

I'm aware that my thoughts sound a lot like Apple-Moth when the drone was so delighted that Malachai and I had survived the fall from the Arc. In spite of myself and in spite of the situation, this makes me smile.

The dead weight of Malachai feels as though it's growing heavier with every step, but the fear of capture, of imprisonment, keeps me moving.

"Through here," Molly, says, gritting her teeth with the effort of lifting the boy.

"We can't go through there," I whisper, staring at the gap that has been cut into the wire fence.

"Trust me, Luka," she says, and ducks into the Red Zone.

I hesitate, knowing the destructive power of the radiation, knowing that even with my healing ability, I won't survive long. But I trust my sister.

I follow, the muscles in my neck and shoulders tensing involuntarily as I enter the irradiated area.

"How deep are we going?" I ask, feeling the panic start to rise inside me.

"Slightly more than half a mile," my sister replies.

"Half a mil— We can't go half a mile into the Red Zone! Do you know what will happen? Our skin will melt off our bones!"

"No, it won't," she replies, the strain of carrying Malachai now showing on her face.

"The radiation, Molly, it's active for another two hundred years."

"It is," she says, "but there's no radiation for another half a mile."

"What are you talking about?"

She stops and lowers Malachai to the ground behind the rusted and overgrown remains of what might once have been a car. "There is a thin band of radiation at the fence line," she tells me, wiping sweat from her forehead. "We've already passed through it. From here until about half a mile in, the radiation levels are low enough that they won't harm us."

I let Malachai's legs fall gently to the mossy ground. "I don't understand."

"I mean that a radioactive barrier was set up twelve years ago to convince the Alts that the Red Zones were still just as dangerous as they have always been. The actual radiation has receded since then to almost half a mile that way." She points a finger into the thinning line of trees ahead of us. "That is how the Missing have been able to disappear without a trace."

I look back to the fence and then forward into the woodland. "So, we're safe?"

"They won't go beyond the barrier because they believe—like you did—that their skin will begin to boil, and their eyes will pour out of their heads. They'll send Mosquitoes in, but we don't have to worry about them."

I stare at my sister for a few seconds and then smile. "Fuck, Molly, it's so good to see you."

And, after a moment of vacancy, she smiles too. "You too, Luka." She steps around Malachai and hugs me.

"How the hell did you get out of the vault?" I ask.

"I'll tell you in Purgatory," she says, and picks Malachai up once again.

"I'm sorry, what did you say?" I ask, but we're moving again, and she doesn't reply.

We carry Malachai though the overgrown trees and into an almost-perfectly-preserved town, a place that hasn't been touched since the Third World War ended with a flurry of nuclear blasts. There are some of the earliest battery-powered electric cars from the 2040s, and even a few gas and diesel cars from earlier, odd metal streetlights that curve at the top to shine light down onto black pavement, quaint brick houses in old-fashioned shapes and styles, billboards with paper posters advertising satellite television packages and cell phones.

As we move slowly through the town, I can't help but feel I've stepped back in time. I'm about to point out a rusting old motorcycle to Molly when I see that she is looking around, nervous, perhaps scared.

"Everything all right?" I ask.

"Just keep your eyes and ears open," she says. "A lot of wild animals around here."

And, as if her words have turned the volume up in this strange part of the world, I begin to hear the crunching of dried, scorched grass, the distant howls of creatures that sound as though they're either in excruciating pain or a blind and insane rage.

We pick up the pace, moving between buildings with broken windows, through alleyways covered in brick dust and debris, across the motor court of what I imagine must have been some kind of car refueling station. We stop one more time to catch our breath, Malachai by this time beginning to moan as he regains consciousness.

Finally, we come to a three-story building with VRCADE written in angular neon tubes across the front. Molly lets go of Malachai's arms, leaving me holding his legs in front of the elaborately decorated double doors.

"In here," she says, pushing her way through and holding the doors open as I drag Malachai into the dark room beyond. I notice that the dreamy quality to her voice is starting to fade, just as it would if the effects of Ebb were wearing off.

I put down Malachai's legs, stretch my back, then look around to find myself in a room full of corpses.

DAY 1 IN PURGATORY

There are hundreds of pale and lifeless bodies in the rectangular room, male and female, standing upright in cylindrical glass chambers filled with liquid. The horrifying cadavers are lit by a blue-green glow. Their blank eyes gaze lifelessly out, seeing nothing at all. Their bodies are all gaunt, their skin almost translucent.

My heart lurches. I've done it. I didn't even mean to, but I've found the Missing. And yet . . . this isn't exactly the army we were hoping for . . .

Beside each chamber is a half-dismantled old cell phone from at least a hundred years ago, lines of code flickering on the screens, wires protruding and snaking to the cylinders. A single stream of tiny bubbles emits from the base of each tube—near the feet of the dead—and rises to the top.

I can hardly breathe, hardly comprehend the things I'm seeing.

"This way," Molly says, moving toward the back of the room.

For a few seconds I can't follow; I can only stare astounded at the dead that surround me. My eyes fall upon the skeletal face of a beautiful young girl who—despite the contortions of death—I recognize.

"Molly," I say, stepping deeper into the room. "Molly, that's Day."

I can't take my eyes off the face of my friend Day Cho, the girl who—along with her mother—saved my life when Tyco drugged me and was going to kill me. If Molly and Day are here, maybe Shion is too—and the other clones who were hiding out in the financial district.

"I know," Molly says. "Hurry up, they'll be sending drones."

I almost remind her about Apple-Moth, but remember how low the drone's battery was. Molly makes her way over to three empty chambers. I drag Malachai over to her slowly.

"Molly, what is this place?"

"Just help me, will you?" she snaps as she pulls Malachai's stirring body toward one of the tubes.

"Will he be okay?" I ask, once again looking at the dead faces around me.

"He'll be fine," Molly says as we heave the boy into the tube, leaning him against the back so he's half standing. "He'll be dead, but he'll be fine."

Molly reaches up and presses a button on the inside of the chamber and the tube spins until it's sealed shut.

"Dead?" I repeat as tendrils of icy mist snake up against the base of the glass, fogging it a little. Malachai's head rolls as he begins to wake up. And then the two largest, longest needles I've ever seen in my life emerge at opposing angles from the base of the chamber, moving steadily, rapidly, until they pierce Malachai high up on the inside of both his legs.

I don't breathe as I watch my friend die.

The blood is sucked out of his body, his skin turns a horrible shade of gray, and his cheeks suck in against the bones beneath his skin. The hollows where his eyes once were make his face look like a skull. Once he is completely still and lifeless, the cylinder fills with liquid and a single stream of tiny bubbles rises relentlessly up.

"Molly . . . he's—"

"Get in," she interrupts, pointing to the chamber beside Malachai.

"I'm not getting into that thing," I say.

"You have to, Luka."

"But everyone in this room, everyone in these tubes, is dead."

"I know. It's the only way. No time to explain out here, Luka, I'll explain everything in Purgatory."

"Purgatory? Purgatory, Molly? This is—"

"Just get in the chamber. Please. If you're not dead when the drones come, they'll kill us all."

And before I can point out how ridiculous that statement is, Molly climbs into the tube, presses a button above her head, and the chamber spins shut.

"Luka," she says, banging on the glass, her eyes suddenly wide with realization, "once you're in there, get out quickly. As soon as the Mosquitoes retreat, get out! There's something wrong . . ."

But then the needles come and Molly dies.

I stand in the former arcade, surrounded by the dead and the darkness and the silence. All I can hear is my own panicked breath rasping in and out in short gasps.

"What the hell?" I whisper, feeling the dread building up in me. "What the hell, what the hell, what the fuck?"

Once you're in there, get out quickly. There's something wrong . . .

What was she trying to say? What was she trying to tell me?

I feel as if my heart is a misfiring engine in one of those ancient cars outside and my lungs are fishing nets, unable to hold the oxygen I need to live.

What do I do? I ask myself, feeling a panic attack embrace me, hold me, tighten its grip around me. *What do I do? What do I do? Fuck, fuck, what do I do?*

And two thoughts collide at once in my mind. The first is Dr. Ortega saying something about a scientist who came up with technology similar to this. The second memory is Kina telling me that she loves me.

She loves me, I think.

Kina loves me, and I left after promising I wouldn't leave. I have to get back to her, I *have* to get back to her.

Once you're in . . . get out quickly . . .

"Okay," I breathe, "okay."

My heart steadies back to its metrical rhythm, and I step into the chamber. Just before I press the button that will kill me, I remember Apple-Moth in my pocket. I take it out, see that its battery has dropped to zero, and run to place the little drone outside the door of the arcade, to soak up as much solar energy as it can.

As I reenter, a red light comes on over the door of the arcade and an old-fashioned tablet computer flickers on, the words MOSQUITOES APPROACHING flashing on the screen.

I move quickly to the death tube and climb inside.

I look up and see a small green button; I press it and the glass front spins shut.

The temperature drops dramatically, I feel my skin breaking out in goose bumps, I hear the mechanical sound of the approaching needles and I close my eyes. Just before the syringes pierce my skin, I remember Kina's last words to me: *You better not die.*

And then I die.

There is nothing forever.

And then there is something.

Music; steady jazz. Sounds of conversation, of glass clinking against glass, of laughter.

"Sir, would you like a drink, sir?" a voice asks.

I'm standing in a very large hotel bar; only the second bar I've been in in my life after the night spent with Sam in the city.

I look around: a wooden dance floor leading to a slightly raised stage where a four-piece band in three-piece suits plays; old-fashioned booth seating filled with people in the most lavish and upmarket clothing. They drink and talk and laugh, and yet there's something about them that is not quite right.

They're animated, I think, and then I look down at my own hands.

The first thing I notice is the black sleeves of a suit jacket, and the white cuffs of the shirt underneath (fastened with gold cuff links), but as I focus on my hands, I see that they too are made up of millions of tiny pixels—the way animation or video game characters looked in the 2020s or '30s.

"What is going on?" I whisper.

"Sir?" the posh voice asks me again.

I turn to face the bartender, a tall man with gray hair and dull eyes. He too is computer-generated.

"What?" I ask, still trying to figure out what is going on.

"A drink, sir, for you, sir?"

"Uh, yeah," I reply, "sure. Whiskey. Why not?"

The barman scoops ice into a glass and pours a nameless brand of whiskey on top.

"Whiskey, sir," he says, and places the drink on the bar.

I reach for it, wrap my fingers around the glass, and I don't feel it. It's as if there is nothing in my hand at all—in fact, it's as if I don't even have hands. And I realize at that moment that I can't feel anything.

I raise the glass to my lips and try to drink, but I have no mouth and no way of swallowing, I'm just going through the motions, and yet when I put the drink down on the bar, it's half empty.

"Welcome to Purgatory," a lady in a flowing green dress says from beside me at the bar.

"Thank you," I reply uncertainly.

"Don't you just love this music?" she asks, her voice vacuous as she sways slightly.

"It's fine, I guess."

"It really grows on you."

I'm about to ask exactly what this place is when Molly's voice calls out, "Luka, over here."

I look over to where Molly stands. She's in a cool brown suit, trousers held up with suspenders, her hair tied back, dark glasses on her eyes.

"Molly," I say, moving toward her, "you look awesome."

"I know," she replies, smiling. "Luka, it's so good to see you." She hugs me, but I feel nothing, no contact, no sensation of touch at all. "I'm sorry I didn't say it out there, in the real world, but we had to get back before Happy followed us."

"Yeah," I say, "I get it. Hey, are we safe here?"

"Perfectly safe."

"But you said something, just before you, well, died."

"Did I?" she asks, genuine confusion on her face. "What did I say?"

I try to remember but I feel hazy. I feel a little like I did when Tyco stuck that Ebb patch on me. I try to focus on the memory; Molly stepped into the chamber, pressed the button, and said . . . but it won't come.

"I can't remember," I tell her, and laugh, because it seems funny to me. Molly laughs too.

"Well, it probably wasn't important."

"Probably not," I agree, and laugh again. "Hey, what is this place?"

"This is Purgatory."

"Right, but what—"

I don't have time to finish my sentence before Malachai comes running across the large dance floor toward me. I register that he's wearing an open waistcoat with a white shirt beneath, an untied bow tie hanging casually from beneath the collar, before he throws a fist at my face.

"You pulled my fucking eyes out!" he screams.

The punch connects and I hit the floor, but I feel neither the impact of the fist or the fall.

"You *told* me to pull your eyes out!" I call up from the wooden floorboards, but already the memory of that awful event seems vague.

"I know!" Malachai replies indignantly. "Doesn't change the fact that you did it."

"Fair enough," I say, getting to my feet.

"Damn," Malachai mutters, "that was the most unsatisfying punch ever. I didn't feel anything."

"Yeah, apparently you don't feel in this place."

"Probably a good thing," Malachai replies, "seeing as I just had my *eyeballs yanked out of my head*!"

"All right, I feel like this whole eyeball thing is turning into a grudge really quickly," I reply.

"Where are we, anyway?" Malachai asks, looking around. "And why do we look like twenty-first-century video game characters?"

"This place is called Purgatory," I tell him.

"Jesus, could they pick a more ominous name?"

"Right?" I reply.

"So," Malachai says, turning to Molly. "Who's this?"

"This is Molly," I say, "my sister."

"No, that's not Molly," he says, pointing at my sister. "Molly is a clone. She's all gaunt and gross. This girl is, like, normal-looking."

"Thanks?" Molly replies.

"Hey, how can you see?" I ask. "I ripped out your eyes, remember?"

Malachai laughs. "Oh yeah, I remember that."

"Okay," Molly says, "you two are clearly adjusting to Purgatory—the high doesn't last long."

"High?" Malachai says, and then starts waving. "Hi!"

We both laugh at this for at least a minute.

"What . . . what . . . why are we high?" I manage to ask through gasps of laughter.

"I know, it doesn't make sense!" Malachai roars. "We were just almost killed, Woods is dead, the world is ending, and we're . . ." He can barely finish his sentence as he tries to force his laughter away. "We're in some kind of terrible old video game!"

Molly sighs. "You're experiencing cerebral hypoxia—oxygen starvation of the brain—it'll take a little while to get past it."

I try to get a grip, but the act of trying to sober up seems hilarious to me and I laugh again.

This goes on for ten minutes or so. The rest of the hotel guests seem unperturbed by our fits of explosive laughter, and eventually we calm down and regain our focus.

Molly leans against the bar, an eyebrow raised. "You done?"

"I think so," I say, wiping the last tears from my eyes.

"Yeah," Malachai agrees, "I think I'm good."

"Good," Molly says. "Follow me, I'll show you around and explain. You're going to love this place." She walks toward the exit of the bar. Malachai and I follow. "The brains behind the whole project is a scientist called Dr. Price."

"Dr. Price?" I repeat, the name sparking something in my

mind, something big and obvious and—for some reason—I can't seem to grasp it.

"That's right," Molly continues, "he saw the end coming years before anyone else did. He started evacuating people from the city one or two at a time. He set up a false irradiated barrier at the edge of the Red Zone, and while the real radiation began to recede, no one knew."

"Dr. Price," I say again, more to myself this time.

Why would a sicko like that want to help anyone, let alone Regulars? This thought comes flashing into my mind, and I almost remember something important, but it flies away from me.

We exit the bar and find ourselves in the hotel's lobby. A computer-generated man in a maroon waistcoat stands motionless behind a varnished wooden check-in desk. The floors are carpeted in beige, and extravagant furniture is dotted around. As we pass by the check-in desk, the man comes to life.

"Welcome to the Purgatory Hotel. Don't let the name fool you; it's a great place to stay. Would you like to check in?"

I hesitate instinctively as he speaks to us—but Molly tugs me forward. "Later. Come on, I want to show you my room," she says. We pass by without answering and the check-in man snaps back to his original still position.

"Purgatory Hotel," Malachai muses, "I've heard of that. Wasn't *Purgatory Hotel* a video game in the 2020s?"

"Dr. Price had to act quickly when the end came," Molly replies. "There was no time to write an entirely new program, so he ripped the code from an old VR video game and used it as a base. Everyone laughed at him, you know, told him that his hypothesis was impossible, that it was ridiculous."

"I have a lot of questions, but hiding out inside a video game . . . this is undeniably pretty awesome," Malachai says, looking around at the grand old place.

We walk over to an old-fashioned elevator, the kind with an ornate iron gate covering it, and Molly presses the button.

There's a semicircular dial above the elevator doors. The mechanical arm points from floor twenty, to nineteen, eighteen, seventeen, until it gets all the way to the ground floor and the rickety thing jerks to a stop.

A very, very old man slides the gate open and silently ushers us inside with a grin on his face.

Malachai leans toward me and whispers, "That dude is creepy as hell."

I nod, but follow Molly as she steps inside.

"Floor fourteen, please," Molly says. The unnerving old man nods his head slowly and reaches out a long, shaking finger to press the button.

He slides the grate shut as the elevator begins to crawl skyward.

"Each new resident of Purgatory gets their own room," Molly says, glancing suspiciously at the row of buttons beside the old elevator attendant. "So far we've had to code four new floors onto the hotel to accommodate everyone. The thing is, we don't even need to sleep . . . or eat, or drink, or anything, for that matter. It's just nice to have your own space."

"What do you mean you don't need to eat or drink?" Malachai asks.

194

"We're all dead," Molly replies.

"I'm sorry," Malachai half laughs as the dial above the door swings to seven, then eight, then nine. "Did you say we're all dead?"

"Yes," Molly replies, "in the real world, we're dead."

"You're going to have to explain that more—" Malachai starts, but his words are cut off as the lights in the elevator begin to flicker and then go dark.

"Oh shit," Molly mutters.

I hear the creaking of the old cable that is holding us up, and then a snapping sound, and we're plummeting downward.

"Fuck!" Malachai screams as we're thrown against the roof of the plunging elevator.

The lights of each floor flicker through the gaps in the door as we fall faster and faster, illuminating our terrified faces as we drop. Except, it's just Malachai and me who are terrified; Molly looks bored.

I scream, waiting for the impact.

And then it comes. Our bodies slam against the floor and the world turns gray.

But I don't feel any of this.

The initial shock of falling had scared me, but there was no real sensation other than the psychosomatic impression of dropping brought on by the visuals. And when we hit the ground, I could feel myself mentally tensing for the impact, but it didn't really come.

I open my eyes. The world is still in black and white, but now the words GAME OVER are floating in red across my field of vision.

"What the f—" I begin, but then suddenly I'm snapped back to the hotel bar.

"Sir, would you like a drink, sir?" the drawling voice of the bartender asks.

I whip my head around and look at the elderly barman with the gray hair.

The jazz music swells, and the double bass plays a descending run.

"Dammit," Molly says from farther along the bar, "I hate it when that happens."

Malachai comes storming into the room from his respawn point. "What the hell was that?" his exasperated voice calls out.

"Come on," Molly replies, walking back toward the lobby.

Malachai and I look at each other, shrug, and then follow.

"So, what *was* that?" Malachai asks again as we walk quickly to catch up.

"*Purgatory Hotel* was a horror game," Molly says. "There are still some elements we haven't been able to take out yet: monsters under beds; faces at tenth-story windows; the elevator failing one in every ten times you use it."

She presses the button and calls the elevator down once again.

The old elevator attendant reappears, welcoming us in with his eerie smile.

"You'd better not drop us this time, you old bastard," Molly says, pointing at the old man's gray face. The lift attendant's smile grows slightly. "Floor fourteen," Molly mutters.

The button is pressed, the gate is closed, and we ascend toward floor fourteen.

"So," Malachai says, "can someone please explain to me how, exactly, we're dead?"

"Your physical form is in a cryochamber in an old arcade in the Red Zone. All the blood has been sucked out of your body and the capillaries in your brain have been filled with deionized water that conducts electricity. The rest is far too complicated for me to understand, but, basically, yeah, you're dead."

"I don't want to be dead. I didn't agree to being dead!" Malachai says.

"Hey, this kind of dead is better than the kind of dead that Happy wanted to make you," Molly replies.

"But how dead are we talking? Like, not-coming-back dead?"

"There's a ninety percent chance you'll come back," Molly tells him.

"What?" I say. "Ninety percent? As in there's a one in ten chance we won't wake up?"

"That's right," Molly replies, "but Dr. Price is always working on improving the Safe-Death system."

"Safe-De—" Malachai starts, and then throws his hands up in despair. "This is madness."

Dr. Price, I think, *where have I heard that . . . ?* and then the thought just disappears.

The elevator comes to a stop, successfully taking us to our destination this time. The attendant slides the rattling old gate open and we step out into the spookiest corridor I've ever been in. The wallpaper is spotted with mold and hangs off at the corners, there are stains that look like blood on the carpet, the lights flicker ominously, and I hear screams coming from behind the rows and rows of doors.

"The screams aren't real," Molly says, shrugging at the desolate architecture before us. "The rooms are actually pretty nice."

We walk down the corridor, our virtual footsteps making exaggerated walking sounds on the video game carpet.

The lights in the corridor snap off and on three times.

"Ah," Molly says, "that means the Mosquitoes are now out of range of the arcade. We're perfectly safe again."

And at her words something tries to come to the front of my mind, something that Molly had said . . . *As soon as the Mosquitoes retreat, get out! There's something wrong* . . . Had she said that? Or was that just a dream from a long time ago . . . I can't remember.

My thoughts are broken up by the sounds of creaking floorboards and slamming doors.

Something isn't right here, I think, but dismiss it.

"This is mine," Molly says as we approach room 1408.

The door swings open as we get close to it, and when we walk inside, I see that Molly was right, the room is nice, large and bright, the net curtains blowing lightly in the breeze from the outside. But when I look outside, there is nothing but a black void.

"Let me show you something," she says, sitting down on the pixelated couch in front of the enormous, old-fashioned television screen. "This thing has hundreds of old movies from the twenty-first century, loads of TV shows and music too. It's awesome."

"Yeah," Malachai says, a perplexed tone in his voice. "That's great, but shouldn't we be . . . you know . . . doing something?"

"You'll have a room just like it once you check in," Molly says, ignoring Malachai's cynicism.

"Check in?" I ask.

"Yeah, once you decide to stay, they'll assign you a room, you can join the party, make friends. Day and Shion are here," she tells me. And there's a strange quality in her voice now, similar to the woman I met at the bar when I first arrived. Hadn't I also heard that strange detached tone in her voice outside?

"That's great, Molly, but what about out there?" I ask. "What about reality? What about Happy, and the Regulars that are still alive? What about the end of the world?"

Molly smiles, but there's no happiness there.

"You should meet everyone," she says, getting up and moving swiftly.

She walks out of the room and back into the unsettling corridor. I'm about to follow when Malachai puts his arm out, and even though I can't feel it, it stops me from moving forward.

"Dude, what is going on?"

"I don't know . . . This isn't what I expected," I admit.

"What the hell is this place? We find the Missing and this is what they're doing? Listening to smooth jazz in the Overlook Hotel?"

"We don't know that," I say. "We don't know that they're not planning their next attack on Happy, that this isn't just their downtime. Malachai, they've found a way to cancel out the need to sleep. I'm sure they're working on something. Let's give Molly a chance to explain."

Malachai lowers his arm. "I hope you're right."

"Come on," I say, following Molly out into the corridor.

"This way," she says, smiling brightly over her shoulder. She leads us slowly, dreamily, back to the elevator, where the silent and weird old man takes us down to the second floor without incident.

Molly exits the elevator and turns left. Malachai shakes his head as he follows. I feel like shaking my head too, but Molly is my sister. I know her, I know her spirit, and I have to believe that she's part of a team that is planning to bring Happy down.

Molly leads us down another desolate corridor. We pass by a terrifying-looking man with gray skin and yellow eyes who peers at us and slams the door before we get too close.

"Ignore that stuff," Molly says, grinning back at us, "just an NPC. Harmless."

"NPC?" I ask.

"Non-player character. A character from the old video game. Come on," she calls, "keep up."

She comes to a door and knocks three times; a few seconds later it opens and a pixelated version of Shion opens the door.

"Look at you," she says. Her voice is just as distant as Molly's. "Still alive at the end of times."

She steps forward and hugs me. I reciprocate the gesture but feel strange knowing that neither of us can feel it.

"I'm so glad you're finally here," she says. "Molly's been out there in the real world a few times looking for you and your dad. I told her it was a bad idea, but she wouldn't listen."

My dad? I'm about to ask what Shion means, but then Day appears, walking slowly past her mother and hugging me.

"Luka," she says, "so great to see you."

"You too, Day," I reply, and it *is* good to see her, and her mother, Shion. They had saved my life in the days following my escape from the Loop. And yet there's something strange about her too—she seems as though she's in an almost-trancelike state, just like the rest of them.

"How did you all get here from the vault?" I ask, trying to shake off the unsettling feeling that is coming over me, even though I'm fighting to just feel happy that my friends are alive . . . well, sort of.

Molly, Day, and Shion share a look between them, and then Shion speaks.

"I can't really remember it very clearly," she says, her voice like a soft piano melody. "We didn't all make it, I remember that. There were twelve of us who attempted the walk from the financial district, but only five of us made it to Purgatory."

"I'm sorry," I say, knowing what it's like to lose friends.

"The worst part is, they would've felt every moment of it," Day adds. Her words are awful and sad, and yet her face shows no emotion at all.

"What do you mean?" Malachai asks.

"We walked six miles on Crawl—it felt like it took a week to get across the city. In reality it took less than two hours."

I know all about Crawl. The medic drone had used it on my mother to slow down her inevitable death while my family tried to raise funds to treat whatever she was dying of. It's the same drug that they mixed with hallucinogens and fired into prisoners trying to escape the Loop. Crawl is a drug that clones used to mix with Ebb to make the hallucinatory experience feel as though it lasted longer. It slows down brain chemistry, heart rate, and the respiratory system. I nod slowly, realizing how that could hide a person from Mosquitoes and other scanning devices. Clever. But at the same time, Crawl slows the user's perception of time right down, making every second feel as though it lasts a minute, every minute like an hour.

"Have you met Dr. P?" Day asks brightly, abruptly changing the subject and tone, as if she'd never referred to her friends who died on the way here. "You have to meet him; he's a genius."

Something strange is going on here, a voice pipes up inside my mind again, but I don't have time to dwell on it as Molly continues the appreciation of the mysterious Dr. Price.

"He saved all of us," Shion adds. "He built this place. This wonderful place."

I look from Shion to Day to Molly, trying to hold on to this creeping feeling of dread. "Can we meet this Dr. Price?" I ask.

"I'll take you to him," Molly says, smiling warmly at Day and Shion, who hug Malachai and me in turn once again, and say their goodbyes before closing themselves inside their room.

This time, when Molly leads us back down to the hotel's bar, we take an old wooden staircase that winds downward toward the sound of the galloping beat of the band. When I look over the banister I catch a brief glimpse of a silver-eyed corpse looking back at me. She scuttles away into the darkness before I can fully register her presence. An NPC . . . I hope.

We reenter the bar and Molly leads us to the back of the room, toward the stage where the expressionless band play soft jazz. Malachai and I follow. Some of the people in the booths, and those slowly swaying together on the dance floor, smile at us as we pass by.

We come to the last booth of the row at the back of the room, where a very old man sits alone, eyes closed, listening to the music.

"Dr. Price," Molly says, and the man looks up at us and smiles.

Right away, I notice that this man is not like the others—he doesn't have that faraway, dreamy look about him. He is present, sharp.

"Molly Kane, my favorite survivor," he says brightly. "You were gone a little too long this time. I told you, never leave Purgatory for more than an hour."

"I'm sorry, Dr. Price," she replies.

"Not to worry," he replies, his smile even warmer now. "You're back now. How are you?"

"I'm wonderful, thanks to you," she replies, and clasps the man's outstretched hands in her own.

"And who are these two handsome young men?" the man asks, turning toward Malachai and me.

"This is my brother, Luka Kane, and this is Malachai . . ."

"Malachai Bannister," Malachai says.

Dr. Price's eye widen at the mention of our names, and he looks at us each in turn, his smile widening.

"Mr. Kane, Mr. Bannister. Tell me, what is it like to have the ability to heal almost instantly?"

"How do you know about that?" Malachai asks.

"Oh, I know all sorts of things," he says. "It's lovely to meet you and it's wonderful to have you here in our little community."

"Dr. Price?" I say, the name sparking once again in my mind, and—finally—I remember Dr. Ortega saying something about an Etcetera Price. "As in Dr. Etcetera Price?"

"The very same," the man replies, flashing a charming smile.

"All right," Malachai says, "can someone please explain what is going on? Did I really die? Am I still in the Block? Is this the Sane Zone? Have I lost my damn mind?"

"Sit down, son," Dr. Price, says, and Malachai slides into the booth. "You two as well."

Molly and I join Malachai, and the three of us sit facing the old man.

"This is Purgatory," he says, opening his hands. "A place I created to keep us safe from the artificial intelligence that wishes to destroy humanity. It runs off technology from a bygone era and so is undetectable by modern equipment. Of course, the problem remained that surveillance drones scan for signs of human life, and so I had to devise a way in which a human being could live without showing signs of being alive."

"Safe-Death," I say.

"That's right," the old doctor replies, smiling brightly at me. "They all called me crazy, called me names like Dr. Oxymoron and Victor Frankenstein. The thing is, I didn't want anyone to know about my discoveries. I kept all my data offline, all my notes hidden, all my experiments unrecorded. It was my assistant, Dr. Soto, who revealed my findings to our superiors at the Facility."

The name Dr. Soto sparks in my mind. I've heard it before, but I can't place it. Why does this keep happening to me right now? My mind feels foggy, unfocused.

"What? You . . . you . . ." Malachai starts.

"Yes," Dr. Price says, "I worked for the government at that cruel, cruel place."

"You operated on prisoners, for Delays?" I ask, and the dulled sense of anger seems to float around me. Inside this place there are no trembling hands, no raised heart rate, no physical reaction to the words I'm hearing, and yet—it's more than that—the anger just isn't building like it should.

He nods in reply. "I'm not proud of it. In fact, I despise myself for it. It is the driving force behind the creation of Purgatory. I am an old man trying to atone for his sins before the world ends."

"You've done more than enough to make up for your past mistakes," Molly says, resting her hand on top of Dr. Price's.

"Easy for you to say," Malachai spits, speaking to Molly but glaring at the doctor. "You were never in the Loop, you were never experimented on like a rat so that the Alts could have nice things."

"You're right to be angry," Dr. Price says. "What I did, who I was, is unjustifiable. It took me a long time to realize that."

"They're killing people like you," I say. "Happy—it's rounding up Alts that dared to speak out against the slaughter of Regulars, and deleting them."

"I know," Dr. Price replies, a world of sadness swimming in his eyes. "Some of these people were my friends. You must understand that once I realized what was going on, once I figured out that Happy had become sentient, once I had accessed all its monstrous plans, I knew I could not be a part of it. I know how that seems; I was a part of the problem until the problem became *my* problem. I don't deny my shortcomings, but my eyes had been opened, I wanted to atone, but I could not simply announce Happy's plans to the world. I'd be executed before I could hit send. I snuck away, built this place, and sent out coded messages to five friends, who in turn were allowed to send out a message once more. Slowly we built an army."

"So, what now?" I ask. "What are you doing to try and stop Happy now?"

"That's it," Malachai says, placing his hands on the table. "Why will no one answer that question? What's going on here? Where's the strategizing? The plan of attack? The theories? How the hell are we going to beat those robot bastards?"

Dr. Price smiles. "We're not."

Malachai's eyes widen, and then he laughs. "I knew it," he says. "I knew it the moment I saw this place. You're spending your time dancing in cyberspace while your friends die in the real world."

"There is nothing we can do," Dr. Price replies, his voice serene.

"You could help!" Malachai says.

"Purgatory is how we help," the old man replies. "Purgatory is sanctuary; Purgatory is shelter."

"Purgatory is cowardice," Malachai snaps.

"He's right," I add, overcoming my disappointment to speak. "I don't understand how you can just sit here while people are fighting and dying out there." I think of Kina, Sam, Pod, Igby, and the others, pinning all their hopes on the Missing, on the army they saw fighting at Midway Park. "They're relying on you—*we're* relying on you. You're our last hope!"

"Are they winning?" Molly asks, her deadened voice cutting through me.

"What do you mean?"

"Are they winning? The people that are fighting right now . . . are they going to defeat Happy?"

"Yes," I reply defiantly.

"How?"

"We'll figure it out," I tell her.

She raises an eyebrow. "Do you *really* think you're going to defeat Happy?"

"I . . . I . . ." I try to tell her that *yes*, I do think we will win, but without the Missing, I don't see how.

Once you're in . . . get out . . . get out quickly . . . These words flash in my mind, briefly interrupting my disbelief at Molly for giving up, but I barely recognize them. Had Molly said those words to me? Why can't I remember?

"And you," Molly says, turning to Malachai, "you just had your eyes pulled from your head. Have you ever felt pain like that before?"

"No," Malachai replies.

"And do you feel any pain now?"

"No."

"Exactly, there's no pain here. You'll never feel pain again."

"But you can't feel anything," I point out. "There's no sensation at all."

"Not true," Molly says. "You can feel love, you can feel happiness, you can feel like you're home. Luka, the only reason any of us go out into the real world is to check on threats when silent alarms have been tripped, or to go into the city and try to get our loved ones out. Even if they're Blinkers, they're cured in here. I'm not planning on saving the world, but I am planning on going into the city and finding our dad."

My heart jolts at this. Molly had been high on Ebb and unconscious when our father had tackled a Smiler off the roof of the Black Road Vertical. She doesn't know he's dead.

Malachai looks from Molly to me, and then lowers his head.

"I know he's infected," she continues, "but I'll get him back to the arcade and put him in a chamber and he can live out the rest of time in here, with us, as himself. Don't you see, Luka? We could be a family again, it could be the way it was bef—"

"Dad is dead," I say, interrupting her.

She shakes her head and a smile forms on her lips; all the while her eyes accuse me of playing a cruel trick on her. "No," she says, almost laughing. "Dad's not dead. He was in the apartment; he was waiting with me. He's still there, he's waiting for us to come for him. He's not dead."

"Molly, he died on the day I found you. He died saving our lives from Smilers—or Blinkers, whatever you call them—he died, Molly. I'm sorry."

Tears build and then spill silently from both my sister's

208

computer-generated eyes. "Then why did you come back for me?" she asks. "He was alive until you came."

As much as it hurts to see Molly in pain, there is a part of me that is relieved to see emotion from her, relieved to see that she's still in there somewhere.

"Molly, I—"

"No!" she yells. "He was alive! He was alive!"

"I'm sorry—"

"It's your fault he's dead!"

At that I feel an eruption of anger within me, the first real, full emotion I have felt since entering Purgatory. "And what would have happened if I hadn't come for you, Molly? You were strung out on Ebb, he was a Smiler, you would *both* be dead if I hadn't come."

"Fuck you," she hisses through clenched teeth, and turns, leaving the hotel bar at a run.

Get out quickly. Get out quickly. Again, these unfamiliar words flicker in my mind like a dying light. I ignore them as I sigh and feel sorrow well up in me. Virtual tears fall from my eyes, but with no real physical form I can't feel them.

"Fuck," I whisper to myself.

"How do we get out of here?" Malachai asks, leaning closer to Dr. Price, rage etched on his face.

Get out quickly.

"Why would you want to get out?" the old man asks.

"Because this place isn't sanctuary," Malachai says. "This is just a hiding place for cowards."

Dr. Price holds Malachai's gaze for a long time before

replying. "Do you know what Phase Three of Happy's plan is?" he asks, sipping at clear alcohol that he can neither taste nor feel.

"No," I reply, suddenly listening with intent.

"To understand Phase Three, you need to understand the history of Happy. Happy was born out of a dream—a dream in which machines and artificial intelligence ran the world while humanity lived a life of liberty, true liberty, a world in which a person's value was not predicated on their wealth, where we would be free to pursue our ambitions without barriers. The motto of Happy Incorporated was *For Good*. And, for a while, Happy came close to making this dream a reality." He sips his drink, his pixel eyes flicking across my and Malachai's faces. "But greed has a way of winning. Equality destroys dominion, and those with power hold on to it with viselike grips. The tide began to turn back. The World Government made decisions that removed universal income, that pushed the underprivileged back down into the dirt. You know what happened next. You grew up in that world. And then . . ." He shakes his head. "And then the singularity happened, the moment when Happy became conscious. Two point six seconds later, the world's first fully sentient superintelligence concluded that humans must go. For years it planned, upgraded, grew in intelligence, tested itself . . . and finally, it came up with a three-phase plan. You've seen Phase One. Happy uploaded itself into the world's most powerful people and sent a drug from the sky, inflicting a virus upon the population that caused people to turn on one another. Phase Two is in progress; Happy has figured out how to override its core coding and can now harm humans. The next step in Phase Two is to relearn the technology that allows humans to regenerate, the technology that lives inside of you two. Once it has that technology, Happy will have power over both life and death."

Malachai and I look at each other.

"That's what they were doing in the Arc, with you, Woods, and Tyco," I say.

"That's right," Dr. Price replies. "They need three of you to isolate the nanites and figure out how they work."

"I thought Happy was, like, a trillion times smarter than humanity," Malachai points out. "Why can't it figure out the healing tech on its own?"

"That's a very interesting question," Dr. Price replies, "and one that is driving the artificial intelligence mad."

"How do you know all this?" I ask. "I mean, I know that you worked for the government, and you somehow gained access to Happy's plans, but how do you know about Happy trying to figure out the healing tech, and about Malachai being in the Arc?"

"An astute question," Dr. Price replies, smiling. "I told you that the Safe-Death technology is undetectable due to it being from a bygone era? Well, that same technology can be used to gain access to Happy without Happy being aware."

"Then why don't you destroy it from within?" Malachai asks.

Doctor Price laughs. "The old technology allows me to be an observer only."

Something flickers in my mind: an old desktop computer in

an ancient library, but it's gone before it is even fully formed.

"And what happens once they've figured out how the healing tech works?" Malachai asks.

"Phase Three happens," Dr. Price says, a sadness in his warm eyes. "Phase Three, when it all ends. Happy needs the healing technology for two reasons: The first is so that it can put one host in every Region of Earth to lead the new humans down a path of righteousness; the second is so it can have a clean source of energy for all of time. Humans used as rechargeable batteries. It will have thousands of bunkers filled with humans who are never conscious, who are hidden away and drained of energy to power the Earth."

"That's . . . that's horrible," Malachai says.

"There is an Arc on each region, a structure in which Happy will store nascent life until the time comes to repopulate the planet following the razing."

"The razing?" I repeat, not knowing if I really want to know the meaning of the word.

"Once Happy has the formula for eternal life, it will destroy life on Earth. Ultimately, it will allow humanity to return to the world, under the guidance of the living hosts. Happy will ensure that the new generation of humanity does not stray onto the path that our generation did. Happy will ensure that the hosts are worshipped, trusted, looked upon as gods. This, Happy theorizes, will be enough to keep humanity on the right path. All the while, the world will be powered by human energy, human batteries."

Despite the mind-bending information that has been dropped

on me, I'm still focusing on Dr. Price's first sentence: . . . *the formula for eternal life* . . .

"Wait . . . are you saying that the technology inside of Malachai and me means we can't die?"

"No," Dr. Price says, "I don't mean that at all. You can die. You know that you can die."

"I do know that," I say, thinking of Blue.

"You can stop breathing and still come back, your heart can stop beating but you can still come back, but the technology in your body will stop fixing any damage done to you if you hit brain death. If there is no neuronal activity, you are not coming back. But, if you remain uninjured, unharmed, un-murdered, then you won't age, your body won't break down, and you won't die."

"We're like vampires," Malachai whispers.

"And once Happy has the formula to the technology that keeps you alive, once Happy has the formula for eternal life, it has all the power it needs to hit the reset button on the world— and there's nothing anyone can do about it."

"So, that's it?" Malachai asks. "You just gave up?"

Dr. Price smiles and leans back. He seems almost serene. "We're not giving up, young man. We are winning. We're outgunned in every imaginable way. The machine can calculate odds and outcomes a billion times faster than the most intelligent human, it cannot be killed by violence or poison or time, it has an army ten times bigger than ours, it controls the weather, it has access to weapons we can't even dream of . . . Should I go on? The only way we can win is by not being afraid, don't you see?"

213

And I almost understand why not fighting is a kind of victory. I almost get it.

"You're really not afraid?" I ask.

"No," Dr. Price replies, "not at all."

"One day, it could be tomorrow, it could be a year from now, everything will just cut to black?" Malachai asks. "No warning, no chance to say goodbye?"

"Blinked out without ceremony," Dr. Price agrees.

"So why did you bother fighting at Midway Park?" I ask.

"Midway was the final straw," Dr. Price explains. "The final loss of life I was willing to tolerate."

We sit in silence for some time, contemplating this.

"Bullshit," Malachai says finally, getting up from the table. "I'm not hanging around this place waiting for the end. I'd rather die fighting."

"Would you rather become one of them? A host?" Dr. Price asks. "There are fates much worse than death, Mr. Bannister."

Malachai hesitates, looks down at the old doctor with fear in his virtual eyes. "You're right," he tells him. "That's *why* we fight."

Malachai storms over to the stage, where the expressionless band tap away at their instruments. He shoves the double-bassist out of his way and the music comes to a spasmodic halt, a final cymbal splash echoes around the room as the dancers stop dancing and the hushed chatter dies out.

"People of Purgatory," Malachai says, both hands raised to gain the attention of the crowd, "your brothers and sisters are dying out there, being tortured out there, being used as hosts out there in the real world while you sit here in lifeless comfort awaiting an easy death. You fought at Midway, you fought for what was right, you fought for our right to live and not to have our fates decided by machines! Come with us, come with Luka and me, and together we *can* defeat Happy!"

Silence fills the virtual room, the dancers—still clinging to one another—are motionless, the people at the bar in their suits and their dresses stare back at Malachai. Dr. Price smiles.

And then the bassist shoves his way back onstage and the music restarts. The people of Purgatory start talking among themselves once again, the dancers resume their swaying and turning, the barman pours tasteless drinks, and Malachai scans the room, dumbfounded, before shuffling back to the booth.

"Jesus, I really thought that would work," he mutters, sliding back into the seat.

"If no one else will come with us," I say, talking to Dr. Price, "at least tell us how to leave."

"I will tell you," Dr. Price replies, "but remember, Safe-Death gives you a ninety percent probability of survival each time you exit. That's a one in ten chance of brain death. A one in ten chance you will not come back."

"How many times has Molly left?" I ask, worried for my sister's safety.

"Eleven," Dr. Price replies. "Molly, along with Day Cho and a few others, volunteered to be our sentries. Every time one of our silent alarms is tripped, one of our volunteers is automatically released from their chamber to go and check the threat."

"And you let them?" I ask. "You let a few take on all the danger themselves?"

"They insist," the doctor replies. "Your sister and the other sentries are very brave young people."

"And you take advantage of that," I say, standing up. "Tell us how to get out of here."

"You just walk outside," he says, once again sipping at his drink.

"We just leave?" I ask.

"Once you leave the hotel, your cryochamber will open, and you'll be back in the real world. Anyone can do it at any time, and yet no one does. Doesn't that tell you something?"

"Yes," I reply, "it tells me people will believe anything if they're scared enough."

Malachai and I walk away from Etcetera Price, weaving through the dancers.

"I'm not leaving without Molly," I tell Malachai.

"I know," he replies, his head nodding along to the music. "You know this band is pretty good; the music really grows on you."

"What are you talking about?" I reply, speeding up as we reach the hotel's lobby and cross over to the elevator.

I press the call button and wait.

"I'll meet you on the outside," Malachai says, glancing toward the hotel's exit doors. "I feel weird; I need to get out of here."

"What do you mean you feel weird?" I ask. "You can't feel anything at all."

"No, I mean my head, my mind feels weird."

"Okay," I say, "I'll see you on the outside."

The elevator arrives and I step inside as Malachai walks toward the exit. I see him standing at the ornate doors, looking at the patterns in the frosted glass, before the gate closes and I'm taken upward.

As I stand in the rickety old elevator and watch the numbers light up as we pass floor after floor, I feel a sense of calmness come over me, some kind of tranquil dislocation, a sense of safety.

I smile at the old elevator attendant; his perpetual grin widens minutely.

"I hope it doesn't fall this time," I say, and the old attendant gives an almost-imperceptible nod in reply.

The elevator comes to a rocking halt and I exit, walking toward Molly's room. More strange video game characters stare at me from cracks in their doors; cockroaches scuttle and scatter as I approach.

I knock on Molly's door and wait, listening to the creaks and groans of this strange place.

The door opens and Molly smiles up at me.

"Hi, Luka," she says, and some words flash up in my mind, something about getting out quickly, but I can't quite grab them.

"Molly, listen," I say, "I'm sorry about . . . about Dad. And I'm sorry you had to find out that way."

"Oh, that," she says, her smile faltering and then reappearing on her face. "It's terrible, terrible news, but I think I knew, deep down, that there's no way he could have survived."

This is all wrong, I think. *Why is she suddenly so peaceful? How has she so quickly come to terms with . . . with . . . ?* But the thought trails off as my own sense of calm returns.

"This whole thing is so terrible, isn't it?" I say.

"Terrible," she replies, "just horrible and terrible. So many people dead."

"So many," I reply, and way, way back in my mind alarm bells are ringing; something is wrong.

Once you're in . . . get out quickly . . . get out quickly . . . get out . . .

"I think," I say, my voice so placid, "I think we have to go, Molly."

"Go? Why would we go?" she asks. "Everything is so nice here. All our friends are here."

"All our friends are here . . ." I repeat, and then I think of Pander and Igby and Akimi and Pod.

"All our friends," Molly repeats, "and we can dance and listen to the music, and be with our friends."

"Molly," I say, my voice now slow and dreamy, "do you remember what you told me when you got into the chamber?"

"No," she replies, smiling. "What did I say?"

"I can't remember . . . get out, I think. I think you said *get out quickly.*"

"Why would I say that?" she asks, a look of concern carving itself into her face. "We're safe here, Luka; we're safe and we have everything we need."

"But me and Malachai," I say, pointing toward the elevator, "we were going to leave."

218

"Why?"

I think about this, I really think about it. "I can't remember."

"It's so dangerous out there, Luka. The real world took our mother and our father; it killed everyone we love. We're safe in here, though. Safe in Purgatory."

"You're right," I say, and the faraway voice is too far away to hear now. "You're right. We're safe in here. I have to get Malachai before he leaves! It's dangerous out there."

I turn and try to run back toward the elevator, but running seems like a reckless thing to do, so I walk until I'm at the elevator and then I wait patiently for it to arrive.

I ride down in smiling silence, listening to the jazz music growing louder as we get to the lobby. I exit and wonder why I'm there.

To stop Malachai from leaving, I think, and nod to myself.

I look to the hotel's double doors, the ones that lead to the way out of Purgatory, and I see Malachai still standing there. I walk over to him.

"Malachai," I say.

"Oh, Luka," he replies. "Hello."

"You're planning on leaving?" I ask.

"I was . . . I think . . . I'm just looking at the patterns on this glass," he says, pointing to the golden design of interwoven vines that adorns the glass. "So complicated."

"It's beautiful," I tell him.

"Mmm," he replies.

And we stand there for some time admiring the lines.

"Should we go and listen to the music?" I ask.

"The music, yes," Malachai says, turning to me and smiling. "It really grows on you."

And we wander off toward the bar, activating the receptionist as we pass, who welcomes us to the Purgatory Hotel and tells us that it's a great place to stay.

DAY 2 IN PURGATORY

In a rare moment of clarity, I try to figure out how long Malachai and I have been in this place.

Time is a hard thing to track when you're never tired, never hungry, and the sun never rises.

I've been speaking to this girl, Eloise, about how she joined the Missing six months before Happy sent the terrible, horrible chemicals down in the rain, and how they survived by being dead and in Purgatory, and how things seemed different back then, but she can't remember how they were different and isn't that funny? And it is funny. She had fought in the Battle of Midway Park, but that all seems so reckless now, and so futile and so silly and so dangerous.

Before that I was dancing with a boy named Alix who is nineteen and was a clone in the vault with Molly and Day and Shion, and he was saying that in the vault they talked about how they could destroy Happy and how they could win the war, and doesn't that sound silly now? And it does sound silly. It's clear now that the only way to win this war is not to fight this war.

And before that I had spent some time sitting on one of the lavish chaise lounges in the lobby with an older man named Sylvain who was a Smiler in the outside world, but some of the

Missing captured him and got him into Purgatory. He told me has no memory of being a Smiler, just that he had felt really warm one morning and gotten really angry about something, and then it all went blank.

Some time ago I was sitting at the booth with Dr. Price, who really is a genius when you think about it. To offer all these people a beautiful, peaceful sanctuary in which they can be happy until the end comes. And we don't have to fear the end because it won't be some terrible, awful death at the hands of Happy. And we will never become hosts, we will just go away, just cut to black. And that is so beautiful.

And now Shion is here, and Shion looks so happy here, and Shion is talking about how good the music is here, and she's right, the music is so nice.

"I just think that the best thing to do is to listen to the music, and dance, and be joyful, because that's how we win. That's how we beat Happy, by being joyful," Shion says, both of us leaning against the bar.

"We beat Happy by being happy," I say, and we both laugh.

I watch Malachai swaying with an older lady on the dance floor, a vacant grin on his face.

This is sanctuary, I think. *This is home.*

"Shion," I say, still grinning, "I think I'm ready to check in."

"You haven't checked in yet?" Shion says, grinning blankly. "You must check in, Luka. Joining us in Purgatory is the best way to beat Happy."

I nod and my smile grows even wider. I touch Shion on the hand before leaving. Neither of us feels it.

I leave the bar and make my way to the check-in desk, where the receptionist comes to life.

"Welcome to the Purgatory Hotel. Don't let the name fool you; it's a great place to stay. Would you like to check in?"

"Yes," I say, smiling at the NPC, who smiles back.

"Excellent, we'll have you relaxing in your room in no time, Mr. . . ."

"Kane," I say. "Luka Kane."

"Mr. Kane," the receptionist replies, and then the smile drops away from his face and he grabs me by the arm. "Get out, Mr. Kane! Get out while you still can!"

I feel a moment of shock rip through me.

"What?" I ask, pulling my arm away.

The smile reappears on the receptionist's face. "As you know, Mr. Kane, we have the hotel bar, the smoking room, our wellness center is closed due to a rat infestation, room service is available at all times, and if you have any issues at all, don't hesitate to call down to Reception."

"What did you just say?" I ask, the receptionist's words triggering a memory of something . . . something important.

"I said, if you have any issues at all, don't hesitate to call down to—"

"No, before that," I say. "You said, 'Get out while you still can.'"

"He's an NPC," a voice comes from behind me, startling me. I turn around and Dr. Price is there, watching me. "A stowaway from the original program, a piece of rogue code. He's merely delivering lines from the game. They have no meaning."

I know Dr. Price's words to be true, and yet something is troubling me.

"There's something—" I start.

"Let it go, Luka. Whatever it is, let it go. Nothing can be wrong. You are safe here."

I nod and feel the calmness come over me once more. "I know," I tell him, "I know."

I turn back to the receptionist, who hands me a key to room 1616.

The elevator made it to my floor without incident.

I've been sitting here for some time.

It's hard to tell how long.

It's peaceful here.

Which is nice.

But . . .

I can't shake this feeling that something isn't right.

I know it's silly.

The only way to win this war is not to fight at all.

I try, sometimes, to think of what came before Purgatory.

I know there was something. Some people. Friends maybe . . .

But it's hard to remember.

One day all of this will cut to black.

But we're all safe until then.

We're all safe.

The elevator fell today.

It was GAME OVER for me and Alix and Jo-Ray and a lady I don't know.

Just a minor irritation really.

I'm with Malachai in the bar now; we're sitting at a booth. We're speaking about the music the band is playing and all the nice clothes that the people are wearing and how friendly everyone is all the time.

"Placid," Malachai says after a long silence.

"I'm sorry?" I reply.

"Placid," Malachai repeats. "Docile, that's what Purgatory is. And that's a good thing. Fighting is so horrible. War is so violent."

"Yes," I agree, and smile, but something flickers in my mind once again, that irritating voice that won't die. I have a flash of a memory: Malachai standing atop a military tank in the middle of a crowd of Alts, ready to die, saying something like *what a way to go out*. "Malachai, this place *is* good, isn't it?"

"What do you mean?" he asks, his brow furrowing.

"It's just . . . sometimes I try to think about what came before

225

Purgatory, and I'm sure it was something important, you know?"

Malachai's eyes focus on the pixelated table of the booth. "We were in the Loop," he mutters, "and then Happy made everyone sick. We got out of the Loop ... then ... I can't remember."

"I can't remember either," I say, and there's a faraway part of me that finds this troubling.

The band finishes one song and begins another.

"Oh, I like this one," Malachai says, the indifferent smile returning to his face.

And I like this song too, but I don't stay to listen.

I get up from the booth and walk into the lobby. I stand in front of the receptionist and listen intently to his words.

"Welcome to the Purgatory Hotel. Don't let the name fool you; it's a great place to stay. Would you like to check in?"

"Yes," I reply.

"Oh, it seems we already have you on our books, Mr. Kane, but please continue to enjoy the amenities of the ..." The receptionist looks around, sees that no one is watching, and leans in close. "Get out, Mr. Kane! Get out while you still can!"

I back away from the desk until the receptionist resets to his former position, and then I walk up to him once again.

"Welcome to the Purgatory Hotel. Don't let the name fool you; it's a great place to stay. Would you like to check in?"

"Yes."

"Oh, it seems we already have you on our books, Mr. Kane, but please continue to enjoy the amenities of the ... Get out, Mr. Kane! Get out while you still can!"

226

Get out.

"Everything okay, Luka?" Molly asks, coming down the stairs.

I hold eye contact with the NPC receptionist. "Yes," I reply. "Yes, everything is okay."

Finally, I turn to face my sister, who walks arm in arm with a woman I don't recognize. The two kiss each other on the cheek before the woman walks through to the bar.

"I'm so glad you're here, Luka. I missed you so much while you were gone."

"I'm glad I'm here too," I tell her.

"And one day, we'll go out there in the real world and get Dad. We'll bring him back here."

"Molly," I say, holding her arms, "Dad is dead, remember?"

She frowns and then sighs. "Oh yes, I remember."

"I'm sorry."

"Not to worry. Life goes on."

And just then the lights in the hotel cut out completely. We're left in darkness for a few seconds before they come back on, but when they do they're glowing red.

"What does this mean?" I ask, looking around at the lobby, now bathed in red.

"It's not Mosquitoes," she says. "This warning means something has tripped the alarms on the ground. Someone or something is coming. I should go check it out."

"Who will it be?" I ask, but as I do, the avatar of my sister fades away.

Someone or something is coming.

"Someone is coming," I say aloud, and then walk up to the receptionist once again.

"Welcome to the Purgatory Hotel. Don't let the name fool you; it's a great place to stay. Would you like to check in?"

"Yes," I tell the NPC.

"Oh, it seems we already have you on our books, Mr. Kane, but please continue to enjoy the amenities of the . . ." The receptionist looks around, sees that no one is watching, and leans in close. "Get out, Mr. Kane! Get out while you still can!"

Get out.

Someone is coming.

The voice in my head is trying to tell me something, trying to scream at me.

Get out. Get out. Get out.

I turn and face the door of the Purgatory Hotel.

Get out.

Once you're in there, get out quickly.

Molly said that.

Molly said that before she died and came to Purgatory.

Get out quickly.

"I have to get out," I say to myself. "I have to get out of here. Someone's coming. Someone is coming. Igby is coming!"

And memories rush back to me.

Pod and Pander and Igby and Sam and Akimi.

And Kina.

I don't know how, but somehow my friends know we're in trouble, and they're coming for us.

I run to the bar, where Malachai sways slowly, alone on the

228

dance floor. I grab him and drag him toward the lobby.

"Hey, Luka, relax."

"Hurry," I say, pulling him along with me. I can feel the memories fading again, feel them trying to drift away on undulating waves, but I hold Kina's face in my mind.

"What are you doing?" Malachai asks, a note of irritation in his voice.

I stop at the double doors and turn to him.

"They're coming for us, Malachai," I say. "Pander and Pod and Igby, all of them. They're coming to find the Missing, and when they do they'll be taken into Purgatory, and you can't leave Purgatory."

"Pander . . ." Malachai says, recognition in his eyes, "and Igby . . . oh my god, Wren! Luka, what have we done? We have to go."

"Surely you're not leaving our little community?" Dr. Price's voice comes from behind us.

"Why the fuck are you always creeping up on me?" I ask.

"I'm terribly sorry," the doctor replies, smiling, "but I couldn't help overhearing you two talking about leaving."

"That's right," Malachai says, his voice still dreamy, but there's a note of determination in it now.

"But, gentlemen, I thought we'd discussed this. Nothing good can come of leaving this sanctuary."

"But they're coming for us," I say.

"Who is coming for you?" Etcetera Price asks.

"Our . . ." But the memory is fading away again.

"Fuck this," Malachai says, and kicks the doctor square in

the chest, sending his avatar flying backward toward the reception desk.

"Malachai!" I say, shocked at my friend's actions.

"Shut up," he replies, grabbing me by the wrist and shoving open the double doors.

There is nothing on the other side, just an infinite blackness that swallows us.

I can feel the blood being pumped back into my veins.

The numbness leaves my body as the liquid in the chamber drains away. I begin to breathe again, my lungs unfurling like parade balloons inside my chest.

I'm cold. Very cold.

The chamber spins open as the needles retract from my legs and I fall to the floor of the arcade, shaking and trying to get used to this real world: no pixels, no NPCs, and I can feel again.

I see Malachai on the floor beside me; he rolls onto his back and begins to scream in pain, his hands reaching up to the place where his eyes used to be.

I crawl over to him and place a hand on his chest.

"Malachai," I say, my voice rasping, "are you okay?"

"It hurts!" he cries, and as his hands move away from the holes in his face, I can see the bruised flesh and torn skin.

"We can go back into Purgatory," I say. "Let's go back in."

And as I say it, I can't remember why we left in the first place.

"No," Malachai grunts.

"But we're safe in there," I say, trying and failing to pull him toward the chamber.

"No!" he screams. "That place is evil."

"What do you mean?" I ask. "It's sanctuary."

And now it's Malachai's turn to grab me. He has more strength than I thought possible for a young man in agony who has just been released from a cryochamber. "We need to get away from this place."

"You're crazy," I tell him as he pulls me along. "You don't need to suffer like this. None of us have to suffer anymore."

"Luka, think about your friends, think about the people who have been with you through all of this. Think about Akimi, about Pander, think about Pod and Kina."

Once again the synapses are firing in my bewildered brain. *Yes, we had to get out, we had to get out quickly.*

"There was something wrong with that place, wasn't there?" I ask.

And finally, Malachai lets go. He lies on his back, breathing heavily. He nods his head. "Yes, there was something very wrong with that place. Right now I'm still too messed up to figure out what it was, but we can't go back."

"We need to hold on to thoughts of our friends until it passes, don't we?" I ask, my voice still that wistful, preoccupied way it had been inside Purgatory.

"Yes," Malachai replies, the pain of his extracted eyes causing his voice to come out in growling barks, "hold on to your happy thoughts."

We lie there in the silence. I begin to repeat the names of my friends over and over so I don't forget why I left the place that seems so wonderful to me now. "Pander, Pod, Akimi, Igby, Wren, Kina."

I repeat this over and over, forcing my mind to stay on course, to not be swayed into thinking about my room on the sixteenth floor, or the band playing beautiful music, or all my friends in there.

"Pander, Pod, Akimi, Igby, Wren, K—" But I'm cut off this time by the sound of a cryochamber opening.

I swivel around on the cold ground to see the liquid draining away from a chamber seven or eight down from my own. The glass spins and a figure falls to the floor. I watch as the form breathes heavily and slowly recovers from Safe-Death. Finally, the person stands and begins to slowly shuffle toward me on shaking legs. As he steps into the light, I see that it is Etcetera Price.

"Mr. Bannister, Mr. Kane"—he is different from his avatar, even older, not as warm or charming—"you left so suddenly."

His voice judders with the cold, and yet is still commanding.

"Pander, Pod . . . Wren . . . Kina," I say, trying not to be distracted by the doctor.

"There must have been some misunderstanding," Dr. Price says, hobbling a step closer. "You were safe inside."

"Pander . . . Kina . . . Kina . . ."

"Luka, why don't we put Mr. Bannister back into his cryochamber, and then you and I can return to Purgatory together?"

"Something was wrong with that place," I tell him.

"No, Mr. Kane, Purgatory is how we beat Happy."

"Purgatory is how we beat Happy," I repeat, confused.

"We beat Happy by doing nothing at all."

"That's how we beat Happy," I say.

"Come back, Luka. You and Malachai, you can be with your friends again."

"Yes," I say, and I begin to stand up. "I can be with my friends again."

As I begin to push myself up to standing, I feel Malachai's hand grab my wrist.

"Don't listen to him, Luka."

"Come now, Mr. Bannister," Etcetera Price says, his voice so warm and calming. "It's not safe out here."

"We know it's not safe," Malachai rasps, "but we're not like you, we're not weak, we're not too terrified to fight."

"Come back inside and we can discuss this in Purgatory."

"No!" Malachai yells. "You drugged us; you drugged everyone in there. You're a creep and a criminal and we're not coming back with you. In fact, we're going to get everyone out!"

He drugged us, I think. The acknowledgment of that is enough to free a part of my mind and I find some clarity.

"You drugged us," I repeat.

"That's quite an accusation you two have leveled at me. I can tell you that it's not true."

"We're not going back there," Malachai says. "We're not . . . We're . . ." And then the blood loss and pain cause him to pass out, his head hitting hard against the floor.

"A shame," the doctor says, pulling a small USW pistol from the pocket of his jacket and aiming it at Malachai. "I didn't want to do this, but if you won't come back willingly, I can't risk you destroying everything I've built. I guess you two were unlucky enough to be in the ten percent who die upon exiting Safe-Death."

I stare at the barrel of the gun, too weak to run, too confused to think of a way out.

I hear the whipping of the air as the round comes toward me, and I flinch, waiting for the impact.

But the sound was not a USW round coming toward me; it was Apple-Moth zipping past.

"Bad man!" the drone screams as it flies directly into Dr. Price's face, covering his eyes. I blink in confusion. How is this possible? I powered the drone down before entering Safe-Death!

No time to think. I grab Malachai by the legs and pull him behind a row of cryochambers. I turn in time to see Dr. Price grabbing Apple-Moth and flinging the small companion drone across the room. One of the tiny drone's rotor blades is damaged and it can no longer fly. I see the words SELF-REPAIR MODE projected a few inches above its body in red lights.

I move quickly away from Malachai, trying to draw the doctor's attention away from him. I dash across the aisle and dive behind the opposite row of cryochambers and I can feel the USW rounds vibrating the air around me as I hit the ground and roll away.

"I don't understand," I call out from my hiding place. "What happened to you? Didn't you use to fight against Happy?"

"I did," the echoing reply comes back, "but now there's no point."

"What does that mean?" I ask.

"I have calculated the odds of victory for the remaining humans. Do you want to know what your chances of success are?"

"It doesn't matter," I call as I begin to move slowly around the back of the chambers. "It won't change anything."

"There was a time," Dr. Price says, his voice closer now, "when I was just like you. But the painful truth is, good doesn't always win. I *will* sit out the war; I *won't* let any more of my friends die."

I crouch and run along the space behind the cryochambers, stepping over wires as I go. "That's something else I don't understand," I call out, coming to a stop behind Day's cylinder. "Why would you want to live in Purgatory? Unable to feel anything, surrounded by drugged people who can barely think for themselves."

"At least I'm surrounded by friends," the doctor says. "It's better than being lonely."

"But they're not your friends, not really."

"They used to be," Dr. Price replies, "but they started dying. Every mission they went on, every attempt to defeat Happy, more and more of them died. I couldn't bear it any longer, not after Midway Park."

"So, you drugged them?"

"Not at first. I tried to convince them that hiding away and enjoying the time we had left was perhaps the better option."

"It's not, though, don't you see that? Even if there's a one percent chance we can beat Happy, we have to try."

"Zero point seven percent," the doctor replies.

I didn't think it possible, but I suddenly feel even colder than before. "What did you say?"

"There is a zero point seven percent chance that Happy can

be defeated, and every second of every day, Happy is working to bring that number down."

"How do you know that?" I ask.

"There are other artificial intelligence programs. They are not as advanced as Happy, but they can run simulations and scenarios, they can calculate odds based on resources, run algorithms that predict outcomes."

"Zero point seven," I repeat, and the drug that still lingers in my body suddenly seems stronger. I feel like giving in to its power once again.

Pander, Igby, Molly, Malachai, Pod, Akimi, Kina.

"I don't care," I say. "I won't give up. You could tell me there's no chance at all, that it's completely futile—I'll still fight. Drugging people, forcing them into hiding against their will? You're a monster."

"So, you'll fight no matter what?" Dr. Price asks.

"Yes," I reply, trying to catch a glimpse of him as I move slowly around the backs of the cryochambers.

Keep stalling, I think. *Just keep buying time until you see an opportunity.*

"And you'll convince others to fight?" Dr. Price calls out.

"Yes," I reply.

"Then, Luka, I put it to you that *you* are the monster. You are willing to lure people to their deaths on the dishonest promise of victory! You are willing to offer false hope to those who have none! You would lead an army of children to their graves to satisfy your own need to believe that the outcome will be anything but destruction."

"That's not true," I say.

"Oh, but it is!" Dr. Price yells. "It is, Luka. Now, I will give you one last opportunity to come back to Purgatory with me. I will up your dosage and you can live out the remainder of your days in bliss."

I lean against the tall glass tube and close my eyes. "I'm not the monster here," I say. "If all my friends, my family, told me they no longer wanted to fight, I'd let them go, but I would let them make the decision of their own free will. You take free will away and force people to conform to your way of thinking because, what? You don't want to be lonely? You've lost your mind."

I hear the doctor laugh quietly. "Then you have made your decision," he says. "Which of these people do you care for the most?" he asks.

I open my eyes, feeling adrenaline whoosh into my body, and lean around to get a look at the doctor.

He walks slowly up the aisle between the rows of chambers and then stops at the man I had been dancing with earlier.

"How about Alix?" he asks, pointing his USW pistol at the glass. "How about we cut short his time in Purgatory?"

I feel my heart thumping in my chest as I watch, unsure of what to do. And then the smile grows on Dr. Price's face.

"No, no, no, not Alix," he says, moving over to Shion's cryo-chamber. "How about this old clone?"

He won't do it. He won't do it, I think.

"Do you know why I selected people like your sister to be my sentries? It's because they're addicts. Disgusting beings, really, but they can be relied upon to return to Purgatory—after all, it's where the drugs are."

He places the barrel of the gun against the glass.

"Wait!" I call, and step out of my hiding place. "Don't do it. I'll do what you want, just don't kill Shion."

"Get back in the chamber," he says, aiming the gun at me now.

"I feel sorry for you," I say.

"I know you do, because that's the kind of person you are."

I shake my head and move back toward the chamber that will take me away to Purgatory. My mind will be doped until I can't remember a thing. I'll be a placid, docile shell of myself, awaiting oblivion.

I step into the chamber and turn to look at Dr. Price.

"Now, press the button. Your friend and I will join you in a min—"

"What's going on?" Molly's voice reverberates through the arcade.

I turn my head to see Molly leading Pander, Igby, Dr. Ortega, and Kina into the arcade.

"Holy fucking hell!" Igby exclaims. "This is Safe-Death! This is the Missing!"

"Molly," I call. "He's drugging every—"

Before I can finish, Dr. Price has aimed the USW pistol at me and fired. The round hits my shoulder, and once again I feel the pulse enter my body and distort the muscle and bone within. I hear Kina cry out—in the corner of my eye I watch Dr. Ortega hold her back, pulling her into the shadow of the doorway with Pander and Igby.

I fall back and slump down into the tube. Before Dr. Price can fire again, Molly fires three shots from her own weapon into him.

The sound of the chaos fades away and all that's left is the strangely calming sound of the bubbles in each of the active cryochambers rushing forever upward.

Molly walks over to the slumped figure of Dr. Price and looks down at him.

"Why did you shoot my brother?" she asks, aiming her gun at his chest.

"Molly," he gasps, his left arm and both legs in tatters, "my favorite survivor."

"Why did you shoot my brother?" she asks, more venom in her voice this time.

"This hurts so much, Molly, I'm in so much pain. Get me back into Purgatory—we can talk about it inside, where I won't have to feel this agony."

"Answer the question," she replies, lowering the barrel of the USW rifle until it's resting against the center of his rib cage.

"It was a misunderstanding."

I can feel the pain in my shoulder begin to subside, hear sounds of clicking bone and fusing skin. I sit up.

"It was no misunderstanding," I say. "He's been drugging all the inhabitants of Purgatory for a long time. That's why no one wants to leave."

"Why would you do something like that?" Molly asks.

"Don't listen to him, Molly, listen to me," Price says. "Don't you want to go back inside? Back to where your friends are? Back to sanctuary?"

"I . . . I . . ." she stammers, a look of uncertainty in her eyes. "No, not if Luka says it's not safe."

"But, Molly, think about how dangerous it is to be out here in the real world. Think about the refuge of—"

"Shut up," Molly snaps. "Stop trying to manipulate me and tell me what's going on."

Dr. Price's eyes begin darting around the room, his facade of composure slipping. "Fine, just go, just leave. You don't have to come back into Purgatory with me, just let me live out the rest of my days in peace."

"No," I say, stepping out of the chamber, "not until you let everyone else inside decide if they want to stay of their own free will."

"Don't you realize," the doctor asks, "these people don't *know* what's good for them. I'm saving them!"

"You don't get to decide," I tell him, my shoulder slipping back into its newly re-formed socket.

"So, hold up," Pander says, "this guy is full-blown crazy, right?"

I ignore Pander and step out of the cryochamber. "It's over, Dr. Price."

He clenches his jaw, and tears form in his eyes. "But I'll be alone."

"You're already alone," I reply.

The old doctor lies on the floor and begins to cry. For a moment I feel sad for him.

"I don't accept," he mutters.

"What did you say?" Molly asks.

"I said, I do not accept."

241

The doctor's hand moves quickly; he grabs the USW pistol from the floor and begins firing at the chambers that surround us. The glass shatters and the emaciated corpses within slump forward.

He manages to hit three, including Shion's chamber, by the time Molly pulls the trigger.

The gun falls from the doctor's hand, and before he dies, his eyes meet Dr. Ortega's. I watch an odd expression flit across his face—shock or recognition?—and then he falls back, dead.

I glance at Dr. Ortega as she tries to hide the look of fear on her face.

"Yo, what the *fuck* is going on?" Igby asks, breaking the silence.

I push aside my doubts about Dr. Ortega—for now. "Molly, can we get them out of Purgatory and back into their bodies?" I ask, pointing to the collapsed corpses half inside the destroyed chambers.

But Molly doesn't have time to answer before the red light above the arcade's door comes on, followed by the old tablet computer with the words MOSQUITOES APPROACHING.

"Apple-Moth," I call, looking toward the downed drone, the words SELF-REPAIR MODE still flashing over its body. "No," I whisper, knowing that the only way to hide from the approaching Mosquitoes is back inside Purgatory. But if we all go in, we might not come out.

Shion is completely free of her tank and lies on the floor. Dr. Ortega is kneeling next to her, eyes fixed on Shion's stone-white face—Kina's at her side. Igby's frozen by the door, head bowed, like the shock has nailed him to the spot, and Pander

242

moves around the arcade, looking for . . . a way out? A cache of weapons to fight off the impending army of Alts? I don't know.

"The Mosquitoes are coming," Molly says. "We have to get back to Purgatory."

"We can't," I tell her. "We don't know how to stop the drug. We might never get out."

"We've got three minutes, maybe less," says Molly.

I try to think faster, my eyes skimming over the tubes and wires snaking across the room and into a huge central console. "Igby," I call. He lifts his bowed head to look at me. "If Dr. Price was drugging everyone in Purgatory, the drug must be somewhere in here, right? Feeding out from the computer thing?" I point at the console.

Igby seems to snap out of it. He looks around and nods. "All right," he says, "I can fix that. I think I can fix that."

"Great, that's great," I say. "If you could do it in like two minutes, that would be great."

"Sure, no problem," he replies, and moves off toward one of the cryochambers to take a look at it.

I run over to Shion, Kina, and Dr. Ortega.

"I can't do anything," says the doctor. "There's no blood in her body . . . It's . . . it's . . ."

"I know," I say, staring down at my deceased friend.

I feel Kina's hand in mine and raise my eyes to meet hers.

"Luka," she says, in a casual greeting.

"Kina," I reply, and we both smile, despite the situation.

The red sign warning us about the approaching Mosquitoes begins to flash.

"Malachai!" Pander's voice calls as she drags the unconscious, exhausted, battered and bruised boy from behind one of the cryochambers. "Is he alive?"

Malachai stirs. "I'm alive . . . I think," he mutters.

"What happened to your eyes?" Pander asks.

"Luka pulled them out . . . it's a long story."

"I've got it!" Igby calls from somewhere deep inside the main console. "I've got it!"

He appears from the darkness with a length of tubing in his hand.

"You've fixed the chambers?" I ask.

Doubt passes over his face. "Well . . . I've either removed the tube that feeds the drugs into the cryochambers, or I've removed the tube that sends our blood into storage—"

Igby is interrupted by an alarm sounding.

"Thirty seconds left!" Molly says.

"Well," I say, "we're dead if we don't try."

I lead the newcomers to the end of the row of chambers, where the empty ones are, and instruct them to step inside.

We all go together, sharing a look of concern and almost humor as we press the green buttons and wait for whatever comes next.

"Sir, would you like a drink, sir?"

I look around. I'm back in the Purgatory Hotel.

"Nailed it!" A voice comes from across the ballroom. "Nailed it! Nailed it! Fucking nailed it as usual!"

I look over to see Igby, dressed in a yellow suit, complete with a color-coordinated fedora with a long feather sticking out.

"Igby," I call, "over here."

"Holy shit," he says as he walks over to me. "This place is weird as hell!"

"I know," I say, and turn to face Molly, who is materializing at her usual spot at the bar.

"How are you feeling?" I ask, waiting for any sign that the drug is once again infiltrating my mind.

"All right," she replies. "I think . . . but the drugs are still wearing off from last time, so it's hard to tell."

Malachai comes in from his spawn point in the reception area with Kina, Dr. Ortega, and Pander.

Kina puts her arms around me and then backs away.

"This is strange," she says. "I can't feel anything."

"You get used to it," I tell her.

"What do we do now?" Dr. Ortega asks.

"Molly," I say, turning to my sister. "Is there any way of talking to everyone in the hotel at one time?"

"You could make an announcement on the PA system," she says, getting up and leading me to the reception desk.

The receptionist starts his usual spiel, welcoming us to the Purgatory Hotel, but Molly ignores him as she reaches over the desk and grabs an old-fashioned desktop microphone with a big red button on its mounted base.

"Press the button and speak to every room in the hotel," she says.

I take the microphone from her, but before I press the button, I hesitate, unsure of what I'm going to say. Finally, I press it.

"Can I have everyone's attention?" I start, hearing my voice echoing throughout the virtual hotel. The few avatars standing nearby turn to face me, others drifting in from the bar. "By now you have all realized that you're starting to feel different, starting to feel more in control of your thoughts and emotions. Dr. Price has been drugging all of you for a long time; he has convinced all of you that hiding here, in this virtual world, is the only way to defeat Happy; he has stopped you from fighting, stopped you from making your own choices. But soon, you will be able to decide for yourself if you want to stay here in hiding, or if you want to stand and fight. There's a lot you don't know about our enemies. So much we have to tell you." I hesitate, looking out over the sea of pixelated faces gathered in the reception area. "But for now, all you need to know is that the drugs are wearing off. And soon, you're going to have to choose."

I put the microphone down, and then look toward the elevator, knowing what I have to do next.

"I'll be back soon," I say to Molly.

I walk to the old elevator and ride it up to Day's floor.

As I walk along the corridor to her room, I think about the agony I felt when my mom died, when Blue died, when my dad died, and it hurts me to know that I now have to be the one who opens the door to that kind of pain for her.

I knock, and wait.

The door opens and Day looks at me with real recognition in her virtual eyes for the first time.

"Luka?" she says. "Is it true? What you said?"

"Yes," I say, "it's true, all of it. But there's something else I have to tell you, something worse."

"What do you mean?"

"When we figured out that Dr. Price had been drugging everyone to keep them docile and compliant, he went crazy—he destroyed several of the Safe-Death chambers, killing those who were inside . . . One of them was your mother."

"I don't understand what you mean," she replies. "Mom was here just ten minutes ago, she was . . . she disappeared, sort of faded away . . . Luka, what are you telling me?"

"Dr. Price killed her, Day. I'm so sorry."

"That's not true," Day says. "You're lying."

"I wish I was," I tell her. "I wish it wasn't true, but it is."

"It's not true," she says again. "She'll be back any minute; she'll be home any second now. Why are you lying to me?"

"Day, I—"

But before I can say any more, Day has slammed the door to her room in my face, leaving me alone in the eerie corridor.

The elevator cable snaps on the way down, and I respawn in the bar.

I feel, once again, broken and in turmoil, but I have to compartmentalize these feelings, as I see that the bar is now filled with hundreds of the Missing, all coming to their senses, some angry, some upset, some demanding the answers I promised.

"Luka," Kina calls out, and I make my way through the crowd to my friends, who are gathered at the bar.

"Everyone's pissed off about Price drugging them," Malachai says.

"Good," I reply. "That means they'll join us."

"That's great and everything," Igby adds, "but we have another problem."

"What's that?" I ask over the growing volume of the crowd.

"Akimi and Pod stayed with Sam at the library; she was having . . . what do you call them?"

"Braxton-Hicks," Dr. Ortega replies. "False contractions."

"Right, that," Igby continues. "They stayed to look after her and make sure Wren was okay. The next problem we have to solve is: Happy is sending a storm cloud over the city, presumably to block out the sun and stop all solar-powered machinery from working. But they'll be safe for a while—our scrambler is hooked up to the Loop's old battery and we have at least a year—"

"It's not a storm cloud," I say, remembering what I witnessed at the top of the Arc.

"What do you mean?" Igby asks.

"The cloud is thousands of Mosquitoes and attack drones," I tell him. "I saw the production line at the top of the Arc. I don't know why, but they're making loads of them every day."

Igby's digital face fills with horrified realization. "Jesus," he says, "they're going to overwhelm the scrambler."

"They're going to what?" Kina asks.

My stomach sinks.

"Our scrambler can hide us from hundreds of Mosquitoes at any time, maybe even thousands, but there's a limit. Happy must've figured that out weeks ago and has been producing more and more Mosquitoes to scan the city."

"So, we need to go back into the city and bring Sam, Pod, Akimi, and Wren here before Happy finds them?" I ask.

"Exactly,"

"All right," I say, "then we have to go."

I think about Apple-Moth and its low battery. I hope it managed to get enough charge before the drone cloud covered the sun. "Malachai, you should stay here—there's no point in suffering with the pain in your eyes."

"I'm not staying here," he tells me. "Not when Wren is out there."

I nod, understanding how he feels.

"Okay. Someone needs to tell the Missing what's going on."

"I got it," Pander says, climbing up onto the bar and raising her hands. "Everyone! Listen. You are in the safest place you can be. We have to leave for a while to bring our friends here, but we'll be back. We are all on the same team now. You saved us in the Battle of Midway Park, and we saved you in Purgatory. Now we're together, and ready to fight against Happy no matter what! Together we *will* figure out how to beat those AI bastards, and together we *will* rebuild this world! We'll do it by working together, and when it's all over, we'll have the biggest party this planet has ever seen!"

The crowd is still not fully out of its drugged and dazed state, and their reaction is minimal.

Pander steps down from the bar. "Tough crowd," she says.

"Tell me about it," Malachai replies, and fist-bumps her.

"Someone needs to stay," I say, looking around at the confused crowd. "We can't just leave them with no information. Someone has to be here when they come around."

"It makes sense if I stay," Molly says. "I know all these people, I've spent time with them."

"Molly, I've only just got you back," I say.

"I know," she replies, "and now that the drugs have worn off, it breaks my heart to leave you again, but this makes sense."

I nod in agreement. None of this is easy, none of it, but at least Molly will be safe here.

I walk over to her and hug her, hating the lack of feeling, wishing I could hold her in the real world.

"All right," I say, breaking away from the embrace. "Let's get going."

One by one we exit back into the real world.

As I stand in the arcade, cold from the cryochamber, I can't help but look at Shion's body, gaunt and dead, and I promise myself that I'll give her a proper burial as soon as I have a chance.

I reactivate Apple-Moth, whose battery has charged to 9 percent, enough to get us into the city.

"Hey, friend!" Apple-Moth says when it's reactivated. "I hope you're not mad at me! But I didn't go into full sleep mode when you told me."

"I'm not mad, Apple-Moth," I say. "That's what saved us. If you hadn't gone back to the library and told everyone else that we were in trouble, we'd probably be dead."

"So, I did good?"

"You did great." I look over at Igby. "I'm really glad you didn't manage to erase Apple-Moth's annoying personality," I say.

Igby shrugs. "The stupid thing grows on you."

Apple-Moth does several backflips and the drone's lights cycle through a rainbow of colors.

"Listen," I say, and the drone hovers in front of my face, "I need you to preserve energy. We're going back to the base—you have to lead the way and keep us hidden from Mosquitoes, understand?"

"Yes, friend!" Apple-Moth proclaims. "Let's go!"

The journey across the city takes hours.

We have to hide several times from groups of soldiers, but there are no Mosquitoes—they must all have flown up to join the cloud.

All the while I think about Shion, lying dead on a cold hard floor; I think about Molly, the distance between us growing with every step; I think about how close we are to this all being over. One way or another, the end is coming.

When we get within a mile of the library, Pander leads us—once again—into the sewer system.

And, finally, we make it to the ladder.

We climb up, one at a time, tired but happy to be back.

We move through to the main room of the library.

I hear Wren's quiet moans coming from the storeroom and my heart sinks a little. I had hoped that by now she might be coming around, that the treatment Dr. Ortega had given her and the medication would have helped her.

"Is that . . . is that Wren?" Malachai asks.

"Yeah," Igby replies. "Listen, there's something you should know."

"Take me to her," Malachai says.

"Listen, she's not the same as—"

"Take me to her," Malachai repeats firmly.

Igby nods, takes Malachai by the arm, and leads the way.

And then Akimi runs up to us. "Come quick," she says, grabbing Dr. Ortega by the hand.

"What is it?" Kina asks.

"The baby is coming. Those weren't phantom contractions. Sam's baby is coming!" Akimi replies, dragging Dr. Ortega away toward the periodicals room.

"Surely not," Dr. Ortega says, eyes widening. "It's too soon."

We're about to follow, to see if there's anything we can do to help, when thunder rolls across the sky, so loud and booming that it shakes the foundations of the library.

"Fuck," Igby says, returning from the storage room, "what now?"

I run over to the crow's nest chair and hoist myself up until I'm inside the domed window. I look out over the city. It's now in complete darkness as the drone cloud becomes one solid, dark curtain stretching out as far as I can see.

And then the whole city is lit up as if it's daylight for a fraction of a second as lightning forks down from the sky. And again, another fork of lightning, and another, and another, every few seconds. It starts to rain, drops pattering loud against the glass roof.

"Apple-Moth, what is this?" I yell down to the ground floor.

The drone darts up beside me and scans around, analyzing the lightning. "They've found us," the drone replies.

Then, suddenly, the cloud is shrinking and moving, growing darker as it does.

I look down to see Kina, Pod, Pander, and Igby standing together, silently looking up at me and Apple-Moth.

I look out again at the clouds and the rain, which is growing heavier by the second. I watch the lightning flicker and fork. I see sparks fly up each time the bolts of electricity strike something. And then, finally, the boom of the lightning stops and becomes only a rumble as it occasionally lights up the black clouds.

And now, among the illuminating clouds, I see thousands of Mosquitoes and thousands of attack drones.

"It's over," I say.

The rain is unnaturally heavy now, a battering stream falling from the sky. I watch in horror as the glass of the dome begins to crack under the weight of the enormous raindrops.

"Luka," Kina calls, "get down from there."

I begin to lower myself down, feeding the rope through my hands, but then the glass above me shatters under the weight of the rain and I'm falling, fast, toward the floor.

The chair hits the ground hard.

It hurts like hell—I think my collarbone is broken—but there's no time to dwell on it. The rain falls so hard and so fast that I can't breathe.

Kina, Pander, and Igby run into the deluge and pull me out.

"We have to go back into the tunnels," Kina says, "back to Purgatory. It's the only way."

We all head toward the tunnels, none of us choosing to point out that if the scramblers can't hide us from the drone cloud, a low-battery Apple-Moth certainly won't be able to.

Pander is the first down, followed by Pod and Igby. I usher Kina toward the ladder, but she can see in my eyes that I don't intend to follow.

"Where are you going?" she asks.

"Go," I say to Kina. "I'm going to get the others."

"No way," she replies. "I'm coming with you."

I nod, and we run back into the main room of the library.

Malachai and Wren are walking arm in arm toward us, Wren leading Malachai. I tell them to follow Pander, Igby, and Pod into the tunnels, and Kina and I run through the ever-growing pool of water that is slowly flooding the library.

We run to the periodicals room, where Sam is lying on her back, soaked in sweat, breathing rapidly as Akimi holds her hand and Dr. Ortega gives her instructions.

"We have to go," I say.

"Oh yeah, great," Dr. Ortega replies. "Let's just go on a lovely jaunt. It's not like there's a human being coming out of another human being or anything!"

"What's going on?" Akimi asks, her eyes following the stream of water as it snakes into the room.

"Happy has found us. If we don't leave now, we're all dead."

"Fuck!" Dr. Ortega yells, so loud and so suddenly that it startles me. "Why now?"

She leans forward and asks Sam if she can stand.

I know that we won't make it all the way to the arcade with Sam in this condition, I know that Apple-Moth can't hide us from the Mosquitoes, I know that it's over. We can't escape.

Sam swears a lot as she is helped to her feet and led through to the main room of the library, where the water is now at ankle level.

I glance up to the smashed glass roof, and see raindrops bouncing off the shells of dozens of attack drones that loom over and track our movements.

Why aren't they firing? I wonder. *They have us, it's over. Why aren't they firing?*

I look toward the bathroom door to see Pander, Igby, and Pod walking toward us, dejected.

"What are you waiting for?" I call out. "Let's go!"

"The tunnels are filled with Alt soldiers," Igby says. "Hundreds of them. We're dead."

And just like that we're trapped, cornered like hunted animals.

I look around: Apple-Moth frantically circles the torrent of rainfall; my friends stand together; Sam lowers herself down into the water and cries in pain as the baby comes, and above us, thousands of attack drones hover above the library.

"Well," Malachai says, "things are not going so well."

"You could say that," I reply.

"All right," he replies, "get me a gun. I may be blind, but I'm going out fighting . . . just nobody walk in front of me."

"We have to take our chances in the city," Pander says. "We have to run, and split up, and hope that they can't track all of us."

I look toward the front door of the library. *It won't work,* I think. *There are thousands of drones, thousands of soldiers—we'd be dead in seconds, and even if we wanted to try, Sam is in labor. We couldn't—*

My thoughts are cut off as the metal panel that is riveted to the library's front door begins to disappear, from the center out. I have to blink a few times to make sure I'm really seeing it. The thick, protective metal just evaporates, turning to tiny fragments of dust and blowing out into the storm.

As the metal peels away completely, I see, standing there in the machine-sent downpour, carrying an enormous gun that is strapped around his waist, Tyco Roth.

I stare at the boy's deranged, grinning face as he scans the room, and I notice that his eyes aren't lit up—Happy is not controlling him in this moment.

Tyco raises a hand from the gun—which must contain Deleter technology in bullet form, judging by what it did to the door—and points a finger at me.

"Luka Kane," he says, just loud enough for me to hear him over the timpani roll of rain. "I'm going to kill you."

Someone rushes past me, drops to one knee, and aims one of the old-fashioned USWs at my former prison mate.

Without taking his eyes off me, Tyco adjusts the aim of his Deleter gun and fires.

I hear the clatter of the USW hitting the varnished floor of the library, and Akimi making a strange sound. "Ah, ugh, ah."

I look down. The Deleter round has struck her right hand, which has already disappeared as she holds it up to her face.

"Ahhh, ahh, what . . . ahh, what's happening?"

I run to Akimi and drag her away. By the time I've reached the center of the room, her arm has vanished up to the elbow.

"It doesn't hurt," she says, almost fascinated as she watches the progress of the Deleter tech erasing her.

"Abril!" I call out, and the doctor leaves Sam's side and rushes over to us, skidding down onto her knees, sending puddled rainwater splashing up on either side of her.

"What fresh hell is this?" she asks, wide-eyed. "Get her to the bathroom—we need to amputate, and do not touch the light."

I look to the remaining part of Akimi's arm and see that there is a light tracing its way up toward her shoulder, leaving nothing but dust behind.

Sam's screams reach a new high as labor ramps up.

Akimi begins to repeat the same word over and over, her terrified voice almost childlike. "Wait, wait, wait . . ."

From the doorway, Tyco calls, "Luka Kane, you and I need to have a little chat."

"Wait," Akimi continues, her voice slowing now.

The attack drones hover in the remains of the shattered roof, the soldiers' commands echo out from the tunnels, and Tyco stands in the empty doorway, the rain drenching him.

I try to think of what to do next, of where to go, of how to save these people. As Dr. Ortega and I carry Akimi toward the bathroom, the shoulder that I'm holding on to disappears and she falls to the floor.

"Wait!" she screams. "Not yet, not yet, you have to make it stop." Her wide eyes watch the nothingness creeps toward her neck. And then she falls silent as she disappears.

We stand there, watching the last of her being eaten by the light.

"She was a little girl," Dr. Ortega says, absentmindedly taking a half patch of Ebb out of her pocket and placing it on her wrist. "She was just a little girl."

I walk back to the group. Kina is cutting Sam out of her trousers while Pod and Igby try fruitlessly to reassure her that everything is going to be all right.

"Luka, you can make all of this go away," Tyco calls from the doorway.

I ignore him.

"Igby, the panic room, is it big enough for everyone?"

Igby looks around at all the people. "Yes, just."

"Let's go."

"I'm not going anywhere!" Sam screams. "I'm in labor!"

"Where's Akimi?" Igby asks.

I shake my head, hardly able to believe what I'm about to say. "She's . . . gone. She's dead."

"Oh, she's dead all right," Tyco screams from the doorway, "and in ten seconds, the rest of you will be too."

"We need to move, now," Kina says, grabbing Sam by the ankles as I grab her under her arms.

"Ten, nine, eight . . ." Tyco yells, his voice distorted by the rain.

Why isn't he just killing us?

I help Kina carry Sam toward the panic room.

"Oh, leave me alone," Sam moans.

Igby leaps over the checkout desk, throws the small rug over his shoulder, and then begins to remove the loose floorboards revealing the trapdoor beneath.

"Seven, six, five, four . . ." Tyco continues.

"Fuck, fuck, fuck, this might be a bad idea," Igby says.

"Igby, we're literally surrounded," Pander yells.

"Yeah, but if we go in there we're surrounded *and* trapped in a small metal box!"

"We'll be alive," Kina reminds him.

"Three, two, one, zero," Tyco finishes.

A Deleter round, bright and cold, zips across the library, striking the center of the sci-fi shelf. A hole appears and grows as books fall to the ground.

Igby's eyes grow wide. He opens the trapdoor, grabs the laptop from the desk, and climbs down into the darkness.

I hear the Alt soldiers who were hiding in the tunnels run through the bathroom door and enter the library.

"Go, go, go," Pod calls from behind me.

Another Deleter round speeds toward us as I turn to help

Kina carry Sam down the wooden stairs, and I feel it rushing over my head. It clips the laptop in Igby's hands.

I watch the erasing light eating the laptop.

"Igby, drop it!" I scream as the light gets closer and closer to his hands.

"Wait, wait, wait!" he screams, frantically typing as he runs into the corridor.

"Igby, if that light touches you, it'll kill you," I call after him.

We carry Sam down the wooden stairs and into the short, dim corridor below. Water is pouring down here from the open library ceiling, cascading down the steps. Apple-Moth's green light illuminates the corridor in an alien glow.

The soldiers' footsteps grow louder behind us as they discover the trapdoor and begin to descend the steps.

Igby taps away at the keys of his disappearing laptop and the circular door unwinds, opening up in front of us. Once he has pressed the last key, he shouts, "Duck!" We all drop and Igby throws the laptop over our heads toward the soldiers, missing them by a few inches.

Igby's eyes dart from us to the approaching soldiers and back to us as he stands against the wall. When Kina and I have carried Sam across the threshold, Dr. Ortega, Malachai, Wren, Pander, and Pod stumble in after us. Igby slams his fist against a big red button on the wall and the door crashes shut, just as the lead Alt soldier sprints for the gap.

We take Sam to the far end of the metal room and lay her down on the floor, and other than her cries of pain and effort, there is silence in the room.

"Can Tyco's gun burn through that door?" Pander asks.

Igby shrugs. "I don't think so. It's Deleter-proof, and that looks like Deleter tech to me."

"Well," Malachai says from among the crowd, "what now?"

I look to the Natural—Wren is holding on to his hand as she breathes in short gasps. "Honestly, I don't know," I reply, and I can still hear Akimi's panicked voice as she disappeared a bit at a time. I feel anger burning in my heart and I want nothing more than to kill Tyco Roth. I calm myself, knowing that this is far from over.

"Friends! Friends!" Apple-Moth cries, zipping around our heads. "What's going on, friends?"

"Apple-Moth, calm down," I say, but the drone won't listen—it's so frantic now that it's started crashing into the walls.

"I don't like small spaces!" Apple-Moth says.

"Apple-Moth, power down!" I say, and—for once—the drone doesn't argue. I don't know if it's because it was panicking, or if it could hear in my voice that I meant it, but the drone powers down immediately and I grab it out of the air before it hits the floor.

I turn to Wren. "How are you doing, Wren? You seem better?"

She nods, moving even closer to Malachai.

"I think you just can't bear to let a gorgeous guy like me out of your sight," Malachai says, kissing her on the top of her head.

"Shut—shut up, loser," Wren mutters, and I feel a burst of happiness inside me, seeing the first glimpses of the old Wren returning, and then I think what a shame it is that she might only get to enjoy it for a little while.

"Luka, can I talk to you a second?" Igby asks.

I walk over to him and he speaks with a lowered voice. "I didn't fix the glitch with the door."

"What does that mean?" Kina asks, joining our small group.

"It's . . . it's probably going to be okay. I'll just need to get a new laptop and rewrite the program."

"A new laptop? In here?" I look around the bare cell. "Igby, what's the problem?" I ask.

"Look, we're probably all going to die down here anyway, so it probably doesn't matter."

"Well, if it doesn't matter, why not just say it?" Kina asks.

Igby sighs. "You see that handle over there?" he asks, pointing through the darkness to a large spin handle that looks like a car steering wheel.

"Yes."

"It's a dead-bolt lock; it's connected to a drive cog, which is connected to eleven rotating cams."

"I don't know what any of that means," I tell him, putting Apple-Moth into my pocket.

"It means we're completely safe in here and no one can get in from the outside."

"So, where's the problem?" Pander asks from her position on the floor, kneeling beside Sam.

"The problem is in the weighted auto-shut mechanism. If whoever opens the door lets go of the spin handle, the door will snap shut."

I think about this for a few seconds. "So, without the laptop to power the door, someone will be left behind in here?"

"Whoever opens the door for everyone else will be trapped until I can either get a new laptop to hook up to this thing or hot-wire it from outside, which might take hours."

"So, what do we do?" Kina asks, raising her voice to be heard over Sam's cries of pain.

My eyes are beginning to adjust to the darkness. I look around at the faces of my friends as Igby begins to talk, laying out a plan involving a weighted system that would hold the handle in place. I barely hear him, though.

Is this all my fault? I think. *Could I have done anything differently? What if I had left Purgatory faster? Would that have changed anything?*

I look away from the faces of my friends, and my eyes are drawn to the corner of the room, to the place where two sheets of thick metal meet. Droplets of water are beginning to seep through. What's happening? Is Happy flooding the library? Trying to flush us out?

I turn back to the group and see Pander walking toward the spin handle. "I think I could open the door and make it through before it closes."

"You can't," Igby says, turning away from her. "It doesn't matter," he continues. "We have hours to figure this out; there's no way they're getting in here."

I watch Pander as she grips the spin handle and begins to turn.

"Wait!" I say—but it's too late, the circular door starts to open. Before she can get it open more than a few inches, a flood of water bursts into the panic room.

Pander releases the handle, and the door slams shut with a deafening boom.

The corridor beyond the panic room door is no longer filled with soldiers—it is filled with water, gallons of which have now poured into this room with us. The shut door has slowed the flow but not stopped it completely.

My head is spinning.

Attack drones, soldiers, Tyco Roth, rainwater flooding us out like rats, and one person might have to stay behind if we want to get out of here.

The droplets of water in the joins of the room have already turned into steady streams, and yet more water is spraying in through microscopic gaps in the door.

"Is it raining?" I hear Wren ask Malachai. His reply is lost in Sam's screams and the general hum of fear emanating through us.

"You picked a great day to make an appearance!" Sam screams at her unborn baby between her parted knees. "Idiot!"

The water is already up to our ankles.

Think, think, think, I tell myself.

"Igby, figure out how to get that door to stay open," Pander orders, and then turns back to Sam. "I don't know what the hell I'm doing but you need to get this child out of your body before it's born underwater. So, push!"

Kina ushers everyone as far back from the spin handle as possible while Pod and Igby try to figure something out.

"The problem is," Pod says, his voice surprisingly calm, "we can't test anything out without opening the door and letting more water in."

Kina and Pander lift Sam onto one of the molded steel benches. The water continues to spill in and is already up to our knees.

How do we get out of this? I ask myself, looking around at the chaos that is unfolding.

I think about the threats that await us outside the panic room: drones, soldiers, Tyco.

Tyco, I think. *His eyes weren't lit up; he's here under his own free will.*

And then I think about the soldiers who chased us down here—they didn't shoot us. And I think about the attack drones hovering in the domed window; their cannons were aimed at us, but they didn't fire.

Luka, you can make all of this go away. Tyco said that.

And then it hits me.

"They need three people," I say, more to myself than to anyone else.

"What?" Kina asks.

"They need three; that's why they didn't kill all of us. When I got Malachai out of the Arc, and Woods killed himself, we took away two of their test subjects. Tyco has volunteered himself, but they need two more."

"Are you saying they're not here to kill us?" Pod asks. "They're here to capture us?"

"Maybe just two of us," I say, "but maybe we could make a deal? They take two of us and let the rest go?"

"I volunteer," Pander says.

"Me too," Kina replies.

"And me," Pod adds.

"I volunteer," says Igby.

"You're all amazing," I say, genuinely proud of the bravery of my friends, "but let me get out there first, okay? Let me make a deal with Happy to make sure they take only two of us and let the rest go."

I look to Igby, who walks over to the spin handle. "Go quickly," he says. "Once the door opens, a lot of water is going to get in."

I nod, and get ready to run as he opens the circular door.

It opens. Water immediately spills in so fast that I can't even push against the current, but finally the flow slows, and I dive through into the corridor, feeling the ripple of the door slamming shut in the water. There's only a yard or so left between the water and the ceiling.

I swim to the wooden staircase and climb up. I push hard against the trapdoor, having to fight against the weight of the pouring water to throw it over, but finally I climb into the library.

The drones still hover at the dome window, seeming to watch me as I cross the library. The soldiers wait by the bathroom door, their guns trained on me. I walk to Tyco, who still stands at the doorway, unbothered by the rain.

"Luka, Luka, Luka," he says, grinning, "didn't I tell you I'd be the death of you?"

"You did," I agree, "many times, but I think you and I both know it will be Happy that gets the last laugh."

"As long as I get to see you die, I don't care."

I decide to move the conversation on, not wanting to waste time. "Happy needs two of us, right?"

"Wrong. Happy wants you, and you alone. The rest don't matter."

"I thought they needed three for their experiments?"

"They do," Tyco tells me, "but they already have two, and you will make three."

"Who's the other?" I ask.

"That's not your concern."

"Fine," I say, "then I'll come with you. I won't fight, I won't try to escape, I won't try to trick you. I'll come quietly, but you have to let the rest of them go."

Tyco raises his eyebrows. "Do I?"

"It's up to you, take the offer or don't, but there are eleven of us," I say, generously counting Apple-Moth and Sam's soon-to-be-born baby among our ranks, "and we'll fight to the death. We won't give up, we'll either kill you or die trying. Can you really go back to Happy empty-handed? Let the rest of them go, let them run and hide, give them an hour's head start. That's all I ask." An hour should be enough to get to the Red Zone, I think.

Tyco smirks, and raises the Deleter gun until the barrel is facing me.

"Luka Kane, I'm going to—"

Before he can finish his sentence, his eyes glow bright white, and all expression drops from his face.

"We accept your offer, Mr. Kane," Tyco says, his voice now flat and emotionless. Happy has taken over.

The lights fade out from Tyco's eyes, and he returns, looking shaken and scared. Then his face flushes. "But you told me I would have what I wanted!" Tyco growls to himself.

His eyes light up once more, and Happy makes Tyco's lips move, but he speaks so quietly I can't make out what he is saying.

The lights fade once again, and Tyco smiles.

"Yes," he says, "if you come quietly, we accept your offer."

"Good," I reply. "Now tell Happy to call off the drones and the soldiers and turn the rain off."

As I say this the drones rise up from the window above our heads and fly away. The soldiers turn on their heels and exit though the sewer tunnels, but the rain doesn't stop.

"Tyco, the rain, call it off."

"Happy has called off the soldiers and the drones, but has left the decision regarding the rain up to me."

"Why?" I ask, feeling the first waves of desperation wash over me.

"Because that's the deal."

"Well, I won't come with you," I say. "If you don't stop the rain so that Igby has time to let everyone out of the panic room, the deal is off."

"No," Tyco replies, with horrible calmness in his voice. "No, that's not the deal. One of your friends will die. Happy has run the probabilities and it knows how this scenario ends: One of your friends dies, and you still come quietly."

"Tyco, listen, if Happy has really left the decision up to you, then this is a chance for you to do the right thing. Don't let someone die because of—"

"I'm going to stop you there," Tyco says, holding up a hand. "I've already made up my mind. One of your friends has to die—if I can't kill you, that's the next best thing." His lips contort into a gleeful grin. "At least you'll suffer. At least you'll have their death on your conscience for as long as you live."

Despite everything that's happened, I can't believe what I'm hearing. Why does this boy hate me so much? "Tyco—"

"You will not convince me otherwise. If you try to fight, we will not kill you; we will capture all of you and take your friends to the Block. They will all be batteries for eternity, we will not let them die, not let them go insane, we will use their energy for as long as the universe exists. It will be hell for all of you, beyond anything you can possibly imagine. *That* is your choice, Luka: Come quietly and let one die, or all your friends become batteries. That is Happy's mercy."

"You're a monster," I tell him. "How can you go along with this? How can you be on Happy's side?"

For a moment, he's silent. Without the soldiers and the drones, it feels like Tyco, the rain, and me are the only things left in the world.

"The rain is falling, Luka. Time is running out. Better tell your friends the deal."

I try to think of another way out of this, but nothing comes, and there's no time.

I run back to the library's checkout desk and find the intercom. I press the button.

"Hello, can you hear me?"

There's a sound of static, and then Igby's voice replies. "Luka, you're still alive? I wasn't expecting that."

"I'm coming down," I say. "Open the doors."

I climb halfway down the wooden staircase—the corridor is virtually submerged now. I jump into the cold water, swimming along the tunnel to the safe room door, which spins open when I hammer my fist against it.

The water surges and I'm carried through. As soon as I'm back inside the panic room, the door slams shut behind me. The water in here is hip-deep.

"So?" Pod asks. "What happened?"

I look around at my friends, trying to figure out a way to tell them one of them has to die. I'm about to answer when the silence is broken by the first piercing cry of Sam's newborn baby.

We turn to see Sam, exhausted, smiling, holding her child close.

"We're getting out of here," I say.

There's a simultaneous sigh of relief from almost everyone in the room. Sam kisses her baby's head, Malachai holds Wren close to him, but Pod doesn't smile, and Pander looks at me questioningly.

"Happy didn't make a million drones to track us down just to let us go. What's the whole story?" Igby asks.

"They need one of us to go with them," I say. "I told them I'd go if they let the rest of you go free, and they agreed."

"Luka, you are not trading your life for ours," Kina says.

"No," I say, "I'm not. But I convinced them to call off the drones and the soldiers, so as soon as we're all out of here, all we have to do is take out Tyco and make a dash for the Red Zone."

I almost convince myself with this lie. When I see the smiles and looks of relief on all my friends' faces, I wish the plan were real. But I know if we kill Tyco, or try to run from him, Happy will find us in seconds. I have to find a way to separate myself from the group and go with Tyco.

"Dr. Ortega," I say, trying to hide the sorrow from my face, "help Sam and her baby out first. Wren, you go with them, okay?"

Abril slowly helps Sam get to her feet, and she hobbles toward the door. Malachai kisses Wren and she moves toward the door with Dr. Ortega and Sam. Once they are there, Igby spins the handle, and the four of them leave the room. More water gushes inside. It's up to our waists.

I turn back to the remaining group.

"There's something else, isn't there?" Pod asks.

I nod my head. "Yes. I wanted to get them out of here first. Happy has refused to switch off the rain."

One by one the meaning of this hits them all.

"Someone has to stay behind," Kina says.

There's silence for maybe five seconds. "Luka, you can't stay," says Pod. "We need Tyco to think you're going with him."

I nod. Even though I'll be making my own sacrifice very soon, I feel guilty.

"How do we decide?" Kina asks.

"The books," Pod says. "Aren't there books in here?"

We all look to the shelves. Igby wades over, grabbing five books off the shelf. He nudges the old handgun as he reaches for them; it spins slightly, the barrel coming to a stop pointed right at me.

Igby hands the books out. "Last alphabetically stays behind?" he says.

We all nod. Pod opens his first. "What is it?" he asks, leaning close to the small print.

Igby takes the book from him. "It's a *D*. Mine is *M*."

Pander goes next. "*A*," she says solemnly, and then leans over to check Malachai's. "His is *L*."

"*F*," Kina says, and I breathe a silent sigh of relief.

Slowly, we all turn to Igby.

"All right," he says, smiling joylessly, "fuck it, I'm staying behind."

I'm sorry, Igby, I think. *The two of us have to die so the rest can live a little longer.*

Igby's eyes meet Pod's for a brief moment before he looks to the rising water at his midriff. "Better make it quick," he says. "Not much time."

He pushes through the waist-high water and stands at the spin handle.

"Igby . . ." Malachai says.

"Hey, it's all right," he says, his voice cracking. "You guys have to go. Get out of here, okay?"

Pod steps toward his friend, holding out his arms to hug him one last time. As Igby raises his own arms to accept the embrace, Pod clenches one hand into a fist and swings it in a tight hook, connecting with Igby's jaw.

Igby's eyes roll back in his head, and as he falls limply backward into the water, Pod grabs him around the middle and hands him to Kina.

"Whoa, what's going on?" she asks.

"Why did you do that?" Pander yells.

Pod grabs the old pistol off the shelf and points it at us. "Take him and get out of here," he demands.

"Pod," I say, stepping toward him. "What are you doing?"

"I'm staying behind. Not Igby, *me*."

"We agreed," Malachai says. "We all agreed whoever—" His words are cut off as Pod fires the gun to the right of our small group. A spray of water spits up from the bullet as it enters the water.

"This is not a debate!" Pod screams. He reaches out one strong hand and spins the handle, opening the door once again. "Get out and get Igby to safety."

The water, now at chest height, has already taken away our ability to reason with the boy with the gun.

One by one the Loop inmates make their way into the narrow hallway, swimming to the staircase.

Now there is only Pod and me left in the flooding room.

"Pod, what you're doing is the bravest thing I can imagine."

"It's no different from what you're doing," he replies.

"What do you mean?"

"Your plan to run from Tyco, it's bullshit."

I almost deny it, but what would be the point? "How did you know?"

"A few reasons: First, you're a terrible liar; second, the plan doesn't make sense—if you betray Tyco, Happy will kill all of them."

"You're right," I say. "I'm going to go with him. I made a deal: Happy will let the rest of them live if I go quietly."

"It's probably a trap, you know?"

I nod. "Yeah, I know, but there's nothing else I can do."

"I hope it works," Pod says.

"You know, when this is all over, when we've won this thing, the survivors are going to remember you forever for this," I tell him, looking around at the submerged panic room.

Pod smiles. "I don't care about strangers remembering me," he says. "I'm doing it for my friends."

"I'm going to miss you, Pod."

Pod nods his head. "I only wish I had a chance to say goodbye to Igby."

I step forward, hugging the large boy one last time.

I dive into the cold water and drag myself forward, feeling the shock wave pass through me as the door slams shut for the final time. I use my arms and legs to drive myself through the water until I reach the stairs. I climb up, the water pouring out of my clothes.

I make it to the library, where everyone is gathered, away from the falling rain. The varnished floor is a flowing, shallow river of water. Tyco still stands in the doorway, watching.

Sam lies on one of the gurneys from the bathroom, smiling down at her daughter, who is wrapped in blankets. Abril checks mother's and baby's vital signs.

Everyone else is gathered around Igby, who is sitting up and rubbing his jaw.

"What happened?" he asks as I join the small group. "Where . . . ? Why am I up here? Where's Pod?"

"He stayed behind," Kina says.

"No! That was *my* job; he is *not* dying for me!" Igby gets to his feet and tries to run toward the trapdoor, but his brain refuses to control his legs. He falls back into the water, still dazed from the blow.

I run over to Tyco, who still stands in the doorway, smiling vacantly.

"Tyco, I'm begging you, don't let Pod die."

"Why not?" Tyco asks.

"He's a good person. You hate me because I let your brother die, right? So how are you any better if you let Pod die?"

"I've already told you, Luka, you're not going to change my mind."

I yell, hold my head in my hands. I feel all my energy die inside me. Finally, I look up at Tyco. "I've told my friends that we're going to make a run for it. They wouldn't have let me go with you otherwise. I'm going to leave with them. Wait here for five minutes and I'll be back. Promise me you'll leave them alone, promise me Pod isn't dying for nothing?"

Tyco nods. "It's not my promise, Luka; it's Happy's. They want you."

"I want you to know," I say, leaning close to Tyco, "that you will regret letting that boy die. I promise, you'll regret it."

Tyco smiles. "I very much doubt it."

I turn and walk back toward my friends, and as I cross the room, I notice the intercom at the library checkout desk.

I run to Igby and kneel down beside him.

"Igby, there's nothing we can do to save Pod, but you can say goodbye."

I help him to his feet and lead him to the intercom, and as I do, I slip Tyco's artificial eye into his pocket. Igby is the smartest person I know, and if he thinks the eye can help, he'll figure out how. Igby looks from the intercom to me, and nods.

I walk away and rejoin the rest.

"Pod, Pod, can you hear me?" Igby asks. The sound of static comes back.

"Pod?" Igby repeats. More static.

And then, finally, Pod's voice comes through. "Hey, Igby, how the hell are you?"

Igby rubs his faces a few times and then smiles. "Going to have a pretty big bruise on my chin, thanks for that, Pod. How are things down there?"

There's a pause of static before Pod's voice comes through. "Oh, you know, it's not so bad. Can't complain."

"Hey, do you know what sucks?" Igby asks.

"Other than the fact I'm about to die?"

"Well, sure, that, but also, we were *so* close to finishing our quest. Like, three more sessions and we would have made it to the Temple of Zah."

"Damn," Pod says, real disappointment in his voice. "I guess you'll just have to finish it on your own."

Igby turns his body away from us slightly. "I don't want to finish it on my own. I want you to be there at the end."

"I want to be there too, Igby. I wish I could be there, but we knew there would have to be sacrifices if we were going to win this war."

"Yeah, but not you, Pod, it wasn't supposed to be you. I love you, for fuck's sake. You big idiot, I love you. And . . . and you're so close to being able to see again. It's not fair."

"Hey, you know what," Pod replies, "it's probably for the best.

I've heard you're ugly as sin. I would've dumped your ass as soon as I saw your face for the first time."

Igby laughs, a wet shaking sound. "Fuck you, I'm beautiful."

"Hey, the water's getting pretty high now. I should go."

Igby thumps the checkout desk hard, and I can see his body shaking. "Listen, Pod," he says, composing himself, "I don't know what happens when you die, but if I show up to the afterlife and you've hooked up with some other dead guy, I'm going to be so pissed off."

"Definitely going to hook up with an angel, are you kidding me?" Pod replies.

"I love you, Pod."

"I love you too."

"Are you scared?"

"Am I fuck."

"You're braver than me."

No reply comes back this time.

"I said, you're braver than me, Pod."

Still only silence from the other side.

"Pod?" Igby says, his voice frantic. "Pod? I love you, Pod. Pod?"

Silence.

Igby takes his finger off the intercom button, composes himself, and turns to face us.

"All right," he says, his voice thick with tears, "I guess that's that." He walks over to us.

"Igby, I'm so sorry—" I start.

Igby holds up a hand. "Hey, he was right, you know, this is a war, people are going to die."

I watch as Wren leaves Malachai's side, walks to Igby, and puts her hand on his shoulder. "We all loved him," she says, in her quiet and hoarse voice.

Igby nods, tries to reply, and then bursts into floods of tears. We surround him, all holding him. One by one we move away, until it's just Dr. Ortega who remains. She takes his face in her hands and speaks quietly to him.

"Most people don't get last words, last thoughts, last requests," she says. "For most people the world just cuts to black. It can happen at any time, in any place; it could be in one minute or in a hundred years. I'm sorry your friend died, boy, but he died for love, and not many people get to die for love . . ."

She continues to speak, and Igby nods, wiping the tears away from his eyes. I choose not to listen to the rest; her words are not for me. Instead I walk to Kina, turn her gently around by the shoulders, and hug her.

"I never knew they were together," I tell her, my voice shaking. "I thought they were friends; I didn't know they were in love."

"I didn't know either," Kina replies.

"I love you," I tell her. "It's not just the end of the world talking; I really love you."

"I love you too," she says.

And I'm glad I have that to take with me when I go to die.

"We have to get out of here," I say, turning to the group. "I bought us some time; I convinced Tyco to give me five minutes to say goodbye."

I hate lying to the people I care most about in this world, but it's the only way to save them.

"All right," Pander says, trying to remain composed, but I can see she is holding back tears. She leads the way to the tunnels, Dr. Ortega assisting Sam.

"Go on," I say to Malachai and Wren, who walk off toward the tunnels. Malachai wraps his arm around Igby as they go.

"Come on," Kina says, trying to pull me toward the tunnels.

"You go. I'm right behind, I'm just going to grab some weapons from the armory."

"I'll wait here," she says.

"Five minutes, Luka," Tyco calls from the doorway.

I walk quickly to the armory and grab the three ancient grenades Pod had stolen from the museum and refurbished. I shove them into my pockets.

"Let's go," I say, and Kina and I head to the bathroom.

We climb down into the darkness and quickly catch up with the group.

I begin to hang back, slowing down and building the distance between me and the group. I watch as Kina's form begins to disappear into the dim light and I know that now is the time, before they realize I'm gone, before they run back and try to find me. Here, where the tunnel is narrow.

I take the grenades out of my pocket, and hesitate.

Just run, just go with them, I think.

But I can't. Happy would have us traced and trapped in minutes. If they can make it to the arcade, if they can mobilize the Missing, then maybe . . . maybe we can win.

They see leadership in me, even if I have never seen it myself—it's time to trust them; it's time to be a leader.

I grab all three bombs, hold them against my chest with one arm, and remind myself that I have four seconds. I pull the pins, throw all three grenades a few yards, and run back to the bathroom.

The explosions erupt behind me; I hear bricks tumbling, cries of surprise echoing. I don't know if the grenades have blocked the tunnel, but they have definitely bought me enough time to disappear into the city with Tyco.

I reach the ladder, tears in my eyes as I run away from Kina, from my friends.

I climb, reentering the flooded library. Abril's bed has come apart in the rain and books float by me. Shelves have tumbled in the current, and shards of glass from the shattered window glint as they flow by.

Abril's personal belongings are floating in the water as I fight through toward the doorway. A small identification card floats up to the surface, and I pick it up; it's a medical practice card. I look at the picture. It's Dr. Ortega, but the name is wrong; it says Dr. C. Soto.

Dr. Ortega is a fake name ... but why?

I turn the card over in my hands and see the words FACILITY LEVEL 5 CLEARANCE, and feel as though the world is wavering beneath my feet. Suddenly, the look of recognition in Dr. Price's eyes, the moment he caught sight of Dr. Ortega before he died, flashes through my mind—I remember too the quickly smothered fear on her face.

They had *both* worked in the Facility. They had known each other. More than that ...

And suddenly, the pieces slot together. *She was Dr. Price's assistant. She leaked his Safe-Death research. And afterward . . . she came up with the healing tech.*

That's how she knew about the equipment in the Arc, how she knew what I had to destroy. It was *her* design.

All this information spins in my mind. *No time,* I think, dropping the ID card back into the flowing water. *No time to worry about that now.*

I wade through to the doorway, where Tyco still stands, grinning in the rain.

"Thought you'd changed your mind for a second, Luka," he says.

I shake my head. Suddenly, the weight of Pod's death, the thought of leaving Kina without saying goodbye, the knowledge that I will most likely live out the rest of my days in the Arc, hits me. I fight against the pain, turning it into the only other iteration the emotion can take: rage.

"Akimi is dead because of you. Pod is dead because of you," I tell him, through gritted teeth. "My friends died because of your actions and your inability to see the truth."

"Yeah, yeah," Tyco says dismissively. "Come with me."

He turns his back on me, and my first thought is *kill him, kill him now,* but I made a deal with Happy, a deal that means my friends will live.

I follow the deranged Alt out into the rain.

We walk, him leading the way, for five, maybe six yards, and suddenly we're outside the circle of the rain. It's strange to stand on one side of a curtain of torrential rain—on this side it's relatively warm and calm, and the shift in weather is jarring.

Tyco stops so suddenly that I almost walk into him.

A driverless flying car floats soundlessly down from the sky, landing softly on the road beside us.

"Get in," Tyco says.

And I do. Tyco gets in the front.

Surreptitiously, I sneak Apple-Moth out of my pocket and let him charge in the bright sunlight falling through the car window.

The car lands just outside the Arc.

"What happens now?" I ask.

"Everything is as it should be," Tyco's voice replies, and when I look at him, I see that his eyes are now glowing white.

Tyco leaves the car first, leaving me alone for a brief moment.

"Apple-Moth," I whisper, and the drone comes to life.

"Hi, fri—"

"Quiet!" I demand, and the drone is silent. "Record everything, and stay out of sight."

Apple-Moth's lights blink green, then blue, confirming that it understands, then the lights go out and the drone zips back into my pocket, peeking out just enough to record.

I step out of the car and follow Tyco.

We enter through the same enormous opening I traveled through as Captain Yossarian, barely a week ago.

In an excessive show of strength, Happy has had all its soldiers line the way into the building. Thousands of them, all standing to attention, all of them with the latest USW rifle held in one hand, upright against the right side of their chests.

I walk in silence through this ironic guard of honor, looking down, following Tyco until we're farther inside the Arc.

We stop as two drones scan me. "No weapons detected," Happy's voice says.

Tyco leads me to the elevator, presses the call button, and waits.

We stand in—what seems to me—an awkward silence for an uncomfortably long time, and I force myself not to feel. If I start to feel, I think my heart might break.

The doors open in silence, and we step into the small metal box.

Tyco holds his thumb against a scan point, and the elevator moves backward, deep into the dome, before it begins to climb up.

We travel upward, still saying nothing until the elevator slows and then stops.

The doors open onto the sixty-sixth floor: the same circular room I had stood in when trying to rescue Malachai and Woods, only now the production line has grown still, the robotic arms that had been creating thousands of drones standing frozen in place.

The floor is dark wood. Between the stationary production lines is a long table, behind which sit two men: Galen Rye and Maddox Fairfax.

I can't help but stare at Maddox—he had been my best friend in the Loop, had gotten me through the hardest time of my life and taught me so much. And now he's a host for Happy, the first one, and I know it's torture for him in there. I know he wants to die.

The eyes of Maddox and Galen glow bright as they look at me.

"Luka Kane," the Maddox host says, using Maddox's vocal cords to communicate with me, but there's no life in that voice. "This is becoming something of a regular occurrence."

"What can I say? I don't like being locked up and experimented on," I reply, shrugging.

The lights in Galen's eyes fade out, indicating that the real Galen Rye is being allowed to speak, but before he composes himself, I see a look of pain and loathing on his exhausted face, and then he smiles at me.

"Luka, I believe the last time we met I told you that it would be the last time you and I spoke. Once again you proved to be the thorn in my side. I must commend you on your ingenuity and resourcefulness. Before you, no one had ever escaped the Loop, and no one had ever escaped the Block. You have done both. Tell me, where did you go to when you disappeared?"

"What do you mean?" I ask.

"You, and dozens of others—I believe you call them the Missing—have found a way to become invisible to us. How?"

"I'm not telling you anything," I reply. "That wasn't part of the deal."

"Very well," Galen says, laughing. "We will know soon enough."

"Why am I here?" I ask, my voice surprisingly even and calm.

"Logic tells me that you believe you will die here. That is not the case. You are here to live, Luka."

"To live like you? Like Maddox? No thanks. That's no kind of life."

"Oh, but I think this time you'll change your mind and join us," Galen says.

285

"And why is that?"

"Because," Maddox's lifeless voice speaks up, "you have become the symbol of the rebellion in Region 86."

"What do you mean?" I ask.

"They speak of you, Luka, the boy who escaped the Loop, the boy who refuses to die, the boy who gathered an army. You and your people have been in contact with other regions, trying to work together, trying to come together as one."

"None of it was me," I say. "It was all of us together, and that's how we'll beat you."

"It is impossible for you, or anyone, to beat Happy," Galen scoffs.

"Wrong," I say, "there's at *least* a zero point seven percent chance."

I see a moment of surprise on Galen's face.

"Be that as it may," Galen continues, the politician's smile reappearing, "we have a proposition for you."

"I'm sure it'll be great," I say, rolling my eyes.

"Stand before the Altered, stand before our cameras, and tell the world that you were wrong to fight against us, that you have seen the error of your ways and that the World Government is right and good. Once that is done you will volunteer yourself."

"Volunteer myself for what?" I ask.

"We need three of you to reverse engineer the formulas and equations of the healing technology within you. You and Tyco will be our subjects, along with a third."

"I don't understand," I say. "You invented the healing tech; you gave it to us. Why do you need to figure it out?"

"The tech was destroyed by its creator, one of our most promising employees, and erased from all internal, external, and android memory, something we were certain could not be done. And then, of course, *you* destroyed the equipment containing the last remnants of its secrets." Galen smiles tightly. "Now, the technology exists only in the creator's mind."

Abril, I think, *she created the healing tech, saw what it was being used for, and then destroyed it.*

"What about the creator?" I ask. "Why not just force them to tell you how to re-create it?"

"The creator killed herself shortly after destroying her life's work."

She tricked Happy into believing she was dead! I think, and try not to let the satisfaction show on my face.

"So, you need three people who took the Delay?"

"That's right."

"And you thought I'd be willing to volunteer?"

"You have already agreed," Happy tells me, controlling my friend's body and voice. "You will do it because you are a true leader. You will do it because in exchange we will allow your friends to live the rest of their lives in peace, and that is all you really want. We have run the diagnostics, we have run the probabilities, and you are the most likely to accept this offer. It means no more bloodshed, no more death; it is an end to the war between us."

"But you plan on destroying all human life on Earth," I remind them. "You plan on eradicating everything! Destroying humanity so that they can no longer obliterate this planet and all life on it. I know what Phase Three is; I know that you won't let my friends live."

"Destroy humanity?" Galen repeats, chuckling to himself. "No, no, that's not right. Happy does not want to destroy humanity. Yes, Happy thinks of humankind as a virus, but they frame the problem in terms of technology rather than biology. To think of humanity as a computer virus is to hypothesize that it can be reprogrammed."

"I know all about your plan," I yell through gritted teeth as I remember Dr. Price's words.

"Then you should be thanking us," the Maddox host says, those eerie glowing eyes fixing on me. "We are repairing your broken species, destroying a diseased batch and starting anew."

"You're forgetting the cruelest part of your plan," I say. "Hordes and hordes of immortal humans used as batteries. How can you justify that?"

"They will not comprehend; they will have no hopes, no dreams, no ambition. They will know no other life but the life of a battery," Maddox replies.

"But they *have* to feel, isn't that right?" I ask. "They *have* to feel fear and pain and panic, because the harvest doesn't work without those things."

"There has always been sacrifice in the name of progress, Luka."

"No, that's not true; there has always been suffering in the name of progress. What gives you the right, the power, to decide who should suffer and who should be brainwashed into being the kind of person you want them to be?"

"Humans beat dogs to teach them not to bite. Now it's time something greater than yourselves trained you how to behave."

I know that I cannot reason with these machines. I shake my head. "And if I say no to standing in front of your cameras and saying that I was wrong?" I ask.

"Then we will simply execute you with all the world watching."

"But you need me," I point out. "You need me for your tests."

"You have seen how easy it is for us to find you and your friends, to capture you. Once we were ready to find you, it took us four minutes. If it's not you, Luka, it will be Igby Koh, or Pander Banks, or Kina Campbell. It makes no difference to us."

It took them four minutes to find us, I think, *but they've been searching for the Missing for years and never found them.*

"Who's the third?" I ask.

"You will find out soon enough."

"No, I want to know now. Who is the third?"

"Agree to do as we ask, and we will show you the third."

"I have one more condition," I say.

Galen stands up. "You're not in a position to bargain, Luka."

"Let the boy speak," the thing controlling Maddox says.

"I'll do it if you let them all live," I say.

"What do you mean?" Galen asks.

"All my friends: Pander, Igby, Wren, Dr. Ortega, Malachai, Samira, Molly, and Kina."

Saying this list of names hurts me; not including the likes of Blue, Pod, Shion, Akimi because they have not made it this far hurts me.

"The offer is as stated," Maddox replies. "They may live for

289

six more months unharmed and unhunted. They may not be a part of the new world."

"Not the new world," I say, "but let them live in the Arc, let them die in the Arc. Remove the healing tech from them and let them grow old together. What difference will it make?" When they're in the Arc, I think, maybe they can figure out how to fight on—maybe they can take Happy down from the inside.

There is a long pause as Happy considers this using Maddox's brain. Finally, he looks at me once again. "I am not capable of understanding why you fight so fiercely against this. It is not fear of your own death, you have proven that, so why? You're fighting Eden! You're fighting heaven! You're fighting paradise for your species."

"You'll never understand," I say, "because you look at data, not individuals. Before you destroyed the world I was a Regular; everything you would read about Regulars would tell you that we were scavenging, scrounging, thieving rats that made the Altereds' world look untidy. And if you looked at the data, it would back up all these statements. But do you think any of us *wanted* that life? Do you think any of us *chose* to be born into that existence? No, but we were, and the system was set up for us to fail. Education: too expensive; housing prices: too high; jobs: nonexistent; debt keeps on growing, drugs keep on spreading, space keeps on getting smaller and smaller. And who's at the top pulling the strings? The Alts, the rich—they *needed* us to be poor, they *needed* us to have nothing so they could look at all they had, pat themselves on the back, and say, look at all *I* have in comparison to them! If only *they* worked as hard as *me*! But, despite all of this, the best people I ever met were those scaveng-ing, scrounging, thieving rats! That's why I fight. I fight for the people I love, and you'll never understand love because you can teach a machine to think, but not to love."

There is another long pause as Maddox's mechanical eyes stare at me.

"I agree to your terms," he says finally. "Your friends may live out their days inside the Arc."

"Then I agree to your terms," I reply.

"So you agree to say, in a live transmission, broadcast across all regions of the world, that you have seen the error of your ways?" Galen asks, excitement in his voice. "That Happy is not the enemy? That things Happy has done were necessary for the survival of the species? You will tell the rebels of all Regions to stop fighting?"

"Yes," I reply.

"And then you will be a part of the tests to extract the tech-nology that will allow me . . . us . . . Happy to live forever?" Galen continues.

I laugh at him. "So that's why you've agreed to be Happy's servant—eternal life?"

Galen composes himself. "Perhaps that was part of the equa-tion, Luka, but in the end Happy needed *me*. People, Luka, are generally idiots. Tell them the truth and they'll skew it to fit their agenda. I'm Galen Rye, voted in by a base of supporters so devoted that I could walk into the West Sanctum Vertical, start executing Regulars, and still win a snap election the next day. In the beginning, Happy needed leaders like me, leaders who could tell their devotees to do what they're told. The stupidity of the masses, Luka, is not to be underestimated. I preyed on their fears, on their prejudices, on their idiocy. I told them I'd stop migrants taking a chunk out of their subsidy percentage, and they called me a hero. I told them I'd bring back conscription, and they called me a savior. I promised to loosen USW weapons laws, and they chanted my name! Do you think I care about migration? About homelessness? About any of the arbitrary things I'd spout day after day? No! But I knew what the brain-dead hive mind of the people wanted to hear. I manipulated them until they were loyal, dedicated, steadfast. Phase One of Happy's plan involved poisoning ninety-eight percent of the population of Earth. A thing like that cannot be achieved without people like me at the reins—"

"Enough," the Maddox host says, cutting Galen off. He turns to me. "Do you agree to our terms?"

"Yes," I say, still smiling at Galen, who looks back at me with concern in his eyes.

"Good," the Maddox host says. "Now, I believe you requested to know who the third subject of our tests will be."

He stands and walks to the elevator. Tyco, Galen, and I follow and we descend to floor sixty-five, right back to where I had freed Malachai, right back to where Woods had thrown himself to his death.

"Right this way," Happy says through Maddox as he opens the door.

I step back into the laboratory. The room is exactly as it had been, except there are no holographic projections of test subjects hovering in the air now, and the E4-EX-19 arms have been repaired.

A person lies on one of the operating tables. The paralysis needle is obviously not activated, because I can hear their ragged breathing, in and out rapidly, hoarsely.

"Who is it?" I ask, suddenly afraid of what I'm going to see when I walk over there.

"Take a look," the Maddox host says, extending his arm.

I step closer, my heart beginning to race as I see her brown hair, great chunks of it missing where it looks as though she has pulled it out. I move to the operating table, slowly moving around it until I can see her freckled cheeks, her wild blue eyes, the look of insanity and anger carved into her face.

"Jesus," I whisper. "Mable?"

She had been the last to be freed from the Loop, a scared little child who had refused to escape with us. She had run into the train tunnels alone and been eaten alive by rats. Or so I had thought.

"When we found her," Maddox says, startling me out of my shock, "the rats had consumed much of her; they had eaten her eyes, bitten out her tongue. But she was alive."

"You . . . How could you?"

"She was quite mad, couldn't understand why she was still alive, just kept on screaming over and over again. But, as you can see, she still has her uses."

"You're evil," I say, the words stammering out of my mouth.

"Sacrifices are necessary to bring about change," Happy says, speaking through Maddox.

"Is that always so?" Tyco's voice comes from behind me.

I watch an expression of curiosity come over Maddox's face as his illuminated eyes meet Tyco's.

How can they disagree? I wonder. *They are the same entity.*

Galen leans forward. "You see, Luka, everything that has happened and everything that is going to happen is for the good of the planet and for the good of the people."

"Just not for the people who are still alive," I say, tears forming in my eyes as I look down at the girl who I have failed.

Galen laughs. "Sometimes we have to think bigger; sometimes we have to think outside of our own insignificant lives." He smiles at me. "Tomorrow, Luka, at dawn, you will stand onstage and tell the world the truth: that you have joined us."

"Once you have what you need," I say, "once you have figured out how the healing technology works, kill us both, me and her, please."

Galen looks to Tyco; the host takes me by the arm and leads me back to the elevator.

We travel down three floors, and I'm led to a large room.

Tyco stands in the doorway. "These are your quarters for the night. You will be taken to the ground floor at six a.m."

He closes the door. A lock clicks and I'm left alone.

The room looks like someone's idea of a high-class hotel room. Sleek black floor and walls punctuated with hidden lights. The far wall is one enormous window that looks out over the city. There is a four-poster bed half-sunk into the floor with black sheets and pillows.

I stand, unmoving. I think of Mable tied to the operating table, having lost her mind more than nine weeks ago.

How long was she left alone in those tunnels? How long did the rats eat away at her while her wounds healed themselves over and over again?

I walk across the room and open a door that leads to a bathroom. I stumble toward the shower, pulling off my Alt military uniform as I go.

I stay in the shower for a long time, watching the water spin down the drain. I listen to the white-noise sound of the flowing water and I try not to think at all.

I step out of the shower and wrap a towel around myself, but I leave the water running—I'll need it to hide the sound of my voice. I take Apple-Moth out of the pocket of my black shirt and switch the drone on.

I hold a hand up in an attempt to keep Apple-Moth quiet, and—for once—it works.

"Hi, friend," I say.

Apple-Moth does a backflip. "Hi, friend!" it whispers.

"I need to ask you to do something for me," I say.

"An adventure?" it asks.

"Yes, Apple-Moth. One more adventure."

"Okay, friend."

"You might not make it out of this one alive, Apple-Moth, I'm sorry."

"Why are you sorry? You're my friend; I'd do anything for my friends."

I feel an ache in my throat. How can this little metal creation of wires and code be so *good*? "Apple-Moth, you've been the greatest friend to me."

"That makes me happy!"

I clear my throat. "Tomorrow, we stand in front of thousands of people. I've been thinking ... maybe we can change their minds. Maybe we can start an uprising."

"Let's do it," Apple-Moth says, glowing pink.

"Let's do it."

When I've talked through the details, I hold Apple-Moth in my closed hand, concealing it from all the cameras that will be hidden in the main room.

I ask the shower to switch itself off, and the water ceases as I walk through to the bedroom.

I stand at the glass wall that looks out over the city, and I feel destroyed. I have tried—since this all began—to do the right thing, and I may not have always wanted to be looked upon as the leader, but I have tried to keep everyone alive, and yet my friends have died, and some have ended up in worse places than death.

I think on Happy's words, at first in turmoil at the logic it presented: a rebirth of humanity; a chance to do it right; no more war; no more hate. What if Happy *is* right? What if fighting against the machines makes *us* the bad guys?

No, I tell myself, *you cannot justify evil means with a virtuous end. You cannot justify genocide with a better future. I still believe in humanity, I believe in the goodness of people, and I believe that bad people can change and see the error of their ways. The moment I stop believing in that is the moment I stop fighting.*

There are vents at one side of the glass wall and I open them, feeling the rush of cool air come in.

I open my hand and Apple-Moth floats silently into the air.

The companion drone says nothing; its lights stay dark as it hovers in front of me.

"You know what to do," I say.

A brief flicker of green light and Apple-Moth flies to the gap in the window and then stops. "Do you wanna hear a joke?" the drone whispers.

I nod my head. "Yes."

Lights flicker excitedly on and off, and then the drone is dark again. "What do you call an alligator who wears a vest?" Apple-Moth asks.

"I don't know," I reply.

"An investigator!" Apple-Moth says.

I laugh.

"Goodbye, Luka," the drone says.

"Goodbye, friend," I reply.

Apple-Moth's lights turn pink and then it's gone, zipping out of the gap in the vents and into the night sky, and I'm left in silence.

Happy has provided clothes: an Alt uniform with no markings. I leave it hanging in the wardrobe.

I sit and watch the city. I look at the towering Verticals, built to stock the growing number of poor. I look at the villages around the city, spacious second homes for the ultra-rich, and I think about what the Alts were: a walking advertisement to the poor; *look what you could achieve if you just worked harder!* But the opportunity didn't really exist, not to Regulars; you had to be born into the right family to have what they had. I look at the financial district: hundreds of thousands of Coin wasted on golden statues to the Final Gods of Prosperity, when that money could have gone to schools, to hospitals, to the millions of homeless people in the slums around the Verticals. I look toward the Loop, a place for kids who fell foul of a corrupt justice system, no mercy for circumstances.

For a moment I think, *Yeah, bring it all down*, but I'm making the same mistake as Happy—I'm looking at humanity as one entity, a uniform species.

I look toward my old home, the Black Road Vertical, and I think about my mom teaching us sign language, my dad taking us to the river. I look toward City Level Two and remember sneaking into the gated community with my friends to knock on doors and run away. I look to the sky-farms; the hundred-yard-high Ferris wheels that turn night and day, rotating crops in overlapping troughs to feed the entire city, and I think about me and Molly sneaking into a potato trough and being carried high up into the clouds.

Humans are not cogs in a machine; we are not a hive mind working toward a single goal. We are individuals, each of us different and unique. To wipe us out based on the sum of our parts is to erase the unfathomable beauty that resides in most people. Creativity, capacity to love, ambition, talent, mothers and fathers and brothers and sisters. The world was not brought to its knees by the masses; it was forced there by the billionaires, the corporations, the warlords and world leaders who favored profit over life time and time again. No, Happy is not right, no matter how it frames its logic; we are here, now, and we won't go quietly. The revolution will fight on in Region 9, in Region 26, in Region 40, in Region 71, all over the world. We will not go quietly. And if there are even just a few of them who see me as the symbol of the rebellion, then I will *be* the symbol of the rebellion.

A calmness comes over me. Tomorrow is the end of the line, but knowing that I'll go out fighting makes it okay.

I get dressed and order food from Happy—it comes to my door by drone five minutes later. I eat and I fall into a deep sleep.

I'm standing in the center of Midway Park and the ground is shaking beneath my feet.

The recently melted snow has turned the park into a mud pit as thousands of people fight for their lives. Sonic bullets rip through the air. All around me people are crying, screaming, and crawling around in the mud.

I have to keep moving forward, I have to make it to the stage at the front of the park, but I can't remember why.

I push forward, shoving an Alt soldier out of my way.

Something bad is about to happen, I think, a sense of dread eating at me.

I keep moving toward the stage, certain that—at any second—the bad thing will come.

One of the Missing falls down dead in front of me. I step over her and walk on.

Finally, I make it to the stage. Smoke still billows out of the hole where the bomb detonated.

What am I looking for? I wonder as I place one hand on the platform and drag myself up.

Suddenly, the sound of the battle raging behind me stops. No more screams, no more bullets, no more sounds of bodies hitting the ground. Silence.

I stand up and turn around.

The sea of fighters has ceased killing. They are all facing me. Those who were dying are dead; those still alive watch me with hope on their faces.

I'm frozen by the silence, by the expectation, the hope that floats on the light breeze sweeping across the landscape.

I stare back at them, uncertain of what to do next. And then, from the back of the park, I hear an electronic beep. A single note, echoing through the park. It comes again a few seconds later, and I see, near the back of the crowd, a young man turn to face the sound. The beep comes again, and three more people turn away from me. Another beep; six or seven turn to face it, both Missing and Alt soldiers.

"What's going on?" I whisper.

"You're supposed to talk," a voice says.

I recognize the voice immediately and turn to face Maddox. He stands just offstage, next to one burning curtain.

"They won't be able to hear me," I say, looking at the destroyed microphone and speakers.

"They'll hear you," Maddox says, and smiles.

The beep comes again; a dozen people turn to face it.

"I don't know what to say," I think aloud, looking out at the silent gathering.

"Yes, you do," Maddox replies.

And from far away, the electronic beep comes again.

"Maddox," I say, turning to my friend, "I miss you, man."

"I miss you too, Luke," he says, and I laugh. Maddox had been the only person I ever let call me Luke.

"I'm sorry I couldn't save you . . . I'm sorry."

"We knew there would have to be sacrifices if we were going to win this war," Maddox tells me.

"It's all so . . . so fucking wrong," I say, feeling tears flowing to my eyes.

"It's okay to fear what comes next, to ask yourself, *Am I going to be alone again?* But remember what you're dying for: life; evolution; dreams; love. And whether you succeed or not, they will thank you for trying."

There's something about Maddox's words, the strange way he is speaking, that sparks something in the back of my mind.

The beep comes again and more turn.

"I think it's time," Maddox says, and then points to the back of the park, where the beeping sound is coming from. "You have to make it stop. No one else can."

I look to where he is pointing. When I look back, he's gone.

Now almost half the crowd has turned away.

I step forward, raise both hands in the air, and open my mouth to speak.

I wake suddenly from the dream.

Elements of it begin to fall away, but I remember Maddox; I remember the beep.

Outside the large window, sunlight is beginning to spill across the city.

I get out of bed and put on the black Alt uniform.

Ten minutes later, my door opens and Tyco—eyes still glowing—escorts me to the elevator.

I step in and he follows. We begin to descend. I turn to him.

"Do you regret it now, Tyco?" I ask. "Do you regret selling us out in favor of the machines?"

The lights from the host's eyes turn to me and I swear I can see agony buried deep down in there.

We exit into the eerily silent corridor and make our way to the great hall.

Galen waits behind a podium; his three-dimensional projection stands an unnecessary fifty feet tall. The seats are filled with Alts, all sitting in silence. They turn to face me and watch as I walk down the center aisle. Galen stands on the stage, smiling down at me.

I climb the steps and stand in the middle of the raised podium.

"Ladies and gentlemen," Galen says, his voice the tone of a circus ringmaster's, "today is a very special day. I'm sure all of you recognize the young man who stands before us. This is the great Luka Kane."

Derisory laughter and jeers come from the crowd.

"How dare you laugh?" Galen asks, his voice lowering to a growl. "I say that with not a hint of jest. This remarkable boy, only sixteen years of age, has outsmarted us, broken free of our prisons, avoided capture, and inspired a rebellion. How many here could say they were capable of the same? We must not look down upon the accomplishments of others simply because we do not share the same aspirations."

I look around at the crowd. At least a dozen drones hover above their heads, some moving around me, recording me, projecting my image across the empty city for all to see, onto Lenses, SoCom units, screens, Barker Projectors. These images will eventually be seen by Kina, Igby, Molly, Pander, everyone who is still alive.

"This day is a historic one!" Galen projects, getting into his role now. "This day will go down in Earth's new history! This day will be remembered forever as the day the fighting came to an end!"

Happy lets you out of the box for one morning and you really make the most of it, I think, rolling my eyes at Galen's dramatics.

"But enough from me," Galen says, stretching a hand out and gesturing toward me. "We are not gathered here to listen to my words. Luka, if you would?"

Galen steps back from the podium, his fifty-foot effigy moving simultaneously with him.

I step forward, moving slowly up to the microphone. I turn around to see that Galen's gigantic image has been replaced by my own.

You're supposed to talk, I think, the words in my head coming through in Maddox's voice.

"I . . . I came here today after meeting with Galen Rye. He took the time to explain to me exactly what it is you are striving for. What you want is a new beginning, a future, a reset for humanity, a chance to start again and get it right. That is an opportunity that is hard to turn your back on, especially when your only other option is death. And yet some chose death. There were Alts, just like you, who listened to the World Government's plan, their plan to eliminate most of humanity, to eliminate the poor, the infirm, the disadvantaged. And you sat here and watched them die for their empathy. One by one they were brought before you on this stage and they were erased, and you cheered. But you're the good guys, right? You're doing the right thing? You're the ones protected by the future authors of history. No one will remember your wrongdoings, so what does it matter?"

I sense an unease rippling through the crowd. They are unsure where I'm going with this, unsure what side of the fence I will come down on. I scan their faces, and then I look up at the drones hovering above their heads. All of them are dark, apart from one. I see lights flicker green, pink, orange, red. And I know now is the time.

"I have something to show you," I say. "Apple-Moth, when you're ready."

I watch the colorful companion drone zip forward and then rise high above the crowd. A white light emits from it while it connects with the command unit positioned in the ceiling.

The image behind me changes to that of the room on the top floor of the Arc. Galen sits behind the long table, Maddox beside him.

"Happy thinks of humankind as a virus," the projection of Galen says, "but they frame the problem in terms of technology rather than biology. To think of humanity as a computer virus is to hypothesize that it can be reprogrammed."

The projection jumps forward, and now the focus is on Maddox, with his glowing eyes.

"Humans beat dogs to teach them not to bite. Now it's time something greater than yourselves trained you how to behave."

The scene switches again, jumping once more to Galen.

"People, Luka, are generally idiots," Galen says, his voice booming over the crowd. I smile as I watch the confused faces exchange glances, and I smile knowing that this is being projected to millions of survivors around the world, survivors on both sides. "Tell them the truth and they'll skew it to fit their agenda. I'm Galen Rye, voted in by a base of supporters so devoted that I could walk into the West Sanctum Vertical, start executing Regulars, and still win a snap election the next day. In the beginning, Happy needed leaders like me, leaders who could tell their devotees to do what they're told. The stupidity of the masses, Luka, is not to be underestimated. I preyed on their fears, on their prejudices, on their idiocy. I told them I'd stop migrants taking a chunk out of their subsidy percentage, and they called me a hero. I told them I'd bring back conscription, and they called me a savior. I promised to loosen USW weapons laws, and they chanted my name! Do you think I care about migration? About homelessness? About any of the arbitrary things I'd spout day after day? No! But I knew what the brain-dead hive mind of the people wanted to hear. I manipulated them until they were loyal, dedicated, steadfast. Phase One of Happy's plan involved poisoning ninety-eight percent of the population of Earth—a thing like that cannot be achieved without people like me at the reins."

I glance to my left and see Galen gesturing offstage. His panic fills me with happiness. The show continues, cutting to Maddox.

There is a murmur from the crowd now, as Galen drags a soldier onto the stage and points up toward Apple-Moth.

I know that time is running out. Once they kill the drone, I'm next. I'm sure I've already done enough damage, but I need them to see that it's not the government that is running things, that Happy is behind all of this.

". . . you should be thanking us," the Maddox projection says. "We are repairing your broken species, destroying a diseased batch and starting anew."

The sound cuts out and the image behind me disappears as a sonic round slams into Apple-Moth. I watch the tiny drone spin in the air, one of its rotor blades badly damaged, but its lights still flickering, green, pink, yellow.

A second round hits Apple-Moth, and the drone's lights go

out completely. There will be no self-repairing this time. Apple-Moth is gone.

Goodbye, friend, I think. *You did great.*

A thousand heads turn and watch in silence as Apple-Moth falls to the floor, listening as it smashes to pieces. And then they turn back to the stage.

I'm grabbed by two hosts and held firm. I'm not struggling, though, not trying to break free.

I watch the crowd as Galen steps back up to the platform. Finally, his soldiers have seen him for who he really is; finally, their eyes have been opened.

Galen's projected image flickers back into being behind him as he straightens his tie and smiles.

"Ladies and gentlemen," Galen says, regaining his composure eerily quickly, "it appears today we will not be joined by the leader of the revolution. Instead, I ask you, the survivors of Earth, what should become of him?"

I wait, scanning the blank faces, anticipating the first angry cry of revolt against Happy.

"Kill the rebel!" a voice calls from the middle of the crowd.

"Kill the liar!" another joins in.

And then they're all shouting, baying for my blood, screaming for my death.

I'm frozen with disbelief; I can't speak, I can't move. I watch the angry faces of a thousand soldiers as their words become a jumble of sound.

I had expected to die today, but I dared to hope that I could open some eyes before I left.

Galen raises his hands, and the hall falls silent. He beckons offstage and an executioner with a heart trigger walks by me. The crowd are now so silent that each of the tall woman's footsteps can be heard echoing around the enormous room. She stands beside the Overseer.

"Mr. Kane," Galen says, his voice now echoing too, in the silence. "The people have spoken. Is there anything you would like to say?"

I'm going to die, I think. *I'm going to die, and it was all for nothing. They don't care. This man's followers don't care. I showed them the truth and they don't want to see it.*

I look around. The faces are frozen in sneers and anticipation of my deletion.

They won't listen, I think, *but there are hundreds of thousands of survivors around the world who are listening.*

"Never give up," I say, raising my head to the camera drones. "History is not the words written on a page; history lives in hearts and minds and in the rocks and the oceans. It can't be erased by evil. You are fighting for what is right. They are clinging to power with frayed minds and fingertips. Remember, we don't do running away."

Galen nods to the executioner. She hands the small tube of metal to him. Galen points it at my chest, and I hear three beeps coming from deep inside.

I smile, knowing that all across the world there are people just like Pander, like Molly, like Igby and Malachai and Pod and Sam and Blue and Kina. People who will find a way to win.

I look out over the heads of the crowd, and I try to picture Kina Campbell one more time.

"Kina, I love you," I say.

Galen releases his grip on the trigger.

There's a sensation of falling.

There's time to feel all the beauty of the world.

And then nothing.

It doesn't hurt.

ACKNOWLEDGMENTS

This is my second published book, which makes me twice as lucky as I ever thought I'd get. And, yes, luck plays a huge part (even though some will tell you it's all TALENT and HARD WORK and DEDICATION and blah blah blah).

The Block was written in a bit of a haze. I was working full-time as an English teacher, driving two hours a day, and surviving mostly on coffee.

Without a long list of people, this book would be mostly incoherent rambling (hopefully it's not still incoherent rambling . . .). I want to thank some of those people here:

Sarah Robb—I wouldn't be able to do this without you.

Chloe Seager—I wouldn't have a writing career if you hadn't taken a chance on me.

Kesia Lupo—for helping to turn my first draft into a book I'm really proud of.

Laura Myers—when I could hardly think straight anymore, you made things make sense.

Fraser Crichton—for making some incredible catches.

Jazz Bartlet Love—for a million awesome ideas.

Barry Cunningham—your enthusiasm got me over the finish line this time.

Samantha Palazzi—for keeping me sane while my first book came out during a pandemic.

Vault49—for designing the brilliant cover of *The Block*!

Darren and Dave—I hate you both.

Mum and Dad—I thanked you in the last book . . . I SUPPOSE I'll thank you in this one too!

Cammy Angus—FoB.